OMNI
BEST SCIENCE FICTION
THREE

Edited by Ellen Datlow

D1295127

OMNI Books
Greensboro, North Carolina

© 1993, Omni Publications International Ltd. All rights reserved.

"Palindrome," © 1987 by Thomas M. Disch.

 Original to this edition:
"Moving On," © 1993 by Bruce McAllister.
"Virus Dreams," © 1993 by Scott Baker.
"The Black Lotus," © 1993 by Simon Ings.
"Some Strange Desire," © 1993 by Ian McDonald.
"A Cartographic Analysis of the Dream State," © 1993 by Pat Murphy.
"Love Toys of the Gods," © 1993 by Pat Cadigan.
"It Twineth Round Thee in Thy Joy," © 1993 by Gahan Wilson.
"Along the River," © 1993 by Ursula K. Le Guin.
"One Night, or Scheherazade's Bare Minimum," © 1993 by Thomas M.
Disch.
"Exogamy," © 1993 by John Crowley.

Cover art © 1993 Michael Parkes.

Reproduction or translation of any part of this work beyond that permitted by
sections 107 and 108 of the United States Copyright Act without the permis-
sion of the copyright owner is unlawful except brief quotes used in reviews.

Printed in the United States of America.
10 9 8 7 6 5 4 3 2 1
ISBN 0-87455-284-2

Omni is a registered trademark of Omni Publications International Ltd.
Omni Books, 324 West Wendover Avenue, Suite 200, Greensboro,
North Carolina 27408, is a General Media International Company.

CONTENTS

INTRODUCTION

Ellen Datlow

Omni, first published in October 1978, was the first glossy mass-market magazine to provide science fiction and fantasy with the forum and format it deserves. Since its premier issue, *Omni* has showcased some of the most entertaining and thought-provoking sf and fantasy of our times. *Omni* was the first American magazine to publish Clive Barker; William Gibson's first professional appearance was in *Omni.* In addition to publishing fiction by the genre's biggest names and important newcomers, we have also published stories by cross-genre writers such as Joyce Carol Oates, Julio Cortázar, Jonathan Carroll, Jack Cady, Harvey Jacobs, Patricia Highsmith, and William Kotzwinkle. *Omni* commissioned and published a science fiction story by William Burroughs.

Omni Best Science Fiction Three consists of all original stories, novelettes, and a novella, with one reprint from *Omni.* Most of the contributors will be familiar to readers of the magazine. Two who might be unfamiliar are Ian McDonald from Northern Ireland and Simon Ings, from Great Britain. Their fiction is imbued with the edge typical of *Omni*'s fiction; their visions of the world are unique, and although McDonald has a definite head start, with several novels and two story collections to his credit, they are both writers to watch in the '90s.

Several of the following stories are focused on sexual themes. Others make at least passing reference to a character's sexuality, something the traditional magazines avoided for many years. I'd like to think that *Omni* has helped the field overcome its resistance to the facts of life and brought to the genre a new maturity and sophistication, and that with these anthologies as well as in the magazine, we'll continue to lead the field in this direction.

Moving On

by Bruce McAllister

Bruce McAllister lives in Redlands, California, and is direc-
tor of the writing program at the University of Redlands. His
first short story was published in 1963, when he was seventeen. Until 1987 his short fiction output was small, but since
then he's had stories in *Omni, The Magazine of Fantasy and
Science Fiction, Isaac Asimov's Science Fiction Magazine,*
the anthologies *In the Field of Fire* and *Alien Sex,* and
elsewhere. His original story "Sister Moon" was published in
Omni Best Science Fiction One and "Kingdom Come," a
reprint from *Omni* magazine, appears in *Omni Best Science
Fiction Two.* His first novel, *Humanity Prime,* was part of the
original Ace Special line edited by Terry Carr, and his most
recent novel, *Dream Baby* (Tor), is based on his Nebula
Award-nominated novella of the same title.

McAllister has the ability to get inside his characters and
make them utterly believable whether they're female nurses
in Vietnam, Franciscan assassins, or lonely, emotionally- and
physically-damaged young men—as is the protagonist of the
following novelette.

MOVING ON

Bruce McAllister

When John Klinger went out to the Mojave Witness, which
he did as often as he could, he took the Bell 420. Flying it with
his one good arm had gotten easier over the past few months,
and he could forget he didn't have two good ones. That was
one reason he took it: He could forget the pink plastic.

He would set the little helicopter down thirty meters from
the shack at the eastern end of the Witness and close his eyes,
waiting for the rotor wash to die down. If it was daytime, he
would get out and check the three kilometers of electrified
chain-link fence for any animals that had blundered into it in
the night and bury them some distance away, thinking about
death. He would stand for a moment in the shack's doorway
looking out at the endless sand the smog still hadn't touched
and wonder how much time he had. He would think about his
parents, the quake-loosened bricks outside his apartment that
had hit him, destroying the nerves in his arm, and what his
twenty-six years of life really added up to.

If it was night, he would sit for a moment in the Bell and
watch the moths—like little ghosts—batter themselves against
the single bulb by the shack's front door. If there was a moon,
he would remember what the Witness itself—the kilometer-
long, open tank of water—looked like with the moonlight on

2

its surface and wish he had hovered over it longer. He would find himself wondering how many weeks or months he had before Central got the funds for a new detector-translator system and his life would have to change: With new equipment he wouldn't be able to justify so many visits, wouldn't be able to come out like this every few days, lying about "recurrent problems."

Then he would go inside, sit down at the little card table in the shack and do what no fixer—no one in his position— was supposed to do: He would read the transcripts of what the Witness—listening day and night for the voices of the *just-dead*—had picked up from the Limbo.

Whether it was simply against policy, or a misdemeanor, or a felony to read the transcripts, he could not remember, but he had been doing it now for months. It was simply a function of the amount of time he spent at this station, when other fixers were always on the move. Since he spent as much time here as he could—attending to the problems of a first-generation system and fabricating problems when he needed to—his "crime" had evolved logically enough, hadn't it? He wanted to be out here away from the city, and so he was—two or three times a week. He'd had a radio for a while, and a video player small enough to fit on the card table beside the coffee maker, and later a few books, but these, he'd discovered, had been "baggage" from the city, and really had no place here. The transcripts belonged when so many other things did not, and one day he had begun to read them. He was the *living,* after all, and they were the *dead,* and here at least—at the Mojave Witness—that was all there was.

Had he been like all the other fixers, the techs who kept the Witnesses all over southern California working, Davis, his supervisor, would have moved him from one station to another throughout the Seventh District, all 200,000 square kilometers of it, and he would probably never have started reading. But Davis knew he liked the desert—*needed* it in his own way—and a fixer as good as he was, winner of Central's Troubleshooter Award three out of five years, got what he wanted. What he wanted was this station. The *voices*—the transcripts in front of him on the table—were the ones that had come *here*. Not to Camel's Back overlooking San Diego Bay, or Camp Pendleton's Witness with its view of Pacific breakers, or Mullholland's, or El Centro's, but here—to the high desert, to the cold dry peace of its winters, to the dreamy heat of its summers, to a place where there were no human voices other than these. Even he wasn't a voice here. He didn't sing. He didn't talk to himself like a desert rat. He didn't play the radio or VCR. It felt wrong to, so he didn't.

Had he loved the city, as fixers like Corley and Tompai seemed to, the transcripts wouldn't have interested him either. For people like them—who liked hanging out in the tech lobby at Central, even had fun playing with the design software on their assigned terminals in their assigned cubicles with the fluorescent lighting—the living were very much alive. And the *just-dead*—their voices, the transcripts of their ethereal babble—were just that: ghosts, gone, moving on.

For him, month by month, the opposite had somehow become true.

The Justice Department, under whose legal jurisdiction the Witnesses operated, required printouts as well as tapes—a hedge against malfunction or criminal sabotage—and so the transcripts were printed on a simple Centric printer even as the transmissions were being received and tapes being made; and one night, alone, reluctant to return the Bell 420 to the Sherriff's Aviation helipad, or himself to his apartment in Corona, he had started reading.

* * *

On August 16, six days before his twenty-seventh birthday, in the meanest heat of the upper-desert summer, he phoned from his apartment in Corona and informed Davis that he'd need another overnighter at the Witness. Davis, of course, swore.

"Jesus Christ, you're spending a helluva lot of time up there, Klinger."

"It's the translator drive, sir. You know how old the boards are." And then he added: "I don't like spending my nights out there any more than you would."

He held his breath.

"Bullshit, Klinger, but when the new system comes in, you won't have to. Try to make it in to Central on Monday at least, will you?"

"Yes, sir."

When the man's image was gone from the phonescreen by his bed, Klinger started to breathe again.

If Central were expecting the new equipment any time soon, Davis would have told him, wouldn't he?

He drove through the heat of the Inland Empire to Sheriff's Aviation headquarters in Rialto, where, if he was willing to listen to McKinney talk weapons for an hour—over coffee, in the snack bar—the old pot-bellied bigot would let him take the Bell 420 again, instead of some county ground vehicle, which was all the JD agreement with the County of San Bernardino required. It wasn't that he didn't like McKinney. McKinney was the one who'd taught him—ignoring his prosthesis kindly—to fly in the days when Klinger would spend his off-hours hanging around the airport like some PD wannabe. Like some deranged uncle, McKinney seemed to want Klinger to have the very best, so of course he liked the man. It was just the constant talking. Sometimes it drove Klinger crazy.

But he listened again, and again McKinney gave him the helicopter, and again Klinger lifted off into the heat of summer.

That afternoon the air conditioning in the shack went out. He didn't need to step outside and check the tap lines that ran to the nearest power-line support tower a quarter kilometer away. Everything else was working. He got down on his hands and knees and pulled the thing apart. A box of spare parts he'd collected over the past months was under the card table, and when he discovered he didn't have the part he needed—an alternator—he got up calmly and plugged in the swamp cooler, the one he'd bought with his own money. He closed the one blind, got out the Reynold's Wrap, and did the window. The equipment could operate up to 400 degrees Fahrenheit without any trouble, so the air conditioner was for the living, and as a consequence, in Central's eyes, didn't really matter. He knew it was the heat that helped keep other fixers away. "You want the Mojave?" Tompai had once said. "You can *have* it. You're already dead, Klinger."

It wasn't true. He'd never felt more alive than he did when he was out here under the stars, cool or sweaty, thinking about life and reading the printouts. It was the morgue of the living—the *cities*—that made him feel like a corpse, and the feeling wasn't getting any better. He went to his apartment— he went to Central—less and less, and the only thing that really worried him was how long he had before the new equipment arrived.

The vast swimming pools with their open water and immense cement walls—the "receivers" large enough to register the oscillation of neutrinos in which the computers could find the "voices" of the *just-dead*—would last forever, but the first-generation hardware, like flesh and bone, was wearing out.

He had the shack's aluminum door propped open with a rock and the holes in the screen door covered with tape, but the tape had lost its stick and the bugs, attracted by his reading light, were getting in anyway. He was dripping sweat on the transcripts as he tried to read.

They were the usual. The babble . . . the technical recitations . . . the private memories . . . .

> . . . *Christ died for me I lived for him I died for him he lived for me* . . . .

> . . . *longitudinal studies of the astroglia provide some support for this idea astrocytes in the rat undergo their final divisions* . . . .

> . . . *but when I went back years later and stood on the hillside behind the house closed my eyes I could see the kids I could hear them playing the way they did the way they laughed and shouted before Dorothy died* . . . .

His eyes were very tired when he came across it:

> . . . *for when I was writing I was in golden places a golden palace with crystal windows and silver chandeliers my dress was finest satin and diamonds sat shining in my black hair then I put away my book and the smells came in through the rotting walls and rats ran over my feet my satin turned to rags and the only things shining in my hair were lice the lice of my life as I knew it then* . . . .

He read it again, sitting up straighter. It was beautiful. It was poetry, some of the prettiest he had come across. He had discovered long ago that in general the dead weren't *poets*.

They were ordinary people, souls floating free of bodies at last, thoughts held together for a little while, lodged, as the textbooks put it, somewhere beyond the electromagnetic, "in one of the particle fields, making their detectable oscillations in low-energy neutrinos bound to the gravitational potential well of the Earth." But nevertheless, people.

More often than not they said very unpoetic things, like:

> *. . . where the hell am I?*

Or:

> *. . . if she had only bought her dresses discount she would have had more money for the trip but would she listen to me no she would never listen to me . . . .*

Or:

> *. . . and then I slipped her panties off and put my face . . .*

This was different. It wasn't even the poetic feeling of the words. Poetry in books—in school all those years—had never interested him. The Bell 420 had more poetry, he'd told Corley once. *Flying* was more poetry than any poem. But here a woman—he assumed it was a woman—had died, and even in her death (especially in her death?) she could speak to herself so beautifully. She could *think* and *feel* so beautifully about life, even after leaving it.

She, too, was flying, it occurred to him. Not with a chopper, but with words.

As he copied it out—on lined notebook paper, with his good hand—he recalled something in the fixer's manual about this too. Whether it was a misdemeanor or a felony to copy a transmission, he could not remember. It was probably a felony.

He went to sleep at last on the cot by the card table, wondering how she had died. He could see her face, but only vaguely, in the dark.

Two weeks later he found her again. He could not have said what it was that made him so sure. Maybe the word *lice,* but probably other things as well. He couldn't check. He hadn't written down her ID. He wrote it down now: A266920.

> *. . . I once slept under a bridge I didn't have lice in my hair like the woman who wrote that book it was like a river below me but it was cement with a trickle of water it wasn't the rivers I dreamt of I once slept in a pipe that time I ran away and that night I dreamt of rivers . . . .*

Later that day, under the same ID, he found:

> *. . . laugh child life laugh life is beautiful was written on the wall under the bridge by the mattress the old blood on it even now I dream that I am only a dream because when I was alive my dreams were as real as that blood . . . .*

Had she been a poet herself—in real life? Someone who'd done well in English in school, like so many girls did when boys didn't? Was this all from *books,* ones she had loved? Had she *really* run away, been homeless, slept under bridges? Or were these daydreams, someone else's stories?

She loved words. He could tell that. But that was all he knew.

He thought about her all day, and that night dreamed about a girl who looked a little like Erika, his last girlfriend— the one two years ago who hadn't, for some reason, minded his prosthesis—but also like a girl he had seen years ago in an old photograph from the sixties or seventies: Flowers in her hair . . . blue eyes . . . an old Victorian house behind her . . . thinner than Erika would ever be.

All a fixer had to know was the machines, a little theory, and "policy." But you didn't spend two years at Polytech for a T.A. in Witness Engineering without picking up the rest. There were a lot of jokes and tall tales—like the one about the ghost that had followed a fixer named Nakamura all the way around the world, from one Witness to another, until he went insane—just because he read a transcript. It was a joke, but also a warning: *Don't fuck with things you don't understand.*

The most exciting thing that ever really happened to a fixer was a solar flare seizure in the photon detectors or an anomalous shutdown of the translators, and even those got to be routine. You heard about sabotage—when the cases were big and ongoing—but he'd never met a fixer who'd actually had to deal with it. And the transmissions behaved the way they were supposed to behave . . . like any "hard" paranormal phenomenon. The ghosts didn't communicate with one another, it seemed; the transmissions came in at random; and finally, a few days or weeks or months after the body's death, they just stopped coming altogether. The point was to record what could be recorded before the "ghost" moved on, which they all did. If the ghost was a murder victim, what a Witness heard might contain enough to help the prosecution. Legally it was as good as a deathbed confession. Except in cases of established pre-death insanity, correlations with fact had been too high for the legal system to ignore.

You could, in other words, testify against your own murderer *after* you had died.

The next night he heard the printer start. Something told

him he should look and because he did, he found her once
more:

> . . . *I send you this I send you the night is*
> *darkening round me the wild winds coldly blow but a*
> *tyrant spell has bound me and I cannot cannot go the*
> *giant trees are bending their bare boughs weighed*
> *with snow and the storm is fast descending and yet I*
> *cannot cannot go clouds beyond clouds above me*
> *waste beyond waste below but nothing can move me*
> *I will not will not cannot go how I wish how I wish I*
> *had even once made words like these for you . . . .*

He sat amazed. It was the most beautiful thing he had ever
read. He copied it fast—seeing those blue eyes, feeling the
brush of a woman's hand on his—and sat waiting for more.
    When nothing else with her code appeared, he got up and
made himself some lunch.

    On Monday, after the meeting for all of the fixers at the
hall at Central, he drove out to Sherriff's Aviation, a portable
computer—the smallest and cheapest he could find at Fedco—
in a Samsonite briefcase on the seat beside him. When he
arrived, he put the briefcase in the cockpit of the Bell and went
in to give McKinney his hour.
    "You ever want to try the new firing range, Klinger—it's
automated—I'll let you fire an H an' K infrared g-launcher, or
a galvanic Ingram—"
    "Sure . . . ."
    "You tell me when and we'll do it. *You* say, Klinger.
You'll be the only fixer who's ever fired a skin-wired machine
pistol, believe me."
    "That would be great, McKinney. I gotta go. Thanks."

    He plugged the old home Osterizer in—the one he'd

rewired for the purpose—set the little jury-rigged timer for random ignition, and over the next hour watched the static appear intermittently and the printer turn words and sentences into incoherent letters—the kind Central and the JD so hated. Then he called Davis, told him the digitizer was acting up again, and smiled when Davis swallowed it, allowing him a maximum ("A maximum, Klinger, you hear?") of three overnighters for the upcoming week.

"Thank you, sir."

He had the air conditioner going in forty minutes and the mini-PC from his apartment sexing the recorder in twenty, its "applepie program" doing exactly what he hoped it would, the PC set to block the Osterizer ignition when her ID registered. As long as no one else got assigned to the Mojave, the PC would be able to work day and night in peace, checking the transmissions for her ID and copying only those transmissions.

That was all he wanted—to have all of her transmissions, his own tapes of them, and to copy them out with his good hand.

On a Wednesday, the next time he went to the shack, he found two:

> ... when I was child on Wiegkland Avenue just across the street from Jordan High School there was a tree that smelled funny and had stiff leaves and everyone carved or sprayed names on it I remember buying a packet of seeds I remember looking for a place to plant them and I remember thinking you can't plant seeds in cement can you—

Real interference from a solar flare or gravity shift had lost the rest on both the shack's receiver and his own PC, but the second was intact:

. . . when I went to see my brother up north
when he wrote me to tell me where but don't tell
anyone else and I got there he said no one knows
where I am and I said I know I know where you are
and he said that didn't matter because no one knows
where you are Linda I said I do he said yes you do
and we laughed and that was the last time I saw him
ever . . . .

He copied them, hand shaking, refolded the continuous
printer sheets and taped the copied transmissions to the wall
over the printer. The first one he had ever copied was in his
wallet. He got it out and taped it up too.

That night, when he closed his eyes, he saw the buckled
asphalt and concrete of the Great Quake of '95. When his
mother's and father's faces appeared, he handled it as he
always did—making himself see moonlight on the surface of
the Witness and nothing else. But this time saw *her,* too, and
found himself wondering what those days had been like for
her. He saw her running down a street, buildings falling. He
saw himself holding her—both of them standing still in the
middle of everything, barely breathing. He saw them kneel on
an endless park lawn where nothing—nothing at all—could
fall on them, where nothing could hurt them.

His sheet was wet in the morning, but he left it. It would
dry in the heat by noon.

The next morning, coffee in his good hand, he picked up
the night's printouts from the tray under the printer and began
to read. He found one and it made him dizzy.

. . . why do you ask for poetry why do you ask
for words less real than those you send me on blind
air when I am not sure I even remember when I
waked I saw that I saw not cold in the earth and the

*deep snow piled above thee come live with me and
be my love but thank you for asking . . . .*

He stared at the words and when the chill, moving
through him like winter wind on the sand, faded away, he
knew why he'd felt it.

Perhaps it was only a voice speaking to the nothingness,
trying to keep itself company. Perhaps she was only speaking
to herself, to someone from her past, someone who had loved
poetry as much as she had. Perhaps it was only one of these
things—

But as he read it again he felt the chill again—

He felt that she was *answering him*—

That she had somehow heard him and was answering
him.

That night he got up suddenly from the cot, turned on the
light and stared at the printer. There was no transmitter—there
was no transmitter at *any* Witness as far as he knew. But there
had to be one somewhere.

Others had tried. The original experimenters had transmitted messages to particular *names,* particular IDs (syntactic
personalities and photon configurations) and to the Limbo at
large, and answers had, at least on occasion, indeed come
back. They had come back tomorrow, or yesterday, five weeks
ago, a year from now. Like telepathy in the old dream
experiments at the Maimonides Dream Center, the afterlife
had no reason to respect time and space. And the ghosts
themselves often had a sense of humor, dark as it was. Asked
about the assassinations of presidents and premiers, they had
sent back:

. . . *Kennedy and Castro and Elvis are alive and
working at Johnny Rocket's . . . .*

Asked about the murder of a little girl named Mary, they

had answered:

> *. . . Mary had a little lamb little lamb little lamb*
> *Mary had a little something someone wanted . . . .*

They had even sent back a bad limerick:

> *. . . There was a physicist named Fred*
> *who tried to talk to the dead*
> *but try as he might*
> *he got it wrong*

One of the senders was of course named Fred.

Somebody had a transmitter somewhere. If she were answering him, he would find it and use it—

Because she was answering him—

Because by answering him she was making sure he would look for it, making sure he would find it, and send a message to her.

He spent much of the next week at Central—asking gently about it, joking about it, making fun of the original experimenters, the foolishness of trying to talk to ghosts. There was no such equipment at Central, he learned from the other techs. Only the R&D geeks at Justice had such things, and maybe even they didn't anymore. In any case, it would have been such an outrageous crime for a fixer to try that it wasn't even listed as one. It was Tompai who said this, laughing. Klinger laughed with him.

It was the poet William Wordsworth she was quoting, he discovered. And Stephen Spender, William Butler Yeats, Langston Hughes. He had found them in the indexes of first and last lines of poetry—indexes he hadn't even known existed—on a computer in the university library in Riverside. It was Emily Brontë she had sent to him last. It was the poetry of others, yes, but it was poetry she had loved.

* * *

Without the ID, he would never have recognized it two days later as hers:

> *. . . when he told me to lie down I said listen motherfucker I've laid down for you for ten years I'm not going to lay down again when he hit me my teeth broke my head snapped back against the wall I put my hands to my face and screamed I was going to cut his balls off before I'd lay down for him for him again when he pulled out the razor and told me to get down on the bed on my hands and knees or he'd cut my lips and nose off like he'd done to someone else I did it I did I got down on my hands and knees and he cut my legs I screamed I tried to get away but he was cutting into my stomach and I screamed cocksucker and then I couldn't scream anymore I couldn't see all I could feel was that tugging in my stomach and I let go and I died . . . .*

When the printer stopped, he stared. He didn't want to look at the words again. He didn't know what he was feeling. It was her, but it wasn't.

How stupid could he have been? *No* life was just poetry—a string of beautiful moments in time. Every life had pain and rage. She wasn't an angel. She was a human being, and as he realized this, he knew he loved her.

He read it again, trying to make his body stop shaking. It would not, and as it continued to shake he felt something shift inside him, the way it did when he'd look at the stars at night and feel free and then, all of a sudden, remember his mother and father.

When he began to cry, it amazed him. What it felt like—after so long.

As he copied the transmission by hand, he watched

another begin:

> *. . . a shudder in the loins the broken wall the burning roof and tower I remember the burning I was a little girl and the city burned for days in all the papers it was history and I was living it but I was a little girl do you remember the fires were you even born then?*

She'd been intelligent. That was clear to him now. She'd been well read. She'd been a romantic, but she'd known the harsher side of life, too. A man—a man she had known—had killed her. *Why?* The man had killed another woman, too—the same way he had killed her. Wasn't that what the transmission meant?

The computers had flagged her by now. They had put together *razor* and *I died* and all the rest multivariately, had a pattern, knew it was a murder. They'd be back-searching the transmissions for the ones with her ID, compiling rapidly.

That night, in the shack, Klinger tried to remember his father's eyes—not closed, in the coffin, but back before the Quake.

As he lay in the darkness, he saw for the first time that when he'd first started reading the transcripts, he had actually been looking for any "voice" that had sounded like his father's . . . or his mother's . . . and how insane that had been.

The Quake had happened five years before he became a fixer.

No ghost ever transmitted for more than a year.

The next morning, bright and early, he called Davis from the shack and told him he was sick and wouldn't be making it in. When Davis asked him how the problem was, Klinger told him he thought he'd finally gotten it straightened out. "Good,

Klinger," Davis said. "We've got a meeting tomorrow. Get well, guy." Davis would find out what was happening if Sheriff's Aviation records ever passed his desk; but they hadn't yet, and it was worth the risk.

She was broadcasting a lot now. There might be a dozen of transmissions on any given day. He wanted to be there for all of them.

The first came in at 11:00 A.M.

> . . . *who are you to tell me you hear me who are you to speak of love to me?*

He felt the chill again. All that was missing was his *name*. If she would only say it: *John. John K.*

He waited.

There were no more transmissions.

As all of the fixers waited the next morning for the meeting to start, Corley played with a portable digitizer in the folding chair beside him and a new kid, just out of Poly, leafed through a medical-benefits brochure. When the kid went out to use the bathroom, Klinger said to Corley:

"Corley, any way I could get a name to go with an ID?"

Corley looked at him.

"You really *are* fucking crazy. Don't you ever *listen* at these meetings? Reading a transcript is a fucking misdemeanor. Anything to do with an ID is a fucking felony!"

"Don't get so tracky about it, Corley. I just saw a TV episode where they had this guy, this fixer, finding out who a transmission belonged to and nothing happened to *him* . . . ."

"Sure, Klinger. You're out of your fucking mind."

Corley gave him a good-natured shove and got back to work diddling the portable as Davis began his check-in, the new kid following him around like a puppy, asking questions as if it were the end of the world.

When the meeting was over, Klinger said to Corley:
"Don't tell anyone I asked?"
"Asked what, asshole?"
Klinger gave him a smile. "Thanks."
"Jesus Christ, Klinger, don't *thank* me. That's as good as accessory."
Corley had been in law school once. He was a talker, knew a lot and had balls. Klinger liked him.
"Sorry, Corley."
"I don't hear you, Klinger. Go fix a mixer, will you?"

When he got back to the shack that evening, the cassette ribbon on the printer had torn and the ribbon alarm was screaming faintly. For one insane second he thought he'd lost transmissions, and then he remembered the PC.
The PC had recorded three. Something was garbling them, but it wasn't the Osterizer—it was something out there—and they were intact enough that he could for the first time *hear* her voice in them:

> *. . . you could have been the man who killed me you could have been (garbled) you could have been (garbled) and never said what I needed to hear in the rooms where (garbled) but you didn't you could have been one of a hundred who said nothing (garbled) when dreams meet and I have known rivers my love . . . .*

And:

> *. . . but sometimes I think of myself as Snow White and God or the man whose hand He chose to take me the swan taking me a sudden blow the great wings beating still above me I do not feel special I*

*have wings but these mean nothing I fly but it means
nothing nothing at all John K. . . .*

As he stared at his name—*John K.*—he knew he had been
right.

He knew what he needed to do. He had known it all along,
of course.

That night, on the cot, he dreamed about her again. In it
he saw her face clearly for the first time. Not a flower child's
face, willowy and ethereal, but the big hands of a country girl
from Oklahoma or Kansas, hands that opened a book of poetry
one day to find the voices of angels, which she memorized so
she would have them forever. Blue eyes, yes, but hair full of
grit, blown by the wind, killed by a boyfriend she would never,
in a fairer universe, have ever had.

Seeing her clearly now, he loved her even more.

And wasn't that why he had dreamed it?

The phone message was waiting for him the next day
when he returned to his apartment for some tools and his
checkbook. Davis wanted to see him immediately. *In his
office.*

The new machine had come, Klinger told himself. He
could feel it in his stomach and the feeling only got worse as
he drove the two hours to Central.

"One of your codes is being duped," Davis said.

"I don't understand."

"Someone's been duplicating the transmissions from
one of your IDs, Klinger. The system in Sacramento has
registered it. Have you noticed any tampering with the fence
or the gate, with the machine itself?"

"No, sir."

Davis stared at him. He was a big man who always looked

20

tired and he looked especially tired today.

"Have you noticed any tampering with the recorder itself?"

"No, sir. I'd have mentioned it to you if I had."

"Yes, you would have." Davis paused and looked out the window at the skyline. "I'm going to meet you out at the Mojave at three today. I'm going to have to have a JD investigator and one of their techs with me and they're going to have to ask you questions. They're going to have to give you a polygraph or a voice-stress analyzer, or both—I'm not sure which."

"Yes, sir."

Davis looked at him again. "What do you do out there, Klinger?"

"What do you mean, sir?"

"You know what I mean. What do you do with all that time?"

Klinger didn't answer.

"You like being alone out there? Is that it?"

"Yes."

"There's nothing wrong with a young man being out on the desert alone doing whatever he wants to do in a shack, as long as he's not breaking the law. You wouldn't be doing that, would you?"

"I don't understand . . . . Why would a *fixer* want to duplicate an ID's transmissions?"

Davis looked away.

"That's the question. There was a fixer last year in San Ysidro who made duplicates of a particular ID's transmissions and sold them—sold them to the people who were being incriminated. No one like that has approached you, have they, Klinger?"

"No, sir."

"I'm just asking. That's the kind of question you're going

21

to hear, Klinger."

Klinger was standing now. His arms were stiff, to stop the shaking; his knees locked. He moved his weight to one leg and balled his good hand, watching Davis's eyes.

The eyes stayed on his.

All he could think to say was, "Thank you, sir." The man meant well. He did feel thankful.

Davis nodded.

"If they don't find any tampering with the gate or the fence, they're going to ask you *a lot* of questions. They're going to check everyone who could've gotten a key to the gate and to the shack, but they're going to start with you. I'll be asking security staff if they know of any way the dupe alarm can be triggered by accident. I'll do what I can."

"Thank you, sir."

He took the Bell to the Witness. They'd find out about the chopper record and any sudden change on his part would look bad. He got there by noon, knowing that Davis had given him a head start, that the shack would be untouched. He removed the PC and the Osterizer from their connections, checked the connections for telltales of any kind, removed the hand-copied transmissions from the walls and from the floor (where he'd laid them out), put everything in a black plastic garbage bag and buried it a hundred meters from the shack, looking around for figures or cars in the distance. He'd considered tampering with the gate or the shack's door—Davis had practically told him to, hadn't he?—but decided against it.

Davis and the other two—both somber men—arrived an hour later. Klinger showed them the gate, the shack's door and window, and told them he'd walked along the fence the full three kilometers and hadn't found a thing. They asked him to walk it with them again. As they did, Davis kept looking at him.

Back in the shack, while one investigator began to dust the equipment for prints—using a pink powder Klinger had never seen before—the other began the questioning: Had he given anyone a key to the gate or the shack? Had anyone—anyone *not* working for Central—been asking him about the Witness recently? Had he seen anyone—ground vehicle, chopper, hikers—in the vicinity of the Witness over the last month? How was his social life? Did he have a girlfriend? Had anyone appeared in his life recently—over the last two months—if so, who? Did he go out drinking—if so, with whom? Did he know of any fixer who seemed "troubled"? Had anyone—any fixer—confided in him . . . about personal problems, resentment over work, financial worries?

When they asked him how he felt about his own life—his parents' death, his lack of family in the southern California area, his isolation in the desert—he stiffened and was sure they noticed.

They'd check his bank account, any credit purchases, and would make a visual inventory of any recent acquisitions like a car or boat or expensive home entertainment system. He *knew* this.

They would have someone watch him. He was their prime suspect, whether they were sure he was guilty or not.

When they pulled out the polygraph—and right after it, the Mark IV voice-stress analyzer—and began to ask him a list of very precise questions like, "Do you harbor any resentment toward your employers?", "Do you have financial problems you feel are not your fault?", "Do you find your work unchallenging?", "Has the man who has been loaning you the Sherriff's Aviation helicopter been asking you for anything in return, hinting that there might be something he'd like?" and finally, "Have you, in whatever fashion and for whatever reason, been duplicating the transmissions being received by this Witness?"—he stiffened again but kept repeating silently to himself the one message he had composed so long ago for her. The message he would, somehow, send to her.

As they were leaving, Davis nodded to him and said they would be getting in touch with him again when they had interviewed others at Central—other fixers.

"Is he staying here?" the tall investigator asked.

"I don't know." Davis turned to him. "It might be a good idea, Klinger, if you didn't stay here tonight . . . ." Davis was doing his best to smile.

"I'd like to stay and work on the printer, sir. The ribbon keeps breaking, and the sound-synthesizer on the alarm is weak. Would that be all right?"

"Is that all right?" Davis asked the men.

"I don't know . . . ." the tall one said.

"He'll be out of here in a couple of hours, won't you, Klinger?"

"It shouldn't take any longer than that, sir."

"All right," the shorter one said, frowning. "Just don't touch the dust."

"And, Mr. Klinger," the other one added, "make sure that from now on the arrangement with the SA chopper goes through your supervisor."

"Yes, sir."

Outside, as he walked them to their car, Davis fell behind and said: "I happen to think you're innocent, Klinger." He let the words hang, the sound of sand, of gravel below them. "But this is a *very* big case. You need to understand that. The ID was a nobody, but the people she touched—one of them anyway—had fingers up into Vegas."

Klinger wanted to ask *Who was she?*—wanted more than anything in the world to ask this—but instead found himself saying stupidly, "So it was a murder?"

"Don't ask, Klinger. I just wanted you to know how big it is, that I don't happen to think you're involved. *That's all."*

"Yes, sir."

As he spoke, his father's face came to him and the old feeling with it.

"By the way, Klinger," the voice was saying beside him, "the arrangement with the Bell is fine. I talked to McKinney about it today. But *do* let me know from now on when you're planning to use it . . . ."

They walked together to the car. Klinger wanted to say something, but didn't know what. He could see them—his father's eyes; he wanted to tell Davis something, and couldn't find the words.

As he made his way back to the shack, the sound of wheels turning on gravel somewhere behind him, he realized that they never would have let him stay—never would have spoken to him as they had at the end—*if he hadn't passed the tests—*

That he had indeed somehow passed them—

As if she had been there helping him, helping him lie, because she wanted it too:

That he be free to find what he needed—that he be allowed to speak to her.

When the car was out of sight, he dug up the bag and brought it back to the shack. Reconnecting the PC, he set the alarm to her code again, and began to wait. When nothing had come by sunset, he lay down on the cot, wondering if the just-dead could see the stars, if they could see anything other than what they had already seen during their lives. When he fell asleep it was easier than he'd thought it would be.

He awoke at dawn, checked the printer, unplugged the PC, and put everything in an old backpack he hadn't used in months. McKinney needed the Bell back at 6:30—for a routine check. He had thirty minutes.

He got there with ten minutes to spare, using them in the main office to make a xerox of the handcopied transmissions so that he'd have a second set—so that no one could take them *all* from him regardless of what happened.

No one paid any attention to him at the machine.

McKinney pointed the way to the lockers, giving him a key and joking about desert bums with their backpacks full of drugs. When he'd stashed the backpack, Klinger sat with him in his office and tried to stay awake. All he wanted was to get the bag back out of the locker, get in his car, and return to his apartment.

"In Nam they had a gunship, Klinger, a chopper that could turn a hamlet into matchsticks—one round per second per square foot. They called them Vulcan mini-cannons, Klinger, and I've got one of them sons-of-bitches right here."

McKinney was beginning to blur. Klinger closed his eyes.

"Now, you can't go flying over cities with a mini-cannon, Klinger—that's against every law there is—but we've got one assigned to whatever chopper we want as 'Riot Control Study #14.' " McKinney laughed, the crow's-feet crinkling at the corners of his eyes. "I take it out to Joshua every Saturday and do a little *controlling* of the jackrabbits there . . . How's this Saturday look for you, Klinger?"

"I don't know, McKinney . . . ."

"Shit, Klinger! You *owe* me a Saturday. You keep stringing me along like this"— he laughed again, but it was serious—"and I'll think you don't love me. What about it? *Saturday.* The floor is covered with them. You'll be the only fixer in candy-assed Justice who's ever fired a Vulcan."

Klinger got up unsteadily, feeling he was going to throw up.

"I'll have to let you know . . . . Something's come up at Central and they've got me on call. Something's been going down."

"You steal something?" McKinney was grinning.

"Yeah. A Witness—" Klinger was smiling back.

"—piece by piece," McKinney finished for him.

It was one of their jokes, Klinger remembered foggily. *If they don't pay you enough, Klinger,* McKinney had said one day, *you can always steal a Witness—*

—piece by piece, Klinger had said.

"They hassle you too much, boy," McKinney was saying, "you can always use the Vulcan on them." He grinned. "Saturday?"

"I'll do my best, McKinney."

When he got back to the apartment, he looked around, saw nothing had been touched, and rolled a joint, smoking it on the porch and looking out at the sky high above the buildings. Then he went back in to clean the grease from the pink plastic of his prosthesis. The grease wouldn't come off. He tried to cut his own hair in the bathroom mirror. It looked worse. Nothing was going right. Nothing at all. He put the backpack under the sink with the PC and the Osterizer in it and then flattened both the hand-copied transmissions of her voice and the Xeroxes he'd made so that they would fit inside the pillowslip on the one pillow he used at night.

That evening, he dreamed of touching her breasts, making her gasp and hold on to him hard, as if he could protect her from everything in the world.

That night the men broke into his apartment.

They began in his living room. He woke to the sound. While one kept at it, turning things over, the other one appeared in his bedroom doorway and kept the light on him, blinding him like some animal caught in headlights. Even in the stupor, even in the blinding light, he knew who they were. One found the backpack easily under the sink. The other one grabbed him, pulled him off the bed and laid him down on the floor, kneeling over him. This one—the one he could see— wore a dark leather jacket, the kind the LA gangs liked. The blinding light went away. The bedroom light came on. The man by the doorway wore a nice suit. Both of them were wearing goggles—not unlike the kind McKinney had shown him, the kind you wore for seeing in the dark, but smaller, lighter-weight.

He didn't try to move, but the kneeling man hit him anyway, the blur of the hand passing into Klinger's brain and making him cry out. He'd never be able to identify them with the goggles—which was the point. Or one of them.

"What we want to know," the man in the nice suit standing by the door said calmly, "is where the *duplicates* are and who exactly you're making them for . . . ."

Before he could answer the kneeling man hit him again, this time on the ear, and Klinger made another sound.

"I don't—"

The hand came again—on the same ear—and he knew they weren't going to let it go, that they didn't need some voice-stress analyzer to feel sure they knew who had made the copies, and *why.*

"So you don't get paid enough. So someone approaches you one day and tells you how much he's going to pay you to dupe some ID—"

"I really don't—"

He was pulled from the floor and put against the wall. He was held with one forearm while the other arm, with its fist, broke his nose, then struck his left eye, then hit him just below where he imagined his heart was, moving lower and lower as he blurted:

"Just . . . the handwritten stuff."

He had to repeat it because his mouth was a mess, because the man was hitting him even as he tried to get the words out.

"What the fuck does that mean?" the man in the nice suit asked.

Klinger didn't know, so he thought hard. "I don't have them here . . . . I've got them at the Witness . . . ."

The man holding him let him fall, and as Klinger lay on the floor he felt—as if it were happening to someone else—his lungs pulling at wet air in a cage too small for them. The man by the door gave him a moment to catch his breath.

"You haven't made a delivery yet?"

"No." Something was drooling from his mouth. He wiped at it with his good hand.

"We're in a hurry, John," the man in the suit said. "*You understand.*" Below the insect-like eyes of the goggles there was a grin.

He couldn't get up. He was sliding back down the wall, taking forever.

"I . . .buried them," he said.

"We'd like you to dig them up."

What scared him most was that they might see the pillowslip, how fat it was, and he would get sick, and, as he got sick, having found what they wanted, they would simply kill him or put him in the hospital for a long time and he wouldn't be able to do it. What he needed to do.

He was sitting up at last.

"There's a pickup . . . the day after tomorrow."

"We don't understand, John."

"At the station . . . the Mojave station . . . . At ten A.M."

"The buyer will be alone?"

"That's . . . what he said."

"Who?"

"I don't . . . know. I was contacted by phone . . . by

telephone."

The man with the leather jacket was moving toward him.

"Jesus Christ," Klinger heard himself say. "He told me he'd pay . . . . I didn't care *who he was.*"

The man in the leather jacket looked at the man in the nice suit.

The man in the nice suit sighed. The man in the leather jacket didn't move.

"We really hope," the man in the suit said, "that you're not *fucking* with us."

Klinger shook his head, the pain making pretty explosions.

"If you can keep our little meeting a secret, John," the man in the suit was saying, "we'll have fewer problems, John."

They were turning to leave.

"They teach you this in law school?" Klinger heard himself say.

The man in the leather jacket looked at the man in the suit. The man in the suit looked back. The man in the leather jacket walked over to Klinger where he sat on the floor and hit him in the nose, which was suddenly heavy enough to pull him into a darkness where there was no woman, no blue eyes, no brush of his fingertips on her soft breasts to make her hold him tightly against the pain of the world.

When he awoke, it was night. He didn't want to move but he made himself get up, find the bathroom, and, fumbling, relieve himself. He took three extra-strength Excedrin IB— the stuff with caffeine—and somehow got into his car and drove to the emergency room at Corona Community.

When they asked him how he'd gotten it, he told them a mugger on Tyler Avenue. When they asked him if he'd filed a police report, he told them *yes.* They called his HMO for approval of the treatment and took two hours to bandage his nose.

He filled the prescription for codeine in the pharmacy at the hospital and went home, setting the alarm for noon.

His face felt huge, as if two people were wearing it. He drove to Sherriff's Aviation fighting the edgy dreaminess of codeine, and when he arrived, McKinney took one look at him and laughed:

"Jesus Christ, who worked *you* over?"

"I need a gun, McKinney." He could still taste the blood, though there shouldn't be any. He wondered if his gums were bleeding, a tooth, a tooth turning gray as it died. "I drive out to the Witness last night because Davis asks me to and some ethnic asshole jumps me at the gas station. *I need a gun.*"

"No reason we can't arrange it, Klinger," McKinney said at last.

He had him in the snackbar, showing him off—bandage and all—over their usual cup of coffee. Everyone was looking, even the veterans who'd seen a lot worse. McKinney was having a great time. "God Almighty. The Justice Department of this fine nation tells us we're supposed to give you boys whatever you need, and, as it happens, my boy, I've got a *personal weapon*—a beautiful Colt Phantom—sitting gathering dust in a case. No paperwork. No fuss. How does that sound? A gift from your old friend McKinney to his best friend Klinger...." Less loudly, he asked: "Did Davis see you like this?"

"No.... I phoned him."

The old man shook his head, whistling. "You got the Phantom as of fourteen hundred hours today, Klinger, but try not to grease anyone. Just wave it at them. When are you going to get that nose fixed?"

"Davis gave me two days off."

"That was white of him."

"I want to see your mini-cannon do its thing, McKinney," Klinger said.

McKinney sat back and frowned. "You sure got a fucking weird sense of timing, Klinger." He was quiet for a moment. "I don't know . . . ."

"You're always talking about it, McKinney. I'm in the mood, *now.*"

McKinney squirmed a little.

"Me and the old lady are supposed to go to Lake Perris with her brother's six kids and I'm supposed to get off early. She's *not* going to like this at all."

"Talk's cheap, McKinney. You want to show me what it can do—I may not be in the mood later."

McKinney stared at him and grinned finally. "You want to get it out of your system, right? Every jackrabbit some ethnic son-of-a-bitch, right?"

"Right."

"Okay. We take the Huey. And get that nose fixed. It's enough to make a person puke."

McKinney laughed. Klinger laughed, too, though it hurt.

The sky was clear as crystal and Klinger wasn't paying much attention to the rabbits two hundred feet below. The distinctive whump-whump-whump of the Huey filled the air and the Vulcan was a mechanical belt-fed cannister that fired a hundred M-60 rounds a second. When they weren't knocking rabbits away like rag-dolls, the rounds were raising little plumes of dust, sand and gravel. The rabbits kicked and kept kicking, lying on their sides, becoming specks as the Huey flew on. McKinney made him listen to stories about "the highlands," the "offensive of '68," "armor at Lang Vei," and "black syphilis." Klinger asked him every question he could about the Vulcan and McKinney answered every one. When Klinger asked if he could fly, McKinney said sure. When he asked if he could fire the Vulcan—why were they up here if he wasn't supposed to fire the thing?—McKinney stalled, but said yes at last, and Klinger felt the gun roar like the biggest zipper in the world. He had to fly with his one good hand, but the grip and trigger for the Vulcan fit his prosthetic crab perfectly. Even McKinney was impressed. They got back at five on the button, Klinger took another codeine for his face, and McKinney handed him the Phantom proudly. Klinger thanked him and slapped him on the back with his good hand. The old man seemed sorry—truly sorry—that their little adventure was over.

Driving ten miles up the Santa Ana wash, Klinger parked the Honda in a stand of eucalyptus, the backpack with its PC and Osterizer and the pillowslip full of its paper beside him. The sun would wake him at dawn. It always did in the desert.

He didn't dream about her.

He knew he wouldn't until it was over.

He got to Sheriff's Aviation at eight the next morning. McKinney never arrived until nine. The vehicle-release sergeant at the helipad looked at his nose as if wanting to ask, but only said: "You want the *Huey,* Klinger?"

"Yes, sir. We took it out yesterday with the Vulcan. Someone in Tidwell's office has this theory, McKinney's supposedly testing it, but I don't think his heart's in it. He wants me to make the run for him today ...." Klinger sighed—as if to say *This is what you do for a good friend*—and forced a smile.

The man nodded, unsure. He picked up the phone, pushed the buttons, waited, and set it back down slowly. "You'll be needing a cartridge belt . . .?"

Time seemed to stop. It was the belt. McKinney and all

33

his eccentricities were one thing, but a belt to a *kid?* Klinger sighed again and said:

"Why do I get the feeling McKinney didn't get the paperwork done on it?"

"Because he didn't," the sergeant said, but the confiding tone was there: *We both know what McKinney is like, don't we.*

"Shit." Klinger sighed again.

The sergeant looked at him for a moment and finally sighed too.

"All right . . . I'll consign you a belt, but make sure he fills out the A-202 sheet when he gets in."

"Thanks, sir."

"Have a good run," the man said, and then added: "Just don't shoot anyone."

It was the best joke the man could think of that early in the morning. Klinger laughed at it.

As he left, he knew she had been there with him again. Even this—the belt—had gone too easily.

As he neared the Witness, backpack and pillowslip beside him, the sun blinded him for a moment to the east and he banked, pulling over the access road that drove for ten straight kilometers across the Mojave floor. It was 9:45. Two minutes later he spotted the car below him—the gray-blue paint job and black tire walls of a Justice car. He pulled ahead, squinting toward the Witness, and when he was almost on top of it saw the second car—a big white Seville parked behind the shack, front and rear license plates missing.

Two figures were out, standing beside it.

Banking south, he watched the two closely, and when he was sure they had seen the Huey, he nosed toward them just as McKinney had shown him to, firing.

The sound of the gigantic zipper filled the air.

He let it chew the sand and gravel ten meters from the car

for three full seconds while the two men dove, scrambled, looking like roadrunners with absolutely no place to go.

When he zeroed in on the car at last, it took only a second. The car collapsed, the doors blowing sideways, the roof disappearing, fragments of metal flying after the men wherever they tried to run.

He banked, circling them, and knew at last why McKinney liked those jackrabbits on the desert floor.

He chased them. He sent short bursts every couple of seconds right behind them and the faster they ran, the slower they seemed to go, tiring, circling back toward the shack because there was really no other place to go. One of them fell as he fired. The figure jerked. Little plumes rose around it. The figure began to crawl on its hands and knees, stopped, fell over, jerked some more, and finally lay still.

Klinger wondered what the man would transmit over the next few days, weeks and months, what word or phrase a Witness somewhere would pick up in the neutrinos and transcribe.

And then the bullets hit me?

I tried to crawl, but couldn't, and then I died.

Just like her: *And then I died.*

Klinger thought of the message he had composed—the one for her, the big-boned girl he could only meet in dreams, because that was what life—and death—had dealt them. He repeated it to himself for the thousandth time as he tracked the other running figure, firing until it too was down, and, without looking at the body, flying on, putting the Huey down at last not far from the shack.

When the rotor wash had died away and he could see again, he watched the cloud of dust from the company car getting larger on the access road.

The car stopped. None of the doors opened. With the backpack and pillowslip under his bad arm and the Colt Phantom in his good hand, he got out of the Huey, stood for a moment, and took aim. Gravel flew a few meters in front of the blue-gray car and the car shot into reverse, fishtailing wildly until it had turned and was speeding back down the access road. Stopping about a kilometer away, it turned back around to face him like a bull. They were probably radioing for backup.

He went inside.

With the PC reconnected and the handwritten pages and the Xeroxes—all he had of her—laid out on the floor, he propped open the door and waited.

There was one transmission—only one:

> ... but when I waked I saw that I saw not cold
> in the earth and the deep snow piled above thee
> come live with me and be my love John who knows
> me so well . . . .

He did not understand. How could she be answering him? He had never sent the message. And now he never would.

He wanted to cry, but found he could not.

He heard the bullhorn before he heard the choppers. And then the choppers drowned the bullhorn out and he got up to go to the door.

A black-and-white sat a few hundred yards down the access road, doors open, a bullhorn—what he assumed was a high-powered bullhorn—peeking around one of them.

For some reason they imagined he could hear the thing over the noise of the choppers and he had to point at his ear again and again—standing in plain sight in the doorway—before they got the idea and radioed for the choppers to stand back.

"Klinger!" the bullhorn said. It wasn't Davis. *"We know what you've got and we know what you can do. This is as far as it needs to go. If we can reach some agreement before the SWAT boys get here, things will go, a lot easier. Signal if you understand."*

Klinger waved the Phantom.

"We see the weapon, Klinger. We've received your signal. We want to know what you want—we want to hear what's on your mind."

He wondered if it was too soon for the marksmen to be there. He didn't have hostages. He wasn't even in the Huey with the Vulcan. They actually had, he realized, no idea what he really "had" or what he wanted. They really didn't.

"I want to talk to Davis," he shouted.

The words were lost in the wind.

Someone had binoculars. He could see them. He could see something shaped like a dish too.

"We can't hear you, Klinger," the bullhorn said.

"Davis!" he shouted. *"I want to talk to Davis."*

"You want to talk to Mack Davis?"

The dish was a directional mike.

"Yes!" he shouted.

They were talking to each other now. One of them had to be a negotiator.

"Davis is a good man, Klinger," the bullhorn said at last. *"He's treated you well—just like a father. He's a true friend."*

Davis was with them. That was obvious. The negotiator knew what he was doing.

"Yes. He's the one I want to talk to."

"What?"

"Davis is the one I want to talk to."

There was more talking behind the open car doors, figures scurrying. He could see Davis stand up, two uniforms shielding him.

"Davis is your one true friend, Klinger. Remember that."

"Yes, he's treated me well!" Klinger had, he discovered, started to cry at last.

Everything fell silent at that moment. The wind was gone.

"Davis is the only one I'll talk to," Klinger said again, sure that they could read his lips—even if the mike couldn't pick him up. They had a lip-reader. With binoculars. They had to.

Then, because he thought he heard the ID alarm go off on the printer, he went inside again.

He'd been staring at the printer for what seemed like forever—it hadn't been the alarm at all, but something else, a sound from somewhere in the desert—when he heard Davis's voice on the bullhorn.

Stepping outside, wondering if a rifle round would hit him in the forehead before he could say a word and he would join her where words didn't matter—he shouted: *"I can't talk like this, Davis. You gotta be in the shack. I'm not going to hurt you, but you've got to be in the shack with me."*

More discussion behind car doors and then, through the bullhorn, Davis answered: *"I'm coming in, Klinger. I am not armed and I really don't think you want to hurt me. I think you care about me as much as I care about you."* More negotiator words. *"I think this is something that's simply gotten out of hand. We're good friends and I'm coming in because I think you want and need a friend right now."*

"I won't hurt you," Klinger found himself saying. He said it quietly. His eyes were blurred. He didn't want them to be.

When the big man, sweating in the heat and his own

nervousness, was inside, Klinger couldn't look at him, couldn't keep the Phantom aimed at him. He was looking at the printer instead, while the big man—he could hear him doing it—sat down slowly and carefully on the old cot. He was, Klinger was sure, looking at the hand-copied pages and the dark Xeroxes laid out so neatly on the floor.

"Klinger?"

"Yes."

"What do you want? People have gotten hurt, but I think I know who they are, and the people out there in the cars and choppers are willing to agree. They just need to *understand.* If they aren't able to understand, Klinger, and understand *soon,* they're going to have to come in. If they have to come in, they're going to have to view this as a hostage situation."

"I want to stay here," Klinger said, his back still turned. It wasn't what he wanted to say, but he couldn't think.

"That's what you want to tell me?"

"No . . . ."

"Did you make those dupes, Klinger?"

"Yes."

"Is that why you wanted me here—to tell me *why?*"

"Yes . . . ."

"I'd like to listen—"

"I didn't want to lose her, sir," Klinger heard himself saying. "You don't know what she is like."

He could hear the big man shift his weight on the cot, searching for the right words—his own, or someone else's.

"She's *dead,* Klinger," Davis said at last.

Klinger looked at him. "No, she's not, sir. She's been answering me."

The big man was shaking his head, blinking. Klinger could see it.

"She's dead and she's *sending,* Klinger. That's all. That's what we do, Klinger: We listen to what the dead send us."

"Could you tell me her name?"

Davis closed his eyes. Klinger looked away.

"Please," Klinger said.

"I don't think so, John. I don't think that would help . . . ."

Klinger took a deep breath. "Please tell them that's what I want. I want to know her whole name and I want the right equipment to transmit a message to her. Tell them that."

The big man didn't seem to be breathing. He was shaking his head. "Klinger . . . Klinger . . . ." The big man took a breath at last. "Her name was Semples...Linda Semples. She was a *black prostitute,* Klinger. A *smash* junkie. Her pimp killed her. He killed her because she was threatening to tell the police about his lab, his friends, the distribution from Victorville to Vegas. She *fucked for money,* Klinger. Or she did once. She was getting old. She was forty years old and the only thing that kept her in business, Klinger—I'm sorry to have to say this, but you've got to understand and accept it or this isn't going to end—was the kinds of things she'd do in bed with a man—"

Davis was looking at his hands, which were clenched white. He would not look up. Klinger knew it must have felt cruel for him to say these things, and he was not a cruel man. Klinger realized then how much he loved the man.

"You're doing this over a dead hooker, Klinger—a dead hooker with a mean pimp. You're doing this over a forty-year-old whore who liked honkies like you about as far as she could piss. I think you can be helped, Klinger, but it's got to stop *here.* She's dead, Klinger. You didn't really understand this—you didn't know a thing about her—otherwise, you wouldn't have done all of this, am I right?"

Klinger was looking at him. He was holding the Phantom, not aiming it, just holding it.

"I'd like you to leave now, sir," Klinger said. "I'll be staying here waiting for her next transmission. I don't know how long I'll be here, but I'll signal when I'm ready to leave.

I'd appreciate it if you'd tell them."

* * *

Davis got up slowly, as if reluctant to leave. He opened his mouth to say something, but nothing came out. He wasn't blinking now. Neither of them was.

When the big man was gone, Klinger sat down at the card table, closed his eyes and recited to himself once again the message, letting the fingers on his good hand move as if he were typing on a keyboard somewhere:

> *. . . to the woman who slept under a bridge who loves poetry who dreams I know you better than you were ever known in life I love you please answer me John K. . . .*

His fingers typed it again and again—although there weren't any keys—although there never would be.

When the door to the shack flew open and three men with shotguns exploded into the little room, Klinger's head was down on the card table, almost asleep. He managed to raise the Phantom just enough to let them know what he wanted them to do, and they obliged.

The blast from the weapon to his right raised him in the air, filled his left shoulder with a winter frost, and set him down on the floor not far from the card table. Lying there, looking up at the corrugated metal of the ceiling and feeling the frost move into his arms and legs, he knew the ID alarm on the printer had never gone off. That was the terrible thing. The pain in his shoulder was nothing.

She had *moved on.*

They always do, he remembered someone—Tompai or Corley or Whirley—saying years, years ago.

He thought of the fixer Nakamura who had fallen in love with a ghost and finally gone insane.

Then he let them help him up in all the blood and get him to the car.

That night, in the medical ward of the county jail, he had the very last dream. Her skin was dark, of course, and she was older, much older than he was. But how could it matter? They talked. They talked about his life and about hers and when they were through, they both fell silent. They didn't touch. They didn't touch each other.

This is the last, she told him.

I know, he said.

You didn't need a machine at all . . . .

I know that now.

I love you, too, John. I always have, John, she said. *And I always will.*

When he repeated the same words back to her—feeling them more than he had ever felt them in his life—he awoke in the darkness of the hospital room and saw clearly how it would all go.

He would heal. There would be a trial. There would be a few months in *another* kind of ward. Then there would be a new job, a very different kind, and, in the end, everything would be right again.

The Black Lotus

by Simon Ings

Simon D. Ings is one of several young British writers who began selling their short fiction in the late 1980s, injecting a burst of energy into British science fiction. His stories have been published by *Interzone,* and in the anthologies *Other Edens 3* and *Zenith 2.* His first novel, *Hot Head,* was published by Grafton in 1992, and he recently completed a second novel, *In the City of the Iron Fish.*

"The Black Lotus" is a believable and terrifying story about the unforeseen consequences of a seemingly harmless biochemical experiment.

THE BLACK LOTUS

Simon Ings

We buried Rudy this morning. It was drizzling: the sky was uniformly leaden.

When the vicar invited Rudy's mother to look at the flowers, Tina Strossner edged forward to the lip of the grave and peered short-sightedly at the daffodils some children had thrown upon the coffin. Then, out the corner of her eye, she noticed the bouquets, ready to lay upon the grave, and she realized that these were the flowers she was supposed to be admiring.

She stepped towards them and her foot slipped on the edge of the grave. Soil fell with a hollow sound upon the coffin.

One cannot help but remember such moments. Long after the eulogies have faded, countless trivial incidents remain. We uncover them again by accident, and with a twinge of embarrassment, as one might remove a crumpled paper poppy from a winter overcoat.

After the service Tina came over to me, to thank me for being there.

"Sorry I was late," I said. "The train was canceled."

"How are you getting back?"

"I've a return ticket."

"Drive back with me."

I looked at her. I could not read her expression.

"I think the weather's clearing," she said; she was trying to encourage me.

"I suppose," I replied. I didn't want to talk. I was feeling light-headed, confused. The fugues had started up again.

"Please." She took hold of my hands. "It would be good to have company."

Tina's sister had laid on a simple funeral meal for us. We ate outside, in the back garden. Above us, the clouds broke up and dissolved. She and I sat by the pool. It was covered in green plastic strawberry netting, "to keep the hedgehogs from drowning." The lawn was thin and brown. Tina's sister had sown expensive seed, but it had proved too delicate, and unsuited to the sandy soil. It was choked in moss, itself brown and dead. You could crumble it to dust with your fingers.

Tina took me by the arm as I was absently digging up a little pile of moss. "Maureen?"

I smiled at her. "It's all right," I said. "I'm awake."

Tina smiled back, embarrassed. "Sorry."

She was worried for me. She shared my medical condition, and so she knew what to look for in the onset of a fugue.

About a year ago—it was the week before Tina was due to go to the Maudsley mental hospital in Camberwell—I traveled to Kingston-upon-Thames to visit her. I smelled the bonfire long before I reached her house: above it, a bulb of black smoke hung motionless against heavy gray clouds.

Tina and I had tea in the garden. The neighbors came over to complain about the bonfire: "All times of day and night!" Mr. Campbell shouted across the fence. "All times of day and night! I'm ringing the council! I am! Ring the council I shall!"

"Why do you say everything twice?" Tina retorted; and, louder, leaning on the arm of her deck chair so that it wobbled

45

dangerously, "Why is everything said twice by you? Like Gertrude bloody Stein."

"For God's sake, Tina," I muttered.

"Come on," said Tina; she stood up and marched to the kitchen door. "Give me a hand with these boxes."

"Those black orchids—Rudy reckons their pollen's dangerous," I explained to her, as we built up her bonfire. "It affects the limbic system."

She showed no interest.

When the bonfire was ready I stood, looking at it: folders full of old papers, broken furniture, split cushions, lace nets, string bags, tattered music hall programs. All this junk was so much a part of life in Tina's house, I couldn't quite grasp that soon it would be gone.

Tina danced round the bonfire, shaking white spirit out of a clear plastic bottle.

"Tina," I said to her finally, exasperated, "it'll burn anyway. It's all cloth and paper." Even as I spoke, I didn't quite believe what was happening. "Look, are you sure about this?"

"Don't interfere."

I stared at her. "You just asked me to help you."

"Don't interfere." Tina reached into her apron pocket for her matchbox. The fire caught very quickly. Why did everything burn so fast? Why did it boil away so eagerly?

I knew I would be next.

You wake up and it is late: you have ten minutes to dress and get out the door to be in time for work. You are still half asleep. You only properly come to on the bus, roused by the scent of wet mackintoshes, perhaps, or a mother saying to her son, "I won't tell you again. I won't tell you again," and even then you're not properly awake, and you feel desperate for a second, because you think she must be talking to you.

How did you get out the house, asleep as you were? You have no memory of your actions. How did you get here?

There is a part of the brain called the hippocampal gyrus. It controls stereotyped action. Some stereotyped actions are built in—smiling, crying, frowning. Others are learned. Tying shoelaces. Washing. Opening and closing doors. Simple domestic routines. Rudy, Tina's son, explained it all to me that first afternoon in the Lyceum.

I met Rudy early in 1988, by accident. He was walking out of McDonald's on the Strand when I sneezed, my ladder slipped, and I dropped a hanging basket on his head. It seemed churlish, when he came round, not to accept his offer of a drink.

Rudy was a biochemist. He had just been awarded a professorship for his thesis on the biochemical processes of pollen allergies. It amused him that my own mild hay fever had been responsible for his accident.

He was applying for money to investigate compulsive behavior.

"You perform simple actions more or less unconsciously," he explained to me. "But sometimes the program gets stuck. You can't stop yourself from performing some simple action, over and over. Think of Lady Macbeth."

"You mean her compulsive washing."

"My grandmother couldn't stop washing herself either," he said, proudly. "This was back in the fifties: no one understood the condition then—they lacked a label for it. The treatments were very primitive."

"She couldn't stop washing herself?"

Rudy shrugged. "It's one of the more common variants."

"What happened to her?"

"She died in 1967. Another drink?"

"Why are you working on this?" I asked, struggling to make small talk out of the unpromising material he'd fed me.

47

"I mean, you're a biochemist. This sounds more like a psychological problem to me, rather than a biochemical one. After all, Lady Macbeth washes her hands repeatedly because of her guilt, not because of her glands—or is it bad of me to quote that back at you?"

Rudy laughed. "No, you're right. There are usually good external reasons why people develop this kind of abnormality. But to develop any drug treatments for the condition, we've got to understand what changes occur in the brain."

I smiled ruefully. "Treating the symptoms again, doctor?"

"Professor." he smiled, then he looked at me oddly. "You're not one of these *holistic* types, I hope."

I run an interior landscaping company. When I met Rudy I'd been in business for myself for about six months, hanging baskets in burger joints. The next few years were kind to me, and thanks to Thatcher and the late eighties boom, my employees and I now tend the bonsais throughout the Square Five Mile.

I started up business in Kingston. Some of the main streets here are pedestrianized. This wasn't good for us at all. Try delivering to a loading bay without giving at least a week's notice. The worst, according to Tracy, who drives the van, are the Corps of Commissionaires—"old geezers with gold braid" who've been invalided out of the army. Tracy had had words with one of them, and I was in our office composing a letter of apology to the Corps of Commissionaires when Rudy came in, bearing a jar, and floating inside the jar, a black lotus.

"*Nelimbo nucifera nigra,*" he announced, voluptuously. He set the jar carefully down on my desk. The scent made me sneeze. It was sweet and appetizing, heavy, but with none of the cabbagy undertaste which plagues most rich scents. I wiped my nose and bent to stare at the dark, variegated purple leaves, the fleshy, pure black petals. "Is it real?"

"Or have I been playing with the food dye again?" Rudy teased me. "No, it's real enough. It's a bribe, you see: I want you to have dinner with me tonight."

Rudy had something to celebrate, and no significant other to celebrate it with. He had staggered away from the Lyceum the day before, reeling under a mixed cider-hanging-basket headache, to find a letter on his desk.

It was from a drug company, and they were offering him the funding he needed to undertake work on compulsive behavior disorder.

He took me to a cheap Thai restaurant in Piccadilly and ordered for us both. I drank Tiger beer and he talked about his work, and because he was so obviously excited, I did my best not to show my ignorance or, later, my boredom.

"I've somehow to disturb the workings of the parahippo-campal gyrus so as to trigger compulsive behavior."

The peanut sauce on my vegetables in batter was thin and gritty. There was a sort of upside-down pudding of beef, steeped in cayenne, but by then I'd discovered that Rudy practiced vivisection, and this rather dulled my appetite.

"I reckon it's all to do with micelles."

"Come again?"

"Micelles. Sorry. Tiny globules of soap. I reckon soap in the parahippocampal gyrus may cause compulsive behavior disorder."

My memories from this point on are all jumbled up. I recall a rubbery vermicelli and a dish of jackfruit swamped in sugar syrup.

Thanks to later events, I remember Rudy's explanation of MIF—the main ingredient in the experiments he was planning. "It's a long-chain molecule which ionizes in a neutral solution to form micelles. Its job is to 'stick' macrophages to the site of an infection." Because Rudy suffered very mildly from hay fever, he would prick his skin with a needle dipped in pollen and then draw off fluid from the site of reaction with a hypodermic. By directly administering this fluid to the diencephala of his laboratory subjects, Rudy would be able to raise their micelle levels. "You see," he explained, "the swelling round the site of infection is caused by a long-chain hormone called MIF—"

"I see."

"—and MIF ionizes in a neutral solution to form micelles!"

"Great."

We left the restaurant and I started to say goodbye, but he shushed me. He had something to say.

It was an apology—a very sincere and self-deprecating apology.

"I remembered it being better than that," he said, meaning the restaurant. "Forgive me. And I've been a pig, I've talked shop all night. This was a rotten evening."

It seemed churlish, after all that, not to let him kiss me goodnight. When he let me go I stumbled. I'd drunk too much beer, and I couldn't work out how. I didn't know whether to be angry that Rudy had got me drunk, or apologetic to have got so pissed at his expense.

He lived nearby, of course—I should have been prepared for that—in a flat off Malet Street. Would I like a coffee? I couldn't work out just how disingenuous Rudy was being. The only way I could satisfy my curiosity was to go along with him and find out.

The front entrance to Rudy's flat gave onto a long narrow corridor. Beyond it, above and behind the shops which fronted the street, lay a vast complex of corridors and vertiginous stairwells.

Rudy led me up a spiral staircase. The wooden steps creaked. The rail shook. It was poorly varnished. I ran my hand along it and I caught my palm on a nail.

Rudy opened the door to his flat. There was a ladder blocking the hall, so I had to squeeze through after him. The hall was paneled in wood, very dark and dirty. I bumped into him. He just stood there, not moving or looking at me, waiting—I don't know for what. After a minute or two of this he said, "Where would you like to go?"

I laughed. Already I was nervous. I said, "Well, where is there?"

After a moment he said, "There's my bedroom," and he took my hand and squeezed it, hard.

Rudy's experiments went well. As winter approached, he came to rely on his mother for sources of pollen. She gave him some black lotuses of his own, because lotuses produce pollen all the year round.

I liked Tina. She was mad. Her living room was cluttered to bursting with the strangest bric-a-brac: an ornamental china brandy cask with a brass tap, a tasseled table lamp with a bakelite stand, an elephant's foot, a rusted pump, countless jugs of no particular vintage or interest, a brass diving helmet with little grilled windows, a set of traffic lights, all of the filters illuminated—the red filter had the word STOP stenciled on it in black paint—a hand plane, wicker baskets, a hand-painted paper lantern, some crepe Christmas decorations, a stuffed fox in a glass cabinet, two workman's lamps, a straw hat, a Chinese dragon mask, some African musical instruments, a pair of polished bull horns, a paper model of an albatross, a policeman's helmet (Tina's great great grandmother was a particularly pugnacious suffragette and this was her trophy), and, screwed into the door of the room, a plaque which read *The English and Foreign Governesses Institute.*

The wallpaper was plastered in playbills, mainly for revue and comedies performed by a local am-dram company to which Tina had once belonged—*The Unvarnished Truth* by Royce Ryton, *Pass the Butler, Daisy Pulls it Off, Pack of Lies, And a Nightingale Sang, Close of Play*—the collection weaved its way drunkenly from wall to wall and disappeared down the hall to metastasie through every room of the house.

"My mother," Rudy explained to me, unnecessarily, "is a compulsive collector."

We visited Tina every week. This was a sop to me, because he knew how much I loved plants. But it was also a way of making me beholden to him—and a way of emphasising the permanency of our relationship.

While Rudy sat picking over his food, muttering about his work, Tina and I ignored the food altogether and winked at one another over the top of whatever exotic plant she had placed that evening at the center of the dining table.

She knew that I did not love her son, that I was a kind of imposter, but my love of unusual plants endeared me to her. Every meal had a different and ever more exotic centerpiece: *Calathea makoyana* with its leaves like raised peacock tails, *Orchis glauca* with petals like burnished steel, *Platycerium alipes,* its asymmetric leaves like ruffled feathers, the notoriously delicate *Calathea lucifuga,* its shoots black and sticky as licorice.

Rudy told me that his grandfather had brought the first black lotus back with him from Palestine after the second world war. But I never could discover the precise circumstances surrounding this unusual and, as far as I know, unique importation.

In speaking of her father's treasured plant, Tina would adopt the diction and manner of herbals and astrological gardening books. Ask her a direct question and she would say to you something like, "Today on Delta channels the blue lotus blooms as in the days when they laid the blossoms beside the dead." The first time I asked her where the black lotus came from she shook her head and said, "The *nekheb,* the true, sacred lotus, has vanished from Egypt."

For the first few months, my affair with Rudy went well. He was an attentive, if clumsy, lover. But in the end his clumsiness grew tough and unbreachable. Now when Rudy made love to me I felt as though I were being laid out on a slab, vivisected by his precise, hampered, hopelessly inhibited "technique."

Why, then, did I not leave him? Boredom and habit, I fear, are my only excuses. Anyway, whatever dissatisfaction I might otherwise have felt with him was more than made up for by the satisfactions of my working life.

New business developments in the City of London fostered a new and lively market for "interior landscapes." This was something I was not slow to exploit. My company's success through 1990 attracted the attention of the more trivial business journalists, and you will find pictures of me, more or less embarrassed by all the attention I was getting, in most of the Christmas '90 gardening magazines.

Rudy's research, meanwhile, yielded some promising results. He came over to my new office in Bow one afternoon to tell me he had induced compulsive masturbation in a capuchin monkey.

"It's established," he announced, plonking a bottle of *Lanson Brut* down on the desk. "Benjamin tossed himself off for eighteen hours yesterday and this morning he was back on the job."

"Perhaps he's bored," I suggested.

Rudy smiled thinly and started picking the foil off the bottle. "The results are still wobbly," he went on, "but this is a significant step—"

He fell silent. I waited for him to go on. He just sat there on the corner of my desk, picking at the foil. When the foil was all gone he started picking at the shreds of glue stuck to the neck of the bottle.

"Are you going to open it, then?" I asked him. He glanced down at the bottle. He laughed and shook himself. "Sorry." He left off picking at it, and turned the wire spool to release the cork. I went and got us some glasses from the cabinet by the door.

"So," I said—he was still unscrewing the wire—"what next? Where do you go from here?"

"First, it would be worth seeing if I can induce high micelle concentrations without having to cut my subjects' heads open first."

I winced.

Rudy, oblivious, went on, "In theory, that shouldn't be difficult. MIF passes readily from the blood into the cerebrospinal fluid."

Rudy had wound the wire spool so far back the other way that it snapped at last. Rudy started and stared down at the neck of the bottle. He moved his face away just in time. The cork blew out and champagne foam went all over my desk.

"Oh *shit,*" Rudy muttered, and he helped me mop up with his handkerchief.

As we drank I thought about what he had said. "You're saying, then, that compulsive behavior can be induced as part of an allergic reaction?"

"Not in the real world. All I can say with any certainty is that high micelle concentrations induce compulsive behavior."

He was fiddling with the neck of the champagne bottle again. I watched him in silence for a few moments.

He saw my expression, glanced down and, with a nervous scowl, put the bottle out of reach at the end of the desk. "Sorry."

I poured the champagne and he talked about his work, and eventually he decided it was time for him to go. "Maureen?" he said, when he was at the door, "would you like to come out for a meal tonight?"

I smiled as warmly as I could. "I'm sorry," I said. "I've something arranged."

"Maybe tomorrow?"

"I'll call you."

"Ah. Right." He stood there by the door, waiting for me to say something, and when I didn't he just sighed and left, closing the door softly behind him.

We still visited Tina Strossner.

The food she made for us never varied: cauliflower cheese with pieces of bacon added to the sauce, served with spaghetti, warmed in the oven in a dish wetted with garlic oil. Dessert consisted of Tina's "special" rice pudding crusted with nutmeg and currants. The entire meal was disgusting.

Tina and her plants were enough of an incentive. For all that my clients sometimes demand quite ostentatious displays, it is rare that my company deals in anything more exotic than hoya or weeping fig. Tina's plants were a continual delight to me.

One night after our meal we left Rudy in the house, smiling blankly at *Newsnight,* and Tina led me to her hothouse. An *Aechea caudata* held pride of place on a table by the door. The impress of older leaves had left dark lines in the pale blue bloom of the younger growth. Nested stars of thick serrated petals guarded magnolia-colored stamens.

Sweat trickled down my neck. I loosened my blouse. The place smelt heady and delicious—the air was full of the unmistakable scent of black lotuses.

Tina led me to two shallow tanks. There were eight black lotuses altogether—descendants of her father's original plant.

Tina said, "According to Iamblicus the lotus is a symbol of perfection. It makes the figure of a circle, you see—leaves, flowers and fruit, a perfect circle. Like the sun's rays."

I bent my head to drink in the sweet, salivatory scent.

"The lotus represents the past, present and future."

"Oh?"

"It bears buds, flowers and seeds at the same time."

I smiled. "Of course."

She reached past me into the tank and plucked a lotus and broke it apart.

I gasped, not understanding what she was doing.

She offered me a fleshy petal. "Eat it."

I don't know why I felt so uneasy.

"It's all right," she whispered, offering it to my mouth. "It's quite edible. You can flavor rice with lotus flowers. The Chinese candy the seeds for New Year."

Afterwards, as we left her hothouse, she took me by the arm and said, "I like your visits. If you wanted to, you could come here . . . ."

"Yes?" I prompted.

She smiled nervously. "Without Rudy."

The first time I visited Tina on my own, she was working herself up for yet another assault on the box room. "I've all those plastic bags to sort out," she explained, "and decide what to keep, what to throw away, and it's been hanging over me for months and I need to find some things. By Wednesday"—she rubbed her hands together with glee,—"we should have all we need for a nice big *conflagration!*"

Tina Strossner's compulsive "clear-outs" were focused upon the cupboards in the box room. This was full to bursting with odds and ends acquired from Tina's aunt, who had been bombed out during the war. Whenever Tina tackled the box room she found the oddest bits and pieces. "They never threw anything away!" It became a kind of litany. I soon realized that this menagerie of personal effects was in the same state of chaos as it had been when she acquired it. Her desire to tidy or order these things was, I soon learned, just another facet of a deeply compulsive personality.

Sometimes I stayed the night with her. I remember one morning she got up early "to do some tidying." She came upon a folder containing her great-uncle's bank statements from 1932. "Maureen," she cried. She burst into the bedroom. "Look at these! Now, where's the sense in *that*?" She thrust the statements at me as if I were in some way responsible for them.

I burst out laughing.

The next day Tina sent me a lotus.

It was pure white.

There was a letter with it. "I bring thee the flower which was in the Beginning," she wrote; "the glorious lily of the Great Water."

I don't think Rudy suspected anything.

Spring came. Rudy's results went haywire. He rang me late at night to tell me about it. Once, shortly after midnight, the phone went and Tina, half asleep and not thinking straight, leaned out of my bed and picked up the handset. I reached over her and hit the rest in time. After that I made a habit of putting the phone down on him; I had no more trouble with late-night calls.

Thinking about Rudy depressed me. I hadn't slept with him for some months, but he wouldn't let things drop. It was as though, deprived of my love, he felt he had a right to my pity. At first I had felt sorry for him. Now I was beginning to resent him, his mincing familiarity, the hang-dog look he gave me whenever I refused a date.

It was becoming increasingly difficult to remember him with any affection. The most disgusting things kept coming back: that box of tissues he kept by the side of his bed, for instance. How he wiped himself dry almost as soon as he had ejaculated, and how he turned away from me while he did it as if he were ashamed, which I suppose he must have been. I remembered, too, how he would never give himself in a kiss. It was as though he was afraid I might taste foul. He would never suck my breasts; instead he took each nipple between his teeth and nibbled at it. When I finally persuaded him to go down on me he licked me fastidiously, like a cat, testing out some unfamiliar yogurty treat.

Perhaps this unwelcome but persistent tape-loop of memories affected me, for I seemed unable to hold on to Tina's affection.

She no longer fed me lotus. "Have you had a nice week, dear?" she would say, burrowing deeper into the recesses of the hall cupboard; and, complacently, "I've been clearing out all sorts of things today!"

Her voice grew more distant as she snaked another few inches into the stygian gloom.

I stared at Tina's feet; these alone remained in the upper realm: pink slippered feet, curling and tapping.

What on earth did she find to do in there?

There was a thump, a crash, an hysterical scream.

"Tina?" I rushed forward to help.

"Leave me alone! Oh! Look what you made me do!" Tina shuffled on her hands and knees in the tight confines of the cupboard and poked her head out; the lines of her face were gray with dust, aging her.

I knew that whatever we had shared had come to an end, not because Tina had chosen that it should, but simply because she had forgotten about it; she was now wholly obsessed with her hopeless, endless clear-out.

A letter from Rudy—unexpected, distant, with an edge

of urgency—awaited me at home. He was, as usual, talking shop, and much of what he wrote was obscure, but I grasped enough of it to know that I would have to see him at least once more.

We drank coffee in his lounge. There were magazines everywhere. An ashtray by the corner of the sofa had been kicked over, and spent Gauloises butts lay strewn across the stained carpet.

Rudy wore an orange T-shirt and old black jeans, holed at the right knee. He smelled of stale smoke. He had put on weight. His face was heavy, with pronounced jowls. His scalp above the right ear was bare, scratched and weeping, where he had been scratching.

He found it hard to express things clearly. He meandered and repeated himself. Sometimes he found it hard to remember that we were no longer lovers. At other times he hardly recognized me.

He drained his coffee almost the second he had poured it into the cup, then went to the window and eased the lace curtain aside. "It's summer," he said, pointlessly.

"Yes," I said.

"A lot of pollen. A lot of hay fever." He turned to me. "Do you get hay fever?"

"Yes."

"Me too." He let the curtain drop. "MIF. I didn't know as much about it as I thought I did. No one did. It turns out there are different types."

"Rudy, you've told me this."

"Have I?"

"But I don't understand what that means."

"It means I'm wrong," he said, unhelpfully. He started scratching his head.

"Rudy, stop it."

He didn't hear me.

I stood up and went over to him and pulled at his arm, but he just kept on scratching.

For some reason I burst into tears. "Christ, Rudy."

"There are four different kinds of MIF."

"Christ."

I turned away from him, went to the window. It was very bright out. I wiped away my tears, hoping he wouldn't see.

"Different pollens trigger the release of different sorts of MIF. Black orchids trigger Type C. Of course, that's my own personal nomenclature—it won't mean anything until the paper's published."

"Rudy, I don't know what you're talking about."

He took his hand away from his head at last. He'd opened up all his scabs. "It means I was wrong and you were right: compulsive behavior dysfunction *can* be brought on by an allergenic response. Type C MIF raises micelle levels in the diencephalon four hundredfold." He made to scratch his head again, then lowered his hand. "That's why my results went haywire this summer. I quit using black lotus pollen, and I found I couldn't induce compulsive behavior disorder in my animals anymore. It's only type C MIF can induce it. Type C is released only when the body's exposed to black lotus pollen. It's the only plant I've found can generate it. That's why my grandmother went crazy, and my mother—"

He left the sentence unfinished.

He knew what had happened to him.

I got up and said I'd have to go.

The corridor swam around me like a muddy river. Rudy didn't want me to go, of course.

"Won't you stay?"

I got to the door of his apartment and leaned up against it, catching my breath.

"*Do* stay."

Getting through the door—I felt like a pupa, prizing my

way out of a carcass. The textures of the stairwell I had to go down tore at my eyes. I hurried down the steps, and they swirled around me.

"Do stay."

I felt crawling things on my back and I knew he was at the door, looking at me. I told myself that I mustn't turn round—if I turned round I'd see his fat, bleeding head poking out the gap between door and door frame—a doll's head framed in darkness like a disembodied thing, a lump of meat waiting to rot. I wanted to throw up.

Rudy's discovery came too late for us.

Tina left the Maudsley two months ago. Her condition has undergone some measurable improvement since then. Aside from her fugues, she is quite lucid. She has a good layperson's understanding of Rudy's work, and this has helped her. Knowing that her problem is organic, a consequence of biochemistry, and not of psychology, has enabled her to come to terms with her condition. There is as yet no cure. Rudy's death will only serve to delay its final development. In the meantime, we can only receive what stopgap treatments there are, and hope we do not deteriorate to Rudy's level.

After the explosion, there was of course talk of suicide. Eventually, however, a verdict of death by misadventure was given. I cannot shut out this dreadful vision—I remember that champagne bottle, and his thumbnail, pick-picking at the foil, and I think about him, in his squalid little bedsit, at supper time. It's seven o'clock. The sun is setting. It's been a hot day. He has opened the kitchen window to let in a light evening breeze. He turns the gas ring on, lights it, then goes to turn on the kitchen light. He reaches for the switch, but his hand does not obey him, and he forgets what his hand is supposed to do. So he stands there, scratching his head, for ten minutes, twenty, maybe an hour. The evening breeze picks up. It blows out the flame on his gas ring. How many more hours does Rudy stand there, ripping his scalp off with broken finger-nails? Five hours, six. It's not exceptional. It's impossible to say what finally triggers the explosion. Perhaps Rudy wakes up in the darkness, and, disoriented, maddened by the searing pain of his bleeding scalp, he turns on the light. One spark is enough.

Rudy has been buried for over three hours now. Tina drives us across the spoiled Surrey countryside, through villages with names like Hurtmore and Noning.

I notice the wing mirror's cracked. Tina must have pranged it again. She was never a careful driver, and her condition does nothing for her technique. Not that I can talk: the doctors grounded me more than a month ago. It seems as though whenever Tina responds to treatment, I have a relapse. And vice versa, of course. A door, opening and closing, repeatedly—

Tina was right: the sky is clear now. In front of us, a wide-bodied jet catches the sun, a droplet of flaming magnesium against the sky's ungraduated blue.

It's getting hot so I unwind the window. I reach out to adjust the broken wing mirror. I catch a glimpse of myself in the cracked glass. The scalp above my left ear is all bare, where I've been scratching my head. I snatch my hand back from the glass and press it to my lap, keep it there with my other hand.

Tina shoots me a worried look. "You want a drink?"

"Christ."

The next village we rattle through has a Beefeater in it. Tina swings the van recklessly up the steep drive and into the gravel car park. We go in and she parks me at a table in the corner.

Coming in here was a bad idea. I can't feel grief, the shock of Rudy's death is too recent; all the drink brings up in me is this tape-loop of memories I'd rather not possess.

Sick, uncharitable memories.

I must not think of this today—today is Rudy's day—but looking back on our brief, abortive affair, I can see now that we did no more than degrade each other.

I can identify precisely the moment when I realized I too had compulsive behavior dysfunction. It was November of last year. I had been working hard all week, and on Friday afternoon I took myself off to London Zoo to cheer myself up.

When it was time to leave I couldn't leave the zoo. I just kept walking around and around—one big long pointless circuit, over and over again. I knew what I was doing but I couldn't help but do it. It was as though I had suddenly become trapped behind the green lenses of my eyes; I felt utterly cut off from what was real or solid.

And I remember, as I walked, I kept passing and repassing a cage of green monkeys—capuchins, the kind Rudy used for his experiments.

They found my predicament hysterical. When I came into view they all chittered at me and pointed in different directions.

The pint is done for and I must get to the ladies'. I look at myself in the mirror. My scalp is all bloody—I must have been scratching myself again. I bathe it as best I can—

I wake up perhaps a minute later to find I've been scratching again and all the scabs are open and weeping.

I still need to pee. I step into a cubicle and shut the door. I reach under my skirt and pull down my knickers and shut the door. I start to piss and I shut the door—

The next I know I'm in the car again. Tina keeps giving me anxious glances but won't meet my gaze. My legs are wet. I glance down. There are dark spots all down my stockings where I've pissed myself.

Jesus Christ.

Tina must have gone into the loo and got me.

I glance at my watch. How much time did I lose?

While we've been driving the sky has cleared. A wide-bodied jet catches the sun, a droplet of flaming magnesium against the sky's ungraduated blue.

It's getting hot so I unwind the window. I reach out to adjust the wing mirror. I catch a glimpse of myself in the cracked glass. The skin above my left ear is all bare, where I've been scratching my head. An eidetic memory hijacks my eyes. A door, opening and closing, repeatedly. I snatch my hand back from the glass and press it into my lap, keep it there with my other hand.

Tina shoots me a worried look. "You want a drink?"

The next village we rattle through has a Beefeater in it. Tina swings the van recklessly up the steep drive and into the gravel car park.

All the drink brings up in me this tape-loop of memories I'd rather not possess. Sick, uncharitable memories, about Rudy, who was, I suppose, my lover. I must not think this way today; today is Rudy's day. But the most disgusting things keep coming back...

I drain my pint and the next I know I'm in the car. How much time did I lose?

Before us, a wide-bodied jet catches the sun, a droplet of flaming magnesium.

Tina shoots me a worried look. "You want a drink?"

"Christ."

Eventually, as my preoccupied mind slides further into its allergenic trance, all grip on the real will fade. Perhaps Tina and I will go for a walk in her garden, and she will show me her hothouse. Sweat will trickle down my neck. I will loosen my blouse. She will feed me a petal of the black lotus.

At last the fugue will end. We shall drive through villages with names like Hurtmore and Noning and Tina will say, "Do you want a drink?" and I will suddenly wake up.

Perhaps by then we will be home. Perhaps Tina will take me home with her and put me to bed.

But if she does, it will not mean anything. Tina is nothing more to me now than a concerned friend. I do not suppose we shall ever be as close as we once were. Rudy's death has destroyed all chance of it. I wish I did not hate Rudy so much, but how can I help it? I resent his death, but, worse, I resent his life. The night Tina fed me her lotus I fell in love with her. Simply by living, Rudy blighted that love: whenever I thought of him, what she and I did seemed somehow monstrous.

I must not think of this today. Today is Rudy's day.

The lotus is past, present and future. The door will open and the door will close and the door will open again. Tina's kiss can wait today. Tina's lotus will not arrive today. This is Rudy's day—

"Where do you want to go?" he says.

I laugh—already I am nervous. "Well," I say, wanting him, "where is there?"

Palindrome

by Thomas M. Disch

Thomas M. Disch is a multi-award-winning author whose novels include *Camp Concentration, On Wings of Song, 334,* the historical novel *Neighboring Lives* (with Charles Naylor), *The Businessman, The M.D.* and *A Troll of Surewould Forest.* He is working on *The Priest: A Gothic Romance,* part of an ongoing series set in Disch's own supernatural Minneapolis (where he grew up). Disch is also a theater critic and a playwright. His short play *The Cardinal Detoxes,* a monologue by a Catholic priest jailed for running over a pregnant woman while he was driving intoxicated, outraged the Archdiocese of New York. The play became a cause célèbre when the Archdiocese, landlord of The Rapp Theater in which the play was performed, tried to evict the theatrical company. The play will have its first publication in *The Hudson Review* this spring.

"Palindrome," the only reprint in this volume (*Omni,* September 1987) demonstrates Disch's sly wit and might give the reader a clue as to why *The Cardinal Detoxes* was vilified by the Church.

PALINDROME

Thomas M. Disch

THE PLANE ENTERS THE CLOUD

From horizon to horizon the sky that could be seen from
the departure lounge was a uniform, luminous gray. It gleamed
like a whale lifted out of the water—one dark, undifferentiated
glistening that followed a curve too vast for apprehension.

The 747's that trundled along the runways to lift off and
vanish into this continuum of cloud were of an only slightly
darker and less luminous gray. The flight attendants wore
uniforms of a rather steely gray trimmed, like the planes on
which they served, with red and blue piping. The two nuns
who had been waiting in the lounge since seven A.M. wore
identical habits of charcoal gray, with black veils draped from
high, white wimples. The men in business suits—who consti-
tuted a majority of the passengers—had chosen, almost to a
man, to wear gray that day, following, it may be, the suggestion of the weather. Even the younger men had supplemented
their denim uniforms with gray accessories—a gray sweatshirt,
a gray cowboy hat, a gray knapsack.

In the face of such consensus the few concentrations of
bright color in the lounge took on the force of wild immodesty:
Sister Incarnation's red guitar case (it had cost twenty dollars
less than the identical case in black); the Hawaiian shirt of the

young man in the wheelchair; the screaming green pantsuit of the woman reading *How to Prosper During the Coming Bad Years;* the lemon-yellow cat basket handcuffed to the wrist of one of the gray-suited men.

The flight was announced, and the passengers boarded according to their sections. The four junior flight attendants performed their preflight pantomime demonstrating the use of the oxygen masks and seat-belt buckles, as the senior attendant, Amanda Conklin, chanted the words of this rite into the PA system. The pilot, Malcolm Jay, announced their destination and estimated time of arrival. Then, as they waited for clearance, the Muzak hummed a medley of resolutely upbeat tunes.

Sister Incarnation—she of the red guitar case—made a snide remark about the Muzak, and Sister Fidelis, sitting beside her in the window seat, pointed out the element of arrogance in her remark. Sister Fidelis's conscience was always on patrol. Duly chastened (for she had been uncharitable), Sister Incarnation began a rosary.

The plane taxied to the end of the runway. The flight attendants made a final passage up and down the aisles to see that everyone's chair was in the upright position with the seatbelt fastened. The engines fired, and the plane rolled forward, bouncing and shuddering. The woman in the green pantsuit, Mrs. Judi Schweers, lowered the plastic eyelid of the window beside her and stared resolutely at the temporarily meaningless print on the page.

The plane tilted upward. They were off the ground. Sister Incarnation leaned across Sister Fidelis's lap to look at the swiftly broadening view—the gray, four-square strips of the airport's concrete, the long ribbons of highway, a patchwork of suburban rooftops and lawns, and then, quite suddenly, nothing at all. They had entered the cloud. Sister Incarnation leaned back in her seat with a sigh.

The woman in the green pantsuit raised the blind from the window and returned to a consideration of real-estate values in a period of double-digit inflation. The flight attendants began to distribute earphones.

HIGH ALTITUDES

Barry Anderson could almost feel the first squirt of adrenaline entering his system as he flicked the toggle up and down by way of proving to Malcolm Jay, the pilot, that the radio was indeed dead. Likewise the radar, the altimeter, and any instrument that monitored the plane's external environment rather than its internal functions.

Barry's airline spent large sums making inventories of the psychological traits of its personnel in an effort to hire as pilots and copilots men of absolutely no imagination, men who could be counted on not to panic in situations such as this, which most people would characterize as impossible. Barry's first reaction was a tribute to that selection process.

"I think the difficulty must have something to do with this cloud we're in," he said in a tone of unconfoundable calm. The added adrenaline had no effect but to sharpen his motor responses.

"Yeah, but Jesus, the radar!" Malcolm said, beginning to whine. Malcolm, despite as good a test profile as Barry, was already rattled. "How do you explain *that?*"

Barry offered no explanation beyond a precision shrug. "We'll just have to keep climbing. Then, when we're over this damned cloud . . . ."

As they climbed, Barry calculated on his wrist computer their probable altitude. Given the slope of ascent, the time elapsed, and the speed (which he estimated, based on the engines' thrust), Barry arrived at a probable altitude of forty-five thousand feet. Malcolm checked the figures and found nothing wrong with them, yet it was quite impossible that they should still be enveloped in such a thickness of cloud at this altitude. Even the highest cirrus seldom formed above forty thousand feet.

"We'd better stop climbing," said Barry.

"And just keep heading . . . where?"

"The way we're headed. Do you have any other suggestions?" Malcolm didn't.

"It'll have to clear eventually."

Malcolm nodded. Like a person deprived of sensory inputs, his mind began to produce reveries of a somewhat inappropriate nature. He remembered a flight attendant he had made out with during a layover in Phoenix. In the cockpit of this very plane. He could remember her large, white, billowy breasts drooping down over the tan of her rib cage, the firmness of her thighs, the coolness of her hands, the tickling of sharp fingernails.

STRANGE WEATHER

"This is some strange weather," said Andy Dreer, pressing his nose to the small window beside him. The window was dotted with smudges left by earlier observations. "Mm," said the man in the aisle seat, who was reading the airline's bound edition of *Business Week.*

Andy figured there was no use continuing the conversation. There was more than a seat between them—there was a generation, and it wasn't about to be spanned.

But it was undoubtedly very strange weather, and while Andy trusted implicitly in airplanes, he couldn't help feeling edgy. They'd been climbing for how long already? And still were, and *still* hadn't come out of the clouds.

The seat-belt sign was still on., but otherwise nothing seemed out of the ordinary. People in the back rows were smoking. The attendants were readying a trolley of coffee and drinks.

He felt the weight of his body shifting. The plane was leveling off. They were still in the clouds, though. It was strange.

He dug into his knapsack for a book. Reading was the second best way Andy knew to get his mind off reality, even if all he had to read was the textbook for classic civilization. Midterms were Tuesday, and so far he hadn't cracked a book. Classic civ was reputed to be a Mickey Mouse course, with test questions like "Zeus, the father of the gods, dwelt on Mount (Blank)," or "Aristophanes ruled Athens from 410 to 385 B.C. (True or False)." There were advantages in attending a junior college in Florida, though the degree was not one of them. The ambience, however, was compatible, and you never had to wait for a court. Not that Andy exerted himself excessively in the direction of tennis. Life, he tended to believe, was but a dream, so who needed to bust his balls rowing?

TILT, SHUDDER, AND LURCH

The plane lurched.

Dr. Tumi smiled, imagining the sudden consternation among the arrows supporting the wings of the plane as it hit the pocket of turbulence. It lurched again, and he frowned. There was a change in the pitch of the engines' low organ tones, a diminution of thrust, as though the 747 were slowing down, like a ship plowing through heavy seas. It occurred to Dr. Tumi that he, together with the other twenty-odd passengers on the plane, was about to die. Planes are not dirigibles; they cannot simply grind to a halt and hang suspended. He'd often wondered how he would respond to the threat, or the certainty, of death and felt rather pleased with himself that he was taking it so calmly. If his fellow passengers should begin to panic (and why weren't they doing so already?), he might not be able to maintain this exemplary serenity, but for the moment Epictetus himself could not have been more stoic.

"Mrs. Vow?"

"Doctor?"

"Did you feel an unusual sensation just now?"

"In what sense unusual?"

71

"Proprioceptively," replied Dr. Tumi, with a literal exactitude he knew Mrs. Vow found annoying. After a pause to consult her own sensations, she answered, "We've stopped climbing and seem to have leveled off. The NO SMOKING light is off, but the FASTEN SEAT BELT light is still on."

"What can you see out the window?"

"We're still in the thick of the clouds, and that's odd. Usually one climbs above them. It's the loveliest part of flying, to my mind—looking down over those landscapes of clouds. They seem so solid. One understands how the Greeks might suppose their gods could live on top of them."

"I always fancied one would bounce about a great deal if one walked on clouds."

"On Tiepolo's clouds, possibly," said Mrs. Vow, "but not on Georgia O'Keeffe's."

For a while they discussed the relative merits of the cloudscapes of their favorite painters. After epistemology, chess, and medieval scientific theories, art history was Dr. Tumi's favorite recreational pastime. Mrs. Vow had done a year of postgraduate work at the Warburg Institute and knew how to describe a painting in the most minute particulars while simultaneously evoking its numinous, unnameable what's-it-ness. Before his blindness Dr. Tumi had not taken much interest in painting, but now that all art had become conceptual to him, he had become a great attendee of galleries and museums. His favorite painters were Held, Stella, and Hodgkins, none of whose work he'd ever seen. He had even, in a moment of extravagance, *bought* a Hodgkins. Mrs. Vow favored more painterly painters—De Kooning, Johns, Diebenkorn. The wonderful thing about their discussions on art was that she never pulled rank on him, never suggested that if he could see the painting in question, he would be of another opinion as to its merits. A saint, no doubt of it; Mrs. Vow was a saint.

The captain's voice boomed out over the speakers, interrupting all conversations. He asked the passengers to remain in their seats with their seat belts fastened. The plane was encountering turbulence, but this was a common occurrence, and there was no need to be alarmed.

"He does sound alarmed, though, doesn't he?" Mrs. Vow observed.

"Mm," said Dr. Tumi.

The cabin tilted forward and to the right, shuddered—as though it were fighting against the tilt—then lurched to the left, but without altering its downward inclination.

"I think we're going to crash, Mrs. Vow. Please hold my hand."

A sudden babble of voices expressed correlative forebodings. Several passengers summoned the flight attendants, but no one went so far as to scream—as though to have done so would have provoked the plane to more dire behavior.

Mrs. Vow exerted a steady, steadying force on his hand. Behind the obscuring confusion of voices in the cabin, the whine of the engines seemed to diminish to a rumble, a purr, a whisper. When the engines ceased altogether, the cabin fell silent, too, as though the same irrational intuition had simultaneously occurred to each passenger—that they were not about to crash (there was no sense of forward momentum) but were instead (and quite impossibly) becalmed. Slowly, in utter silence, the cabin righted itself, as though it were a ship riding a long swell.

"Can you see *anything* from the windows?" Dr. Tumi whispered.

"Nothing," said Mrs. Vow. "Clouds."

"Do you know, I wish someone *would* scream. This is unnatural."

"No, Doctor, there I draw the line. I don't believe I have ever in my whole life screamed. Not as an adult, in public. And don't you scream either. If we're all to die, let's try to do so with some dignity."

"We don't seem about to die, however. It's very strange."

"It is very strange," Mrs. Vow agreed, in her most disapproving tone. She seemed to hold Dr. Tumi responsible for what was happening. She let go of this hand. "Excuse me, but I must go to the toilet."

THE CLOUD ENTERS THE PLANE

Until the first dewlike droplets formed on the beige plastic louvers of the ventilator above Mrs. Schweers, grew to teardrop size, and dripped onto the open pages of *How to Prosper During the Coming Bad Years,* no one in the plane had noticed—or at least thought to comment on—the very muggy atmosphere within the cabin. The larger oddness of this seeming suspension of the laws of aerodynamics had blinded them all to the smaller oddity of the suddenly so much higher humidity.

"What in heaven's name is happening?" Mrs. Schweers demanded, holding out the spattered pages of her book in evidence to the gentleman across the aisle. "Why is the air blower *leaking?*"

In the seat behind Mrs. Schweers, Sister Incarnation looked up at the ventilator and saw that there were indeed droplets of condensation upon its louvers—and upon the ventilator above Sister Fidelis as well. Already enough moisture had fallen to the lap of the sleeping nun that her habit was speckled regularly with polka dots of dampness. The extent of this precipitation did not really amount to a "leak," but that there should be any at all was unsettling. Why would a ventilator *ever* drip water? Sister Incarnation had taught general science to legions of fourth and fifth graders, but her sense of the workaday applications of the principles she taught in general science was rather scrappy. She seemed to recall that condensation had something to do with rapid cooling, and that accounted for air conditioners so often drooling in a similar way.

"Amanda!" Mrs. Schweers called out volubly, using the name by which the senior flight attendant had introduced herself at the beginning of the takeoff recitation. "Amanda, will you come here, please?"

Reluctantly (for she'd been grateful for the pilot's instruction to stay seated till the plane's difficulties had been sorted out; she was feeling weirdly groggy) Amanda Conklin unbuckled her seat belt and made her was up the aisle to Mrs. Schweers's bulkhead seat. "What seems to be the matter, ma'am?" she asked, leaning down and fixing her eyes noncommittally on the woman's garish pantsuit. Mrs. Schweers had not properly begun to express her sense of being owed an explanation before her individual alarm became general. From each of the ventilators above each of the seats billows of fog issued into the cabin, opaquely white and quite coherent in shape, like thought balloons in a comic strip. There was a general outcry among the passengers, followed by a certain amount of milling about in the aisles. The plane responded as though it were a light-ballasted boat, tilting and righting itself as the passengers shifted position.

Sister Incarnation joggled the shoulder of her sleeping companion. "Sister Fidelis, I think you had better wake up."

The joggle did not suffice. Sister Incarnation poked, but still Sister Fidelis could not be roused. "Sister Fidelis? You must wake up, Sister! Please!"

The nun's head slumped to the side. Sister Incarnation could hear a far-off rumble of a snore, faint as the signal of a radio station at the threshold of receivability.

THE COPIED CAT

David Woody had remained in his seat during the first outbreak of panic, not so much because he was handcuffed to the travel basket of His Nibs, a celebrity cat insured for two million dollars. His Nibs, after starring in two feature films in which he had played a feline detective, had gone on to earn even bigger bucks as Dyna-Food Corporation's answer to the late and much-lamented (though not by Dyna-Food) Morris. Usually David didn't mind acting as the manager of an ill-tempered, professional cat. Only at times like this did he feel resentful toward His Nibs, times when people would give him odd looks and he could not explain to them that he was handcuffed to a cat basket for entirely aboveboard, monetary reasons, not because he was some kind of kook.

"May I have your attention, everybody?"

David gave his attention to the Hawaiian-shirted paraplegic, who had struggled up to support himself on the armrest of his aisle seat and was waving an aluminum crutch over his head to get attention. "Please!" he insisted, when David alone of the five other first-class passengers afforded him more than a glance. "There is something strange happening in this airplane and we are not being informed about it. I suggest— will you all please *listen* to me!—I suggest that a delegation be sent forward to the cockpit to *demand* an explanation from our pilot."

Amanda Conklin strode briskly down the aisle toward the troublemaker. "Sir, if you would *kindly* return to your seat." With a nurse's unthinking intimacy she placed her hands in the young cripple's armpits and lowered him back into his seat. His crutch overturned a tumbler of glistening ice cubes. "You can be sure that Captain Jay will be making a general announcement as soon as the situation warrants it," she went on as, down on one knee, she scooped the ice cubes back into the tumbler. "In the meantime we must all try to keep our wits about us and stay seated. Any unnecessary movement may be—"she stopped herself from saying *dangerous;* her duty was to promote a sense of calm and order "—upsetting to your fellow passengers. Now, if you do feel the need to *share* your concern with someone else, that's understandable. I'm sure *this* gentleman—" she made eye contact with David, who with the very slightest shake of his head tried to nix her matchmaking. Amanda smiled complicitously "—or *this* gentleman—" she indicated an older man across the aisle who was staring strickenly at the crossword puzzle in the airline magazine "—would have no objection to coming and sitting beside you for a few minutes."

"I'll sit by myself," said the paraplegic, "thank you very much."

Amanda walked back to David's seat and stopped. "What a beautiful cat," she said. "Is it a Persian?"

David looked where Amanda was looking, at the vacant window seat beside him, which was no longer vacant. His Nibs had somehow gotten out of his basket and was snoozing contentedly on the folded jacket of David's gray suit. How could he have gotten loose?

Then he realized—and in the same instant Amanda realized as well—that the cat on the seat beside him was not His Nibs (who was a tawny, almost gingery tom, not this shimmery, hoarfrosted shade of silver). This was not, in fact, any kind of cat at all. It was Amanda who proved herself the braver, for she reached down and touched the simulated cat, which instantly dispersed into tendrils of vapor that spilled over the edge of the seat like water spilling from the basin of a fountain.

A LOCKED-ROOM MYSTERY

Amanda's outcry and subsequent emotional collapse went unremarked outside the first-class cabin, for another and much stranger happening had absorbed the attention of the tourist-class passengers—except Dr. Tumi, the one passenger most directly affected. Even he, however, realized that there was something in the air.

What was quite literally in the air was the seated, slightly slumped body of Mrs. Vow. She hung, like a Dalí Madonna, just before the door of the bathroom that she'd entered some minutes earlier, at about the height of someone seated on the fourth rung of a ladder. Her dress was hitched up and her panty hose pushed down, just as they might have been had she been seated on a toilet instead of, as now, being suspended in midair without visible means of support. Like the simulated tomcat in the first-class cabin, this spectral Mrs. Vow had been reproduced in monochromic black and white, but unlike the vanished cat she did not revert to mere wisps of vapor upon being touched (tentatively, by Andy Dreer, who'd been waiting to be next inside). Rather, a kind of ripple passed through her image, as though it were a reflection (albeit three-dimensional) in a pool of water that had been disturbed by the first scattered raindrops of an impending storm.

"Holy torpedo," said Andy Dreer, with unfeigned reverence. "Did you see that?"

Clearly, many of the other passengers had seen it—were seeing it still—but none wished to discuss their perceptions with Andy. They sat staring at the wraith of Mrs. Vow with the entranced, furtive expressions of hotel guests who have tuned in to a pornographic television channel by accident and find themselves unable to tune away. It was Andy who made the connection between the image suspended in the air of the cabin and the woman who'd gone into the bathroom ahead of him. He steeled himself against the dread of violating a taboo so publicly—and knocked on the locked door of the toilet. "Ma'am? Are you in there? Ma'am, can you hear me?" When there was no response, he knocked more forcefully and called out more loudly: "Hey, is everything all right in there?"

Maynard Ellis, who had been sneaking a cigarette at the back of the cabin and lecturing himself on the importance of *not panicking* (especially as he was the only black and the only male among the flight attendants), recognized in Andy's behavior a problem he had been taught to cope with. "Sir!" he said, bustling down the aisle officiously, breaking stride to stub out the cigarette in an armrest ashtray in the smoking section, then bustling forward again. "Sir, please try to be . . . calmer. There are other washrooms that aren't occupied." (In fact, there were not, but Maynard did not know that.) "Use one of those."

"That's not the problem," Andy explained. "The problem is, there's a *woman* inside there, and I think she's fainted."

Maynard was able only with difficulty to fix his attention on Andy's definition of the problem—i.e., that a woman had fainted in the toilet—rather than on the problem presented by his senses to his disbelieving mind—that a semitransparent woman was hanging right in front of him, her knees level with his nose.

"Do you have a key for the washroom?" Andy prompted.

"Right. Yes. I do."

Looking closely, Maynard could see that the ghostly woman's stomach would rise and fall ever so slightly, as though she—or it—were breathing.

"Then could you *get* it?" said Andy.

"Right. Sure thing."

While Maynard returned to the service area for the master key that unlocked the bathroom doors, the image of Mrs. Vow tilted sideways, like a helium balloon that has slipped from the mooring of its string, and drifted slowly along the aisle in dreamlike pursuit of the flight attendant. All the passengers—excepting the five or six who were dozing—regarded the passage of the spectral woman with the hushed, unwavering attention they would have given a bomb squad's investigation of a ticking suitcase. She—or it—did not remain inflexibly bent into the posture of micturition. It assumed instead the attitude of a body floating in a stream—of Millais's *Ophelia,* in fact, as Mrs. Vow would have observed had she been present to describe the scene to Dr. Tumi. Its hair and panty hose rippled in the invisible current like filaments of cigarette smoke.

Maynard, returning with the bathroom master key, was obliged to hunch down as he passed under the visionary figure to avoid brushing against it. Despite this precaution, his near passage set up eddies in the stream of air supporting the wraith so that its arms and legs flailed about, as a corpse might in going through rapids. One spectral hand encountered the grille of a ventilator above an unoccupied seat. There was a swooshing sound, as when a vacuum cleaner sucks up the edge of a carpet, and then—slowly at first, then quite quickly—the entire body was siphoned up into the ventilating system.

What they found when they unlocked the bathroom door was not the unconscious Mrs. Vow. They found nothing but a small puddle of what resembled a strawberry milk shake in the aluminum basin of the sink. Maynard rinsed the vomit— what else could it have been?—down the drain and cleaned every surface of the washroom with paper towels. *People,* Maynard reflected, *who think that flight attendants have a glamorous job should consider the statistics on airsickness.*

"I saw her go in here," Andy insisted.

Maynard shook his head with affable denial. "Then she must have come out again when you weren't looking."

"I was standing right in front of the door. And anyhow, you saw yourself, the door was locked. How do you explain that?"

More than anything else, Maynard needed to be left alone. "I'm sorry," he said. "You'll have to excuse me. I've got to go to the toilet myself."

He entered the washroom, closed the door in Andy's face, locked it, and sat down on the lowered toilet seat and began to cry. He cried quietly and, as fast as they welled up, wiped away the tears with tissues from the dispenser bedside the mirror.

Meanwhile, unseen by him, helices of vapor, delicate as the root hairs of a seedling plant, began to rise from the drain of the sink and to twine before the mirror in the first tentative hypotheses whose sum would become, for a certain time, isomorphic to the form of the distraught and groggy Maynard Ellis.

THE SLOW COLLISION

It was now twenty minutes since Malcolm had left the cockpit to answer nature's—and Amanda Conklin's—call. Barry Anderson understood, in a theoretical way, that in situations of extreme crisis or threatened disaster, people are prone to cash in their last few chips of consciousness at the exchange of sex. Yet as many times as the sinking of the *Titanic* had been made into a movie, that aspect of catastrophe always got bumped by "Nearer, My God, to Thee." Barry didn't object to Malcolm's temporary dereliction of duty (what were they supposed to do, after all?); he just wished he'd be speedier. Barry wanted a cup of coffee. He was as sleepy as a four-year-old at a midnight showing of *Tristan und Isolde.* If there'd been a road, his eyes would definitely not have been on it.

Though there was not a road for Barry to look at, there was a tiny, greenish something up ahead in the gray of the cloud. A dot. It was set square in the middle of the lane Barry would have been driving in if this were a road and he were a bus driver. The dot grew and took on the features of another plane. Of, in fact, another 747.

Here it comes, Barry told himself. *This is it.* All the earlier strangenesses must have been a hallucination provoked retro-actively by his present panic. Or else the collision had already happened, and his dying mind had thrown up a defensive screen of false memories to prepare itself for the unfaceable fact of death. He seemed to recall having seen a movie to that effect on *The Late, Late Show* long, long ago.

This seemed a better theory than any Barry had come up with so far, but fortunately the airplane in the air lane ahead did not behave in a manner to bear out his theory. Instead it coasted to a stop at what would have been a polite conversational distance if the noses of the two planes had been human noses. And there it sat, as this plane was sitting, motionless in midair, an affront to reason and the law of gravity.

"You can't do that," Barry explained to the untenable 747. "It isn't—" he paused to savor the idea "—allowed."

Barry noticed two things about the plane—or counter-plane—in front of him. He noticed that the airline's emblematic markings—as much as could be seen of them from this angle—were rendered in faintly contrasting bands of gray and darker gray instead of in red and blue. And he noticed that the cockpit of the other plane was empty. So much, therefore, for the possibility that he was seeing some kind of freak reflection formed by the cloud; for if the plane ahead were a mirror image, a mirage, then where was Barry's image in the window facing him?

Just as he posed this question to himself, Barry saw the door to the cockpit of the counter-plane open and a woman enter. A cat was cradled in her arms. She approached the window, bent down, and looked ahead, wrinkling her brow as though puzzled by what she saw.

Was it he that she saw? Barry wondered. To find out he raised his right hand in the manner of an Indian saying "How."

The woman—it was Mrs. Vow—waved back. This was the opportunity His Nibs had been waiting for. With only one of her arms confining him, he sprang loose and dashed back to the first-class cabin to take refuge in the shadowy, cat-proportioned realm formed by the rows and rows of empty seats. He kept thinking that lights would come on, a camera would roll into position, and a bowl of his sponsor's food would be set down before him. But none of these desired events took place. The woman who'd awakened him and taken him from his seat was walking up and down the aisles, calling out the familiar and ever-to-be-dreaded warning call of her kind, "Pussy! Pussy! Here, Pussy!"

A DIALOGUE BETWEEN FAITH AND REASON

Mrs. Vow had decided she was dreaming but could not decide when the dream had begun. The entire plane flight could not be a figment of her unconscious mind. She could remember too clearly all the details along the way: packing the suitcases, the delay in the departure lounge, her conversation with Dr. Tumi after takeoff. The only discontinuity (but it was so inconsiderable, the merest hairline fracture) had been those few moments in the bathroom when she'd felt faint. If she had in fact fainted . . . . But did one ever in a dream—especially so strange a dream as this—did one ever *know* oneself to be dreaming? Not in her experience, but then, she usually forgot everything about her dreams within moments of waking.

More to the point, could she stop dreaming? Could she will herself awake?

"Wake up," she told herself experimentally, feeling an utter fool. Nothing changed. The tourist-class cabin remained as empty of its passengers and flight attendants as it had been when Mrs. Vow had stepped out of the bathroom.

"Wake up, damn it," she said with more vigor. "This is all a *dream!*" There was no need, she reasoned, to act reasonably if there was no one observing her. If this were a dream, it would be quite all right to scream. So she did: "*Wake up!*"

There was a loud sneeze, followed by an outraged cry of "Get *off* me!"

His Nibs leapt from his comfortable perch in the lap of Sister Fidelis, sighted Mrs. Vow approaching, and took cover under seats 25G, 24G, 24H, 23H, etc.

Sister Fidelis, in very ill temper, got to her feet (she'd

83

slumped sideways in her sleep, which is why Mrs. Vow had not noticed her before) and brushed at her habit energetically where the cat had been nestling. "I do believe," she said, more to herself than to Mrs. Vow, "that cats can tell when a person is allergic to them. It's an instinct they have. How else can they always—" The fact that the cabin was almost empty finally impinged. "But good heavens—we've landed! Why didn't someone wake me? Where's Sister Incarnation?"

"I wish I were able to answer your questions," said Mrs. Vow. "I'm as much in the dark as you. But I *don't* think we've landed."

Sister Fidelis frowned, as though Mrs. Vow had just been guilty of an off-color joke. "Of course we've landed. That much is obvious. Though I can't understand how Sister Incarnation could have gone off and left me asleep in my seat. And where is the stewardess? She took my bag from me, and I've no idea what she did with it."

"We two appear to be the only people on the plane. Three, counting the cat."

Sister Fidelis darted a look of theological odium at Mrs. Vow.

"Cats are not *people*."

Mrs. Vow laughed and then—too late to avoid giving offense—stifled her laughter. She decided she'd best let the disgruntled nun explore the plane for herself and come to her own conclusions. If this were a dream, then whatever the nun did or said was really a manifestation of her own, Mrs. Vow's, unconscious mind. As now, when she glowered at the sealed exit door in the areaway between the tourist- and first-class cabins, she was expressing Mrs. Vow's general sense of entrapment by the circumstances of her life. But why a nun? Something to do with sexual repression, surely, though Mrs. Vow was not conscious of any present dissatisfactions in that area. On the contrary. Dr. Tumi was the kind of lover—

Bacchus, Solomon, and Galahad in equal parts—one did not expect to encounter outside the pages of a Silhouette romance. Perhaps it was simply her *name* that engendered the idea of a nun. If so, then she might provoke an interpretable response by introducing herself. "My name is Mrs. *Vow,*" she said, significantly. The nun stood by the window nearest the sealed exit, peering querulously into the enveloping cloud.

"And what's yours?" Mrs. Vow prompted.

Sister Fidelis looked up, bristling at this most pertinent and impertinent of questions like a proper Turandot or Rumpelstiltskin. But at last good manners won the day, and she answered, "Sister Fidelis."

"That means *faithful,* doesn't it? As in 'Adeste Fidelis.' My given name is Maisie, after the novel by Henry James. My father taught English at Princeton and worshiped James. I always wondered, if there had been a second daughter, would he have saddled her with Casamassima?" That was, in fact, a fib; she'd never wondered any such thing. But in a dream— and in talking to strangers on planes—one is free to invent another life for oneself.

"I'm afraid I don't know what you're talking about," said Sister Fidelis. "And this joke has gone on quite long enough. I'd like to get off this plane. Now!"

It did not seem well-bred, even in a dream, to tell someone you believed yourself to be dreaming, since that would make the other person no more than a figment of your own imagination. There had to be a kinder way to suggest to Sister Fidelis that they were not really on a plane but rather on another plane of existence. Perhaps she could find, in her father's phrase, "internal evidences" within the cabin of the 747 by which it could be shown not to be real. And there was, now that she thought about it, a thinness to everything about her, a lack of texture and nuance—as though the whole interior of the aircraft had been formed by some absentminded geometer from vats of pink and baby-blue putty. But no, that proved nothing, for planes were designed on purpose to give such an impression, by way of lulling the passengers' anxieties.

While Mrs. Vow continued in this vein of epistemological reverie, Sister Fidelis trespassed cautiously into the first-class cabin, thence into the cockpit, where she saw what Mrs. Vow had seen earlier: the other 747 that had been parked nose to nose with this one. The odd thing was that though she could see the other plane quite clearly, a thick ground fog prevented her from seeing the runway on which the two planes must be resting. For they could not simply be hanging suspended, motionless, in the middle of the air, like a pair of humming-birds trying to kiss.

His Nibs followed Sister Fidelis into the cockpit, jumped up into the pilot's seat, placed his forepaws on the back of the seat, arched his back, and purred ingratiatingly. It was time for lunch. But the woman in the delicately scented gray clothes paid him no heed and tried only to swat a nonexistent fly that lighted first on her forehead, then on her stomach, and then on each of her shoulders in turn.

FORBIDDEN LOVE
"And then—"

Then her narrative ran aground on the impossibility of her explaining to this poor man what she had seen next. What they had all seen. "This will sound incredible," she said, by way of preface.

"More incredible than all the rest?" Dr. Tumi asked.

She nodded. Then remembering that he couldn't see her (and did not know, therefore, that she was a nun, for in the rush of becoming acquainted they hadn't introduced themselves), Sister Incarnation answered, "Yes. Or no—not more than *all* the rest. Because I haven't got to the other things, such as the way people are falling asleep in the midst of everything."

"Yes, I've heard them snoring."

"We may be the only two still awake. Which is why I came to talk to you."

"And I'm grateful that you did. But don't let me interrupt. Please, go on." Quite as though he could see, he placed his hand on hers where it was grasping the end of the armrest. His fingertip rested on the ring by which she'd become a bride of Christ.

Reluctantly, from a sense of simple duty (for the man deserved to know what had become of his companion), Sister Incarnation described the apparition of Mrs. Vow outside the washroom and its passage, down the aisle and into the mouth of the ventilator. "Of course," she concluded, "it could only have been a hallucination."

"But all of you saw it?"

"We all saw something. No one took the time to compare notes as to what exactly they saw. But they did open the door to the washroom right afterward, and . . . and there was no one there. And later I heard one of the flight attendants say the same thing had happened to the pilot and . . . Miss Conklin. Apparently they'd gone into a washroom . . . together."

"So far that is the most probable part of the whole story."

The crinkle lines around his eyes laughed in a way that was both good-humored and suggestive, and Sister Incarnation realized that despite his years and his blindness he was an uncommonly handsome man. He must have become blind late in life, since those who are born blind rarely develop that liveliness of nuanced expression that is at the root of the idea of "good looks."

"My name is Ettore, by the way," he said with a tightening of his grip on her hand that could be interpreted as a handshake. "That's Italian for *Hector.*"

"Mine is . . . Mary." It was not a lie, only a partial truth.

"So," he said, relaxing his grip and creating, by the backward inclination of his head, a more comfortable emotional distance between them. "How do *you* account for all this?"

"Account for it!" She could actually laugh at the suggestion. But then, with the laughter, an idea came to her. Not a likely idea, but one that she, as a nun, could not dismiss out of hand. "Well, it might be—now it's your turn to laugh at me, Ettore. It might be that we're in the hands of God."

"And we are the cards, so to speak, with which the Almighty is practicing his sleight of hand?"

"I must admit that this isn't how I was brought up to expect God to behave." She ran her right hand, unseen, down the length of her black veil. "But then," she continued, "He is under no obligation to conform to my expectations. There is a book I've always meant to read. It's a large paperback in the theology section of our college bookstore, and I don't recall the author, only the title, which is *The Cloud of Unknowing.* Could we have entered the cloud of unknowing? To which, I suppose, one can only answer, Who knows?"

His smile rippled through his expressive flesh like sunlight flitting across the floor of a forest—evanescent yet ever present.

"My own nonexplanation would be that we've entered the fourth—or fifth or sixth—dimension. It amounts to much the same thing as the cloud of unknowing, doesn't it? As who would say, 'Here in terra incognita, wonders never cease'?"

"Perhaps the oddest element in all of this," Sister Incarnation added, "odder even than the disappearances of people from their seats and from the washrooms, is the way that there's been no *panic* among those of us still left behind. My companion on this trip—who, by the way, was one of the first who *vanished* from the plane—is a teacher at the same school where I teach. And she likes to pose this problem to her classes: What ought one to do if one knew for a certainty that the world would be coming to an end within the next hour?"

"That is a question everyone has had to consider in the nuclear age. And what does she propose for life's final hour?"

"Oh, there's no single answer. She says we should all proceed at our usual tasks at our usual pace, whether that be teaching a class or reading a book or whatever."

"I'm not such a stoic myself. I can still remember how I spent the forty-eight or so hours of the Cuban Missile Crisis, and it wasn't writing a budget proposal. No, if I felt convinced that the world was coming to an end, I'd try and have one last good fuck while there was still time." He paused long enough for this to register as an invitation, then asked, "How about you?"

Everyone else on the plane was sleeping, and *he* was blind, and God didn't seem to be keeping up his end of the bargain, since nothing in Roman Catholic theology could explain the present situation. And for all these years since she'd taken her vows, the single sin she'd had to confess over and over was her *regret* for never having had sex with Gerald McCarthy when the opportunity had presented itself on the evening of May 24, 1967, and wasn't that a ridiculous sin to be damned for? How did the saying go? As well hang for a sheep as for a lamb. Deftly she removed her wimple and dropped it into an empty seat.

"That's always been my feeling, too," she said, with the bravado of innocence. "Why not go into the cockpit? There's no one there, and it's roomier than the washrooms."

He held out his hand to her, and she took it with the most intense, the tingliest sense of *accomplishment.* Just like the tremor of self-wonder she'd felt when, despite all her forebodings, she'd passed her road test and gotten her driver's license. Now she would experience the substance of which that had been the mere emblem. Her life had turned out to have a major surprise.

TERRA FIRMA

For a few moments after waking in the seat beside Sister Fidelis she could remember the main outlines of the dream. To have been vowed to chastity so long and still to harbor such concupiscence! And with a blind man! How strange his tongue had felt when he—

But to remember, to linger over such imaginings was sinful, though the dream itself was innocent. She willed herself to think of other matters. As the plane tilted to the right, circling in for a landing, she leaned across Sister Fidelis to look at the city's self-formed map of roofs and roads.

"Why, look at the dome of the ballpark!" she exclaimed. "It's just like ours at home."

"It *is* ours at home," said Sister Fidelis dryly. "If you hadn't been asleep, you'd have heard the announcement. We've had to turn back. The pilot won't say why, but we're not supposed to worry."

"You mean that I've slept through the entire drama?"

"I sincerely hope so."

Meaning, Sister Incarnation understood, that she hoped the drama was over and was not to have a tragic denouement. Sister Fidelis was distrustful of airplanes.

"I had the strangest dream," she said brightly, trying to divert her companion from thoughts of a crash landing. "And it all took place here on the plane."

"Really?" said Sister Fidelis guardedly.

"But for the life of me I can't remember any of the details."

Sister Fidelis made a cough of polite disinterest and turned to face the window. The plane was now skimming the gray, cloud-mirroring waters of an artificial lake. She, too, had had a dream, but one too sinful to speak of. Yet too vivid to forget, especially those last moments when she had stood outside the window of the cockpit, a voyeur to the act of sexual congress between Sister Incarnation and a naked, white-haired man, the same who now was seated (clothed) some five rows back talking to the woman in the tailored suit. She had been in the dream, too, but in the capacity of a guardian angel, reminding Sister Fidelis of her vows.

The wheels of the plane connected violently with the runway, the cabin shuddered, and the passengers breathed a collective sigh of relief.

THE NAME OF THE GAME

In a place that was not really a place, being outside of space as we know it and similarly situated with respect to time, two macrocosmic entities—which will be designated here, for convenience's sake, as demiurges—had concluded a lively game of Palindrome and were feeding their resulting macrocosm into RAM.

"Well, that was fun," said the first demiurge. (The dialogue that follows must be understood as being in the highest sense approximate; demiurges do not speak colloquial English, except when they manifest themselves in an angelic or demonic character.) "As often as I've run through this one, I've never hit on *that* solution. And it yields a really terrific score."

"Even so," said the second demiurge, who was some eons younger and had had little firsthand experience of this particular recreational pastime, "I'm not sure it's a valid solution."

"Of course it is. The exit line is a perfect palindrome that is now true in this universe and in no other. If you don't believe it, I'll run through the endgame for you."

"Just explain how you got to the exit line."

"Nothing simpler. Once the nun with the red guitar case gets back to her convent—you remember her name, don't you?"

"Sister Incarnation?"

"Mm-hm. That should have given the game away from the start. Especially with that other nun sitting beside her muttering, 'Blessed is the fruit of thy *womb.' Womb* and *tomb* being such apposite rhymes, and the whole palindrome hinging on the one word *Tumi.* "

"Oh, I see that. But how do you justify the initials *U* and *T?* The doctor's given names are Ettore and Alessandro."

"Yes, but his *son* will be christened Ulise Tennyson Tumi. Whence *I'm U. T. Tumi,* a perfect palindrome."

"His *son?* "

"As I was trying to explain, when this Sister Incarnation gets back to her convent, she'll find out she's pregnant. And nuns, of course, never have abortions."

"How can she be pregnant if her fling with Tumi took place on the 747 in the *erased* macrocosm?"

"Because her genes were unspooled and reassembled *after* the moment of conception."

"Okay. But that still leaves the *naming* of her anomalous offspring unexplained. I mean, here's this nun in a convent with no idea how she got pregnant. All she remembers is a vague dream she had on an airplane. How does *she* know to call her son Ulise Tennyson Tumi?"

"Ah, that's the romantic part. You see, when Sister Fidelis learned of her companion's pregnancy and was apprised of the 'dream' that the distraught mother-to-be offered as explanation for her condition (a dream that corresponded in significant details with her own), she undertook to track down Dr. Tumi as being the likeliest candidate for the honor of paternity. How Dr. Tumi reacted to Sister Fidelis's visit (the rules of the game do not permit him to retain any recollections of his life in the erased macrocosm, even as dream fragments) and how he courted and came to be married to Sister Incarnation—all that is quite droll but scarcely worth the bother of working out in every detail."

"Hey, I thought you were just crowing about the score we racked up," objected the younger demiurge.

"Oh, it's a good score—for such a piffling game. Consider, what have we actually *done?* Created a subuniverse in which a fated air crash has been averted and in which one individual is to be born who does not exist elsewhere in creation. Scarcely the stuff that destiny is made of."

"But who's to say that this U. T. Tumi won't turn out to be another Albert Einstein, another Jean-Pierre Rampal, another Vince Lombardi?"

"Although the odds favor his being another Miniver Cheevy, unnoticed in his life and forgotten after his death. A mayfly."

"But with his own special subuniverse created just for him. Surely that's part of the beauty of the game."

"Indeed. But I do wish I could persuade you to expand your event horizon and move on to the *next* level of difficulty. Palindrome II is—"

"Wait a minute. We're getting a readout that says GAME ONE INCOMPLETE."

"Oh, drat. I hope we won't have to go back to that first macrocosm and trim the wreckage of the plane with corpses. That's not a demiurge's work."

"That *couldn't* be it; we *erased* that macrocosm, we didn't just tinker with it." The demiurge pressed the key marked with a question mark. Within the core of the sun there was a corresponding turbulence, then on the screen before the demiurge a message appeared: EPIGRAPH REQUIRED.

"Oh, if that's all that's the matter," said the first demiurge, "I have just the thing. Some quatrains from Cowper's *Olney Hymns.* They're familiar but quite apt. Here, let me key them in."

The first demiurge sat down before the screen (whereupon a star in the Coalsack Nebula went nova) and typed:

God moves in a mysterious way,
    His wonders to perform;
He plants his footsteps in the sea,
    And rides upon the storm.

Deep in unfathomable mines
    Of never failing skill,
He treasures up his bright designs,
    And works his sovereign will.

Ye fearful saints fresh courage take,
    The clouds ye so much dread
Are big with mercy, and shall break
    In blessings on your head.

Judge not the Lord by feeble sense,
    But trust him for his grace;
Behind a frowning providence,
    He hides a smiling face.

"ABLE WAS I ERE I SAW ELBA"

Once the epigraph from Cowper had been added to their completed macrocosm (for the delectation of the Supreme Creator, who loves to be praised in verse, provided it is rhymed), the two demiurges returned the game to the macrobox marked PALINDROME I:747, put it back on its shelf, and took down the macrobox beside it, PALINDROME II: THE BATTLE OF WATERLOO.

They fed the game disk into their macroprocessor. Throughout an infinite subset of multiverses, time slipped into reverse. Suns sucked up their dissipated energies. Black dwarfs glowered red again. Novas surrendered the planets they'd incinerated, and the great fleets of ships that had brought the all-conquering armies of Napoleon to the British

Isles in A.D. 1822 retreated to the shores of Normandy and were deconstructed by hordes of French workmen who grew ever giddier at the reapproaching victory of Waterloo.

The battle itself was unfought. Wellington's sword was returned to his hand and Blücher revived, together with the dead of both armies.

Once again it was the morning of June 18, 1815. The emperor stood at the crest of a low ridge facing Mont-Saint-Jean. On the slopes below him he could see the array of his own troops, seventy-four thousand strong. Beyond them the long red line of Wellington's army invited attack, like a bride attired for her bridegroom.

He felt supremely capable. Today he would prove that the months of enforced retirement to Elba had not unmanned him. His glory would surpass that of Caesar or Alexander, and this little village of Waterloo would be the keystone of that glory.

Low in the sky above Mont-Saint-Jean a gray cloud appeared. As it moved down the slopes toward the French troops, like the dust raised by the hooves of an invisible cavalry, the emperor gave the order to attack.

Battle of the Sexes

by Ursula K. Le Guin

The next four stories focus on conflicts between the sexes—human and alien. Their genesis as a group came about by serendipity, as do most of my thematic short-shorts.

Ursula K. Le Guin's "Along the River" was submitted through her agent, and although I loved the story I didn't know how I could fit it into *Omni* because of its brevity. But I decided its theme of conflict between the sexes just might inspire some other *Omni* contributors. First I approached Disch, sending him Le Guin's story so he could get a feel for what I was looking for. He promptly sent me an unpublished story he had on hand, "One Night, or, Scheherazade's Bare Minimum." Then I called John Crowley and he agreed to write a story; it was called "Exogamy." By happenstance, during the same period I was editing an erotic horror anthology and had requested a story from Gahan Wilson. He sent me "It Twineth Round Thee in Thy Joy," which didn't quite fit the vision I had for the anthology but did seem to fall nicely into the thematic group already assembled. When it was decided to publish a third *Omni* anthology with original fiction, I thought "Battle of the Sexes" might make a nice break from the longer material.

Ursula K. Le Guin's Hugo and Nebula-Award winning novel *The Left Hand of Darkness* explored human sexual politics and the question of gender difference. Le Guin continually returns to this important theme in her writing. Her most recent book is *Searoad* (HarperCollins). Le Guin's most recent appearance in *Omni* was the story "The First Contact With the Gorgonids" (January 1992).

ALONG THE RIVER

Ursula K. Le Guin

The mdambres used to lay eggs and let the sun hatch them. Often the eggs got addled, or eaten by eefoots, and if they did hatch out, the hatchlings had to bring themselves up, and so had no conversation or manners at all. But when the mdambres learned how to make their children out of clay and bake them, it changed everything.

They had to make the children very carefully, and keep the oven fires at the right temperature, watching day and night, cooking the children little by little, so that they would learn how to come alive, how to move, and eat, and sleep, and speak. In doing all this, the mdambres became proficient in the social arts. That was when they started to call themselves mdambres, which means "people" in their language.

The mdambres with flippers and big teeth could light fire by biting flint with their teeth, and they were good at chewing down trees. Their flippers were useful for building big things like ovens, though not so good at shaping little figures out of clay. So they cut the wood and built the fires under the ovens. The mdambres with fingers and toes were better at shaping clay, so they made the children and watched them cook, turning and basting them and making sure they didn't burn, while the others watched the fires. So the ones with fingers and toes called themselves the cooks, and the ones with flippers and big teeth called themselves the firelighters.

It only took one firelighter to light a fire and keep it burning. The firelighters had spare time, and all mdambres like making things out of clay, so they went on and built mud-brick kitchens for the ovens to be in, and houses for the kitchens to be in, and dikes and walls around the houses to keep out the floods of the river and the incursions of eefoots. They went on that way, the firelighters building and the cooks cooking, and nobody bothered to lay eggs any more. Pretty soon the baked ones were the only kind of mdambre. They made their children and baked them, taught them manners, protected them with walls, fished and cut wood and tended the gardens, and enjoyed sex and conversation, as is the way of people.

The careful work of making and baking the children took a lot of the cooks' time. It seemed like they were always in the kitchen. Back when the mdambres laid eggs nobody ever had much to do except fish and chew trees and putter in the garden, but things were different now.

The firelighters kept the fires burning, and also kept on making houses and dikes and walls, always larger and finer. One would build a tower onto the house; a neighbor would build a taller tower; then they would throw mud at each other from the windows, shouting jokes and insults. Or one would build a wall around a garden and others would come knock it down with their flippers, shouting that that was their garden. Or one would chew down a lot of trees for the oven-fires and float the logs down the river and build a big woodpile, and then another would get even more wood and build a bigger wood-pile. Pretty soon the forests along that part of the river were getting thin, and it was easier to steal wood than go chew down trees. The firelighters had to keep watch in the towers and drive thieves away from the woodpiles by throwing balls of mud at them. After a while all the firelighters went around armed with mudballs. All the houses had tall towers and all the towns had huge woodpiles and high walls.

The firelighters had always been the best swimmers and caught the most fish. The cooks had always been better at gardening than fishing, and these days they hardly fished at all any more, being busy making and baking children. Besides, they had to keep the children away from the river. Young children who were still raw or halfbaked couldn't swim. In the water they would turn back to mud. But they could help the cooks tend the gardens, and the firelighters did the fishing. It all worked out fine.

In one mdambre town the firelighter who had the most dried fish in the biggest house with the tallest tower announced that she was the chief. The other firelighters agreed. Then the chief came to the kitchens with all the other firelighters and said to the cooks, "Make more children with flippers and big teeth."

"Why?"

"We want more baby firelighters."

"What for?"

"To fish, to cut wood, to build walls against the enemy, to fight in the mudball wars, and to light the sacred fires."

"There are plenty of people to cut wood and light fires," said the cooks, "and we have enough walls, plenty of fish, and too many mudballs."

"You do not understand," said the chief firelighter. "You're busy all day long doing nothing but baking children, tending gardens, cleaning things, and talking. You do not live in the great world. You do not understand what is important."

At this the cooks were puzzled. They talked together, as is the way of people.

"They must know what's important, since they're out of town a lot, swimming up and down the river, and have time to make so many mudballs and throw them at each other," said a female cook.

"But what's important about that?" asked a male cook.

"Well, everybody needs work to do," said an old cook.

"But I want to make my first child with fingers," said a young cook, "so it can help in the garden, and bake grandchildren for me. Then I'll make the next one a firelighter to fish for us."

"What is a chief, and why is this chief person telling us what to do?" asked another.

All the cooks asked the firelighters, "Why are you telling us what to do instead of talking together with us, as is the way of people?"

When the chief and the other firelighters heard that they got angry. They roared. They came into the kitchen and put out the fires of the ovens. They beat the cooks with their flippers and bit them with their big teeth till they bled. They took the halfbaked children and broke them into pieces. They threw the raw baby cooks into the river, where they turned to mudstains in the water. "You cannot cook unless we light the fires!" they shouted.

And when a cook tried to relight the fire by rubbing two sticks together, they broke the sticks and his fingers with their flippers.

Since then the towers of the chiefs of the mdambres have grown to be the wonder of the riverbank. Their towns are great and marvelous, full of the stink of drying fish.

The firelighters are very large and strong, because the cooks make them so. They make them with huge flippers that can build mighty walls and towers and hurl mudballs with deadly force. They bake and rebake them till they are hard as stone. All the eefoots along that part of the river have been killed. All the forests are gone, and wood for the fires must be floated down the river from the mountains. All the mdambre towns are at war because they raid each other for wood. The largest, strongest firelighters are warriors.

The cooks make themselves small. They make themselves with fine fingers, good at making and baking children, gardening, cleaning houses, healing wounds, and the other things that, like conversation and manners, the mdambres consider unimportant.

Once a cook made a very large, very strong baby cook. As soon as they saw it the firelighters made a law against large, strong cooks. The chiefs had discovered that although they could not make children, they could make laws, and did not even need ovens for them. The new law said that large, strong baby cooks were illegitimate. The illegitimate baby was thrown in the river and turned to a stain of brown mud in the water. The cook that made it was executed by mudball. Many cooks helped the firelighters throw the mudballs, because it was the law, and they believed that only their firelighters could protect them from their many enemies in the great world outside the kitchen.

Only the ones with flippers are called mdambres, now. The ones with hands and the children who aren't baked yet are called cookies.

One Night, or, Scherazade's Bare Minimum

by Thomas M. Disch

Thomas M. Disch's most recent story for *Omni* was the short-short "Egg and Chips," commissioned for the theme "Man's Best Friends" (November 1989). Here is his modern variation on a very famous tale.

ONE NIGHT, OR, SCHERAZADE'S BARE MINIMUM

Thomas M. Disch

"And this," Sara's abductor explained, throwing open the French doors of a room filled with potted plants and hanging ferns, "is the oda."

"An 'oda,' like in crossword puzzles?" Sara marveled.

"I wouldn't know about that." He sounded miffed.

Sara shuffled over to the barred window. With each step the delicate golden chain hobbling her ankles clinked on the marble parquet. In the distance, silhouetted against the lavender twilight, was the dome of the Taj Mahal.

"So this is Agra! That's another word that's always cropping up in crossword puzzles."

"And *this,* my little gazelle—" He unsheathed the long curved sword that dangled from the sash about his waist. "—is a scimitar. The number of wives and concubines who have been beheaded by this blade is many as the stars in the firmament."

"I'll remember that in case you ever propose."

"The Emir of Bassorah does not solicit the favor of his

beloved. The arrows of his desire fly directly to their target. The moment I saw you pass through customs at the Rome airport, I said to my vizier: That one! I must possess her for my pleasure tonight. Hijack the plane, abduct her, dress her in costly raiments and bring her to my divan. I spoke, and he obeyed."

"Okay, but before you possess me or have me beheaded, aren't I entitled to tell a story? I've never been a hostage before, and I don't know a lot about Middle Eastern culture, but that's the basic tradition here, right?"

When the Emir of Bassorah heard his abductee speak in this impudent manner he smote hand upon hand and cried, "There is no Majesty and there is no Might save in Allah the Glorious, the Great." And he sat down on the biggest pillow on the oda's floor and folded his legs into a half-lotus position, which was quite an accomplishment for someone of his girth, but people in traditional societies where there is nothing to sit on (not even in the bathroom!) have to learn to be flexible. And he said to Sara, grudgingly: "All right, those are the rules. Tell me a story, like unto the tale of the loves of Al-Hayfa and Yusuf, and if it amuses I may let you live one night longer. Mind you, I'm not promising anything. I'm merciful, but I'm also capricious."

"Well," said Sara, trying to get comfortable on another pillow without ripping the delicate gauze of her harem pants, "I don't know the story you mention, but in the creative writing course I took at NYU our instructor told us that basically there are only a few stories that anyone can tell. It's all a matter of ascending action and descending action, and how they relate to the objectives of the protagonist. He drew some diagrams that made each archetype clear: if I had my notebook here—"

"Listen, my little American pomegranate, I want a story, not a lecture. A tale full of marvels and wonders and sex and violence."

"Okay, okay, I'll tell you a story about . . . um . . . Ed Walker and Sally Morton. Ed was a marketing executive for a major manufacturer of . . . um . . ." Sara cast about for inspiration. "Ceramic tiles! And Sally was a young woman he'd met at a party in . . . Babylon (the Babylon on Long Island, not your Babylon in the Middle East)."

"And she was very beautiful?" the Emir inquired.

"Stunning. On the street people often confused her with Vanna White."

"And her breasts?"

"Her breast were watermelons."

The Emir licked his thick lips. "Ah, very good! Continue."

Sara continued her tale, which was freely adapted from a story she'd written for her creative writing class at NYU. It had a minimal plot, but her instructor had praised it for the way it revealed the hollowness at the center of Ed's and Sally's lives and for its moments of low-key humor and its accurate observation of everyday life in a business-oriented environment.

As Sara's story unfolded with all deliberate speed, the pointy toes of her listener's golden shoes began to beat time to a faster tempo. At last he broke out: "By the beard of the Prophet, enough of this doleful twaddle! This is not fiction, this is accountancy!"

Sara glared at the Emir and, in a tone of ill-concealed resentment, said: "Sire?"

"I want romance! Mystery! Adventure!"

"Your word is my command," said Sara, and she bethought herself. The Emir of Bassorah was, as might be expected of someone in his position, a male chauvinist pig. The story she had been telling, though it had got her an A in the creative writing course and received some highly complimentary rejection slips from major quarterlies, was probably

106

not suited to the emotional needs of a man of his temperament and social position.

So, instead of telling her own story, Sara began to retell, as well as she could remember it, "The Ballad of Jim Beam," a story by Barry McGough that had appeared in a Pushcart Press annual. It was about a famous short story writer in Oregon who had writer's block and whose marriage was on the rocks because of his alcoholism. On the surface of the story nothing appears to happen—the man and his wife go fishing for bass, without success, drink a bottle of bourbon, and argue about their autistic child—but underneath the surface McGough was opening a whole supermarket of cans of worms.

As an indictment of American culture in the '80s, "The Ballad of Jim Beam" was scathing, but the Emir of Bassorah, unlike so many of his Middle Eastern compatriots, seemed indifferent to the framing of such an indictment, for he yawned a mighty yawn, and scratched his crotch, and began to reach for his scimitar, which he'd placed on another pillow beside the one on which he was sitting, for it's hard enough for a fat man to assume the half-lotus position in an unencumbered state, but to do so with a scimitar lodged in his cummerbund is virtually impossible. Just try it some time.

"Wait!" Sara said, sensing the Emir's displeasure, "I've just thought of another story you might like better. About a magician."

"And is he afflicted with arthritis?" the Emir demanded. "And does he cringe like a beaten dog before his wife's rebukes?"

"No, a real magician, who is extremely rich and has strange powers, called Shahbankhan the Munificent. He can shrink down as small as a pea and swell up to the size of a . . . I don't know, something enormous. And he can fly anywhere in the world on the back of hummingbird."

"How could he do that?" The Emir's hand drew back

from the jeweled pommel of the scimitar.

"The hummingbird had a teeny-tiny saddle."

"Yes. Go on."

Sara continued her tale, throwing in some new wonder or marvel whenever the Emir showed signs of restlessness or inattention. When his eyes drifted to the window's view of the Taj Mahal, she introduced a veiled maiden who ministered with great skill to the pleasures of Shahbankhan and then mysteriously disappeared. When he began to scrape at the dirt under his fingernails with a golden nail-clipper, she had Shahbankhan fall into a pit of vipers.

All the while the klepsydra, or waterclock, on the wall was dribbling away the minutes of the night. One o'clock found Shahbankhan contending against an army of invisible skeletons. At one-fifteen he was in Samarkand in pursuit of the legendary Blue Scarab of Omnipotence. At one-thirty in Zagzig being plied with a love elixir by an Egyptian enchantress. The Emir listened to it all like a drowsy but querulous child, and the night dripped on endlessly.

It was only a few minutes before dawn, but Sara was at her wit's end. Had it been like this for the original Scheherazade? If so, it was small wonder that so many other wives and concubines had chosen the scimitar to such tiresome and demeaning service. Sara would have much preferred just to give the old fart a blow-job and be done with it. But when she hinted at this possibility, in a narrative aside, the Emir's hand edged toward his damned scimitar. He had a rapist's mentality, unable to conceive of sex as other than a metaphor for murder.

A thousand and one nights of Barry McGough would be bad enough, but a thousand and one nights of rehashing superhero cartoons was an intolerable prospect. Enough! Sara thought, for she was a woman of resourcefulness and courage though not really a great storyteller, notwithstanding her A in creative writing. That had been a tribute more to her looks than any gift for narrative.

She knelt down beside the Emir. Her crimson lips brushed the immense pearl popping from the flesh of his earlobe like a nacreous wart. "And then," she whispered, "the fair enchantress removed the veil from her swanlike neck and, ever so gently, covered the eyes of the guileless magician, so that he was blindfolded now by silk as well as by love." Deftly, Sara demonstrated how this was done with the veil that swathed her own swanlike neck. Then, quick as a mongoose, her hand grasped the pommel of the Emir's scimitar. She lifted it from the pillow on which it rested and raised it high above her head—not an easy thing to do, for scimitars weigh more than you might think, but Sara worked out regularly at Jack La Lanne's and was surprisingly strong. And then, with a sense that she was revenging the grievances of every hack writer who'd ever lived, she beheaded the Emir of Bassorah.

After she'd cleaned up the mess and hidden the Emir's body under a pile of pillows in the oda's farthest corner and found a vase big enough to accommodate his severed head, she tested the various keys on his keyring in the locks of the various locked doors of the harem until she found what she was sure must be there, the "Bluebeard" room in which he had stored the personal possessions of his earlier victims. Sara's own clothes were uppermost in the heap. It was a great relief to change from the constricting and *scratchy* harem clothes into something sensible.

Then she looked through the numerous purses arranged on a malachite display case and took those credit cards that hadn't yet expired.

And then, feeling just like a princess in a fairy tale (but also a bit like the nameless wife in Barry McGough's novella "Born to Shop") she took a taxi to Agra's main bazaar and had the spree of her life.

It Twineth Round Thee In Thy Joy

Gahan Wilson

Gahan Wilson may be better known for his macabre cartoons in *Playboy* and *The New Yorker* than for his prose, but his twisted humor translates just as well into either medium. His stories have been published in various horror anthologies. Wilson's current project is a collaboration with Roger Zelazny called *A Night in the Lonesome October* (forthcoming from AvoNova) His most recent appearance in *Omni* was the short-short "Mr. Ice Cold" (April 1990), which was picked for *Best New Horror 2.*

"It Twineth Round Thee In Thy Joy" is an alien sex story.

IT TWINETH ROUND THEE

IN THY JOY

Gahan Wilson

Ehnk Nahk S'Tak'n softly settled down on the coiling of his legs, but his eye never left the diary as his smallest frontal tentacles gently turned its yellowed, fragile pages while his midbrain deciphered and his aftbrain recorded the words written in faded ink upon them.

The first part of the diary was the routine sort of record any tourist might have kept in order to refresh himself so that he could enrich the anecdotes and brags he intended to inflict upon his home folk once he'd returned from his wanderings.

It began by describing the delights and wonders of voyaging first class on an interstellar ship, including a lengthy account of a conversation the diarist had had with a celebrity while seated at the captain's table. This was followed by a brief description of his arrival on New Mars, some details of his stay in the best hotel in its capital, and a list of historic sights he'd seen there with the more impressive ones carefully underlined.

Then the first hint of the strange turn this heretofore prosaic journey was to take appeared in the account of the diary writer's meeting with an ancient New Martian guide in the hotel's café, and S'Tak'n' found his interest quickening as he read the guide's intriguingly vague description of a legendary, deserted village which climaxed with the following tantalizing comment:

"Understand, sir visitor, that there is no specific statement as to what is there," the old guide told me as he leaned over his still-living meal, 'Tis only said that it is all one could wish for in this life.''

The diarist, who S'Tak'n judged to be a rather prissy sort of fellow, paused to express his disgust at the sight of the guide's meal stirring loathesomely as he forked it, then announced his decision to abandon his original plans and form an expedition to the village. S'Tak'n's mouths worked themselves into a variety of ironic grins as the old script spelled out to him the story of a desert trek very like the one he'd finished within the last half hour. It was exactly the same geographically, but differed significantly in most other respects from the one he had just completed since it had occurred a full three hundred years before.

He paused, lowered the delicate document, and observed the New Martian bearers he had hired going about their tasks. They were, under the astute direction of the head guide, efficiently and carefully cutting their way through the thick, complex tangle of the desiccated vine which completely filled the narrow street leading form the city's gate to its interior.

Moving their tall, excruciatingly thin bodies with the careful economy of movement so typical of them, they were guiding the tightly-focused, scarlet rays of their beam guns cagily since they did not wish to start a general conflagration, but had already cleared the way to the street's first turning, and the lead members of the party were disappearing under two overhanging balconies of bright pink stone. It would not be all that long before they had carved a tunnel all the way through the twisting tangle of wood to the central square of the city and S'Tak'n might make his way there with ease and see for himself if the heart of the mystery lay there as the aeons-old rumors, hinted at in the diary, held it would.

The diary had been plucked from the vine, or rather from the fingers of a mummy complicatedly entwined within it, by Soonsoon, the guide of the expedition. He had presented it to his employer at once, without opening it, but S'Tak'n had not been unaware of Soonsoon's many covert glances full of speculation as the New Martian watched him reading it. S'Tak'n beckoned with a wormish wiggle of the tentacles atop his head, and, striding like a wading bird, the guide approached him.

"What was that in life?" S'Tak'n asked, gesturing delicately in the direction of the mummy.

"A humanoid," Soonsoon said in the dry, whispering voice typical of New Martians. "Perhaps an Earthling. He has the most amazing death grin I have ever seen. It appears to stretch even beyond the lobes of his ears. I do not know whether it is due to joy or dehydration."

S'Tak'n nodded, waved the guide back to his clearing of the vine, and resumed reading the diary with increased curiosity since it had begun to describe the clearing of an identical . vine in this identical street. Three hundred years had again made a considerable difference in the time the task required, however, and the diarist's progress had been slow and laborious in the extreme:

It has taken us three full days to chop our way within the village's square. There is a large fountain at its center and from a distance it seemed as though the bright, curling green coiled round it might be the body of a gigantic serpent, but as we drew closer we saw that it was, in truth, the living beginnings of the vine whose dead branches filled the rest of the city with their frozen writhings.

I went to touch it, but the old guide took hold of my arm with his spidery fingers and whispered, even more softly than was usual with him, that it might be best if someone else risked the first contact. He beckoned and one of the carriers bravely stepped ahead of all the rest. We all leaned forward eagerly to watch as he reached out and laid both his palms upon the smooth, glistening swell of an uppermost coil.

I started and felt the old guide's fingers dig into my wrist as we saw the green vine stir beneath the volunteer's touch. The thing was not only alive in its origins, it was clearly sentient!

"Pull back!" commanded the old guide. "Leave it!"

The bearer looked over his shoulder at him, and there was something indescribably piteous in his expression, but otherwise he did not move. The vine continued to stir, and as the rest of us watched in horror, we saw fresh, almost luminescently green new tendrils pop out from its shiny skin and writhe upwards even as they thickened. More and more appeared and steadily, layer upon layer, wrapped themselves possessively, even quite caressingly, about the bearer.

That unfortunate's body had now begun to tremble most oddly in all its parts, and as his long mouth opened, he started a steady, monotonous, high-pitched wailing which was far and away the loudest sound I had, up to that moment, ever heard a New Martian make.

I turned to the old guide and was astonished to

observe that his eyes had lost the haughty squint so typical of his race and were now positively bulging from their sockets as he stared at his compatriot.

"This cannot be!" he cried, totally abandoning his customary whisper. "There is no female! This cannot be!"

I stared at him a second longer, then turned my attention back to the bearer and saw that a most remarkable transformation was beginning to take place.

I have, in the several weeks of my stay on the planet, found very little difficulty in becoming entirely familiar with the physical structure of the New Martians. It is highly visible, as their clothing consists merely of short, diaphanous togas whose main purpose seems not to be modest concealment or protection from the elements, but to carry and display their insignia of rank.

Though they are extremely tall and thin to the point of emaciation, and the glittering red polish of their featureless, poreless skin is at times a little disconcerting, they are, by interstellar standards, constructed along lines very similar to my own species, having four limbs and a head attached to a central torso in the same general fashion as are as my own.

Now I saw that there were very important aspects of the New Martian anatomy which were ordinarily concealed from view. Under the strok-ing—I can think of no other word that would apply—of the constantly increasing number of ten-drils enwrapping the trapped bearer's form, drip-ping slits were opening between his ribs and along a line running from his groin to the base of his throat.

From each and every one of those slits, with a languid, almost graceful turning, delicate pink spirals were beginning to emerge.

I had no doubt, no doubt at all, that I was observing a sexual arousal.

"How awful!" I exclaimed, and was surprised to realize that I had said it aloud.

The head guide turned and looked at me with interest.

"I am not surprised to hear you say that," he said, after a pause, his voice returned to its usual whisper. "The sexual functionings of species other than one's own often do seem revolting."

He paused again, and I observed considerable concern and puzzlement in his expression.

"But I must admit that this particular manifestation is, however," he continued, "highly disturbing even to myself, who reproduce in a like manner, since it is markedly unusual in two important respects: it is ordinarily quite impossible for us to become sexually activated in the absence of a female, and I have never heard of the emergence of more that four *wanoon* simultaneously, not even in the most erotic legends. Here we have all fourteen functioning at once. His state of arousal must be incredible."

The wailing of the bearer—who was now totally encaged in the ever-increasing accumulation of new green vines—reached an extraordinarily high, trilling note, and then abruptly cut off.

For a long moment the head guide and I stood and watched as the bearer's thrashings diminished. Then, very slowly and carefully, we approached and peered down at him, only to pull back in horror when his body suddenly twisted in several enormous final spasms, then sagged inside its vegetable cocoon with the complete and unmistakable stillness of death.

"Is this the way it is with your kind, then?" I asked. "Is the sexual act fatal for the male?"

"No," said the head guide, his whisper grown so quiet I could hardly make it out at all, "it is not. This is a third, and by far the most depressing, variation from the norm."

A few hesitant steps nearer, and we saw that a new, different sort of tendril had begun to grow from the constantly extending vine. These differed form the previous forms by terminating with a sort of bulb which, even as we watched, opened and showed itself to be a dark, deep-purple flower with a ring of what I took to be pointed pistils and stamens ringing the deep interior of its cup.

Something about the flowers had given me the dim but unmistakable sensation that they were oddly sinister, and when I leaned closer I saw clearly what before had frightened me only vaguely—that the pointed things in the central cavity were not pistils and stamens at all, but a ringed multitude of sharp, tiny teeth. I had barely managed to assimilate that grim new aspect of the vine before the flowers began, first one by one and then in nodding waves, to attach themselves systematically to the dead bearer's flesh.

I felt a soft, insistent, increasing pushing and turned my head to see that all the New Martians in the party had gathered close behind us and were steadily pressing against our backs in order to peer over our shoulders at their dead comrade.

When I looked again before me I felt a cold

chill run through my body as I saw that the petals of all the flowers had spread and flattened and were now squeezing and kneading the dead bearer's skin. They looked like evil, purple stars as they began to pulse together as regularly and smoothly as a baby sucks, and I observed that every one of the vines leading from their bases had now become swollen and veined with red.

"Observe," whispered the old guide, almost dreamily, "They are drinking him dry. See how he shrinks."

What he said was true. First, only the skin reaching to the points of the petals sank like little craters in a moon, but these depressions spread and joined, and soon the whole form of the bearer began to steadily decrease and shrivel before our fascinated gaze. The eyes sunk into their sockets even as they withered; the lips dried and wrinkled back to reveal the teeth they had heretofore concealed; the very joinings of the bones beneath the skin became more and more clearly defined.

As the body of the bearer slowly collapsed, new tendrils of the vine, doubtless encouraged by the end of their long drought, groped eagerly out beyond him in search of new nourishment. I stared transfixed and observed one of the revolting things pawing in my direction.

A coiling green branch of it paused just before me and I gaped stupidly as one of its leaves gently touched my fingers, then slid forward and flattened itself on the back of my hand. The leaf was warm and faintly throbbing and I felt a loathsome but seductive glowing spread insidiously from its touch.

I found myself swaying and sagging where I

stood, as an extraordinary languor spread through my body like some interior version of the vine, but then I saw my hand—all on its own, with no command form my conscious mind—begin to stretch out longingly towards the nearest green swaying of the damned thing, and a thrill of total disgust woke me suddenly from my trance. I cried aloud and pulled my hand quickly back, and the spell was broken.

"We must leave this awful place!" I shouted.

I do not think that any one of the New Martians so much as heard me, so deep was their fascination with the growing plant. Their breathing was now clearly audible and was now coming in unison, each one like one great, hissing inhalation; their bodies exuded a thick, strong odor which was at the same time both bitter and sweet.

There was a terrible moment when I found I could not retreat because of the steady forward pressure exerted by the crowd of blankly staring creatures behind me, but then I discovered it was possible to edge sidewise, and I began a crablike scramble along the front of the mob, carefully arching my body back from the constantly exploring, greedy tendrils which, nevertheless, managed to flick at my flesh and clothing as their reach from the expanding vine grew longer and longer.

I had hardly left my space when a bearer who had been directly behind me shuffled forward. His mouth flopped open and he began a monotonous keening which was instantly taken up by all the others save for the head guide, who reached out towards him vaguely, half trying to stop him.

The bearer evaded him easily, and his moaning

changed to a wavering howl, an awful sort of
singing, as several dripping slits opened in his chest
and I observed the pink corkscrews, which I now
knew were called *wanoon,* begin to rotate, dripping,
into view. As they continued to emerge and spiral,
the New Martian, shuddering and jerking in ever
more violent spasms, began to lower his body
clumsily into a squirming tangle of juicy new vinelets
even as they reached up to gather him into their
writhings. The guide let his hands fall slowly back
to his sides, continued to stare ahead with increasing
fascination, and—softly at first, but then more and
more loudly—began to join the others in their
endless moronic ululating.

   In spite of all my efforts, I was totally unable
to quell an increasing trembling as I worked my way
past these hypnotized creatures. They were now, to
the last one, starting to shamble forward, and though
I greatly feared their mindless shoving would push
me into one mass or another of the monstrous purple
flowers, my struggles succeeded. I finally managed
to force my way clear of them all and stagger some
yards down the path that had been chopped through
the old, withered growth of vine before I collapsed,
flopping like a rag doll onto a desiccated tangle of
wood.

   After my breathing became less than a painful
gasping and the pounding in my chest receded to a
tolerable level, I was able to gather myself together
enough to look back.

   I was appalled to see that so many of the New
Martians had thrown their bodies into the fresh
green sproutings of the vine that they had filled its
first shoots altogether and their companions had

been forced to shuffle slowly along the sides of the noxious plant so that they could eagerly follow the unfoldments of its steady growing.

As soon as those who had shouldered themselves into the lead judged that a sufficient tangle of new vines had sprouted to absorb them, they would throw themselves into the fresh green mass with its sprinkling of gaping flowers and leave those behind them in the shuffling line to wait for the next enthusiastic budding which the absorption of their bodies would produce.

For a short time I was so exhausted that I could only lie back on my complex hammock of dry twigs and watch this grotesque parade of New Martians and growing vine steadily work its way in my direction. But as the gap between us grew smaller and smaller I managed to summon the strength to pull myself up, stagger to my feet, and somehow, before completely losing consciousness, lurch down the entire length of the tunnel we had all foolishly carved through the ancient growth of this fiendish vegetation during the last few days.

When I woke I found that this diary had tumbled out of my pocket as I fell and was lying in the chill New Martian sun, spread open to my last entry, and I confess it struck me as looking more than a little pathetic on the ancient paving of the street. After staring at it vaguely for a while, I pulled it to me and began to put down this account of the vine for no particular reason.

It occurs to me only now, as I reach the end of this record, that I may have been writing a warning for the next visitors unfortunate enough to find their way to this accursed place and its hideous inhabitant.

If there is to be some reader of these pages, some traveler following after me, I beg you to leave now, while you are still on the outskirts where you will have found whatever husk remains of my body. In particular I implore you: do not go to the center of the village, to its well. *Do not look on the living vine!*

Some time ago it grew around the first bending of the road leading from the arched entrance of the village wall. I have watched its slow creeping under the twin pink balconies as I have lain here patiently on the cobbles. I have been writing and watching it near.

It moves a good deal slower now that it is not being constantly fed, but that is not what intrigues me most about its new mode of progress. What interests me most is that it did not come straight for me, as I expected, but rather circled round me in a graceful coil which was as large and spacious as the confines of the street would admit.

Even then it was leisurely in closing the gap; in sealing me in. I calculate I may have watched for as long as half an hour before it grew the last few inches and twined itself together.

Then, in a manner so slow as to be almost unobservable, the encirclement has thickened, the space about me gradually lessened.

Now, at last, the vine is all about me, touching my curled body gently on all sides. I am at the very center of a bower of purple flowers.

I could have left at any point heretofore. I've tried to tell myself that I stayed because I knew I could never make the journey through the desert on my own, but I'm well aware that's a lie.

I stayed because I wished to.

I want the damned plant as much as it wants me.

Sighing very softly, licking his many lips, Ehnk Nahk S'Tak'n gently closed the diary and looked up to see the venerable guide, Soonsoon, looking curiously back at him.

"We have cut our way to the center of the village, sir visitor," Soonsoon reported with a tiny bow.

S'Tak'n flowed erect. He looked briefly at the arched entrance of the village and through it to the coral desert which stretched endlessly open beyond; then he looked back the other way to where the village road curved under the twin pink balconies on its way to the well.

"What do you wish to do, sir?" asked Soonsoon, after a respectful pause.

"Why, go to the center, of course," exclaimed S'Tak'n. "And find the root. And hope it's still alive!"

Exogamy

by John Crowley

John Crowley lives in the Berkshire hills of Massachusetts. He is noted for his subtle blending of the real world with the fantastic in novels such as *The Deep, Beasts, Engine Summer,* the award-winning *Little, Big,* and *Aegypt.* Four shorter pieces are collected in *Novelty.* His story "Snow," published in *Omni* (November 1985) was nominated for both the Hugo and Nebula Awards.

EXOGAMY

John Crowley

In desperation and black hope he had selected himself for the
mission, and now he was to die for his impetuosity, drowned
in an amber vinegar sea too thin to swim in. This didn't matter
in any large sense; his comrades had seen him off, and would
not see him return—the very essence of a hero. In a moment
his death wouldn't matter even to himself. Meanwhile he kept
flailing helplessly, ashamed of his willingness to struggle.

His head broke the surface into the white air. It had done
so now three times; it would not do so again. But a small cloud
just then covered him, and something was in the air above his
head. Before he sank away out of reach for good, something
took hold of him, a flying something, a machine or something
with sharp pincers or takers-hold, what would he call them,
claws.

He was lifted out of the waters or fluid or sea. Not his fault
the coordinates were off, placing him in liquid and not on dry
land instead, these purplish sands; only off by a matter of
meters. Far enough to drown or nearly drown him though: he
lay for a long time prostrate on the sand where he had been
dropped, uncertain which.

He pondered then—when he could ponder again—just
what had seized him, borne him up (just barely out of the

heaving sea, and laboring mightily at that) and got him to shore. He hadn't yet raised his head to see if whatever it was had stayed with him, or had gone away; and now he thought maybe it would be best to just lie still and be presumed dead. But he looked up.

She squatted a ways up the beach, not watching him, seeming herself to be absorbed in recovering from effort; her wide bony breast heaved. The great wings now folded, like black plush. Talons (that was the word, he felt them again and began to shudder) the talons spread to support her in the soft sand. When she stepped, waddled, toward him, seeing he was alive, he crawled away across the sand, trying to get to his feet and unable, until he fell flat again and knew nothing.

Night came.

She (she, it was the breasts prominent on the breastplate muscle, the big delicate face and vast tangled never-dressed hair that made him suppose it) was upon him when he awoke. He had curled himself into a fetal ball, and she had been sheltering him from the nightwinds, pressing her long belly against him as she might (probably did) against an egg of her own. It was dangerously cold. She smelled like a mildewed sofa.

For three days they stayed together there on the horrid shingle. In the day she shaded him from the sun with her pinions and at night drew him close to her odorous person, her rough flesh. Sometimes she flew away heavily (her wings seeming unable to bear up for more than a few meters, and then the clumsy business of taking off again) and returned with some gobbet of scavenge to feed him. Once, a human leg that he rejected. She seemed unoffended, seemed not to mind if he ate or not; seemed when she stared at him hourlong with her onyx unhuman eyes to be waiting for his own demise. But then why coddle him so, if coddling was what this was?

He tried (dizzy with catastrophe maybe, or sunstroke) to

explain himself to her, unable to suppose she couldn't hear. He had (he said) failed in his quest. He had set out from his sad homeland to find love, a bride, a prize, and bring it back. They had all seen him off, every one of them wishing in his heart that he too had the daring to follow the dream. Love. A woman: a bride of love: a mother of men. Where, in this emptiness?

She listened, cooing now and then (a strange liquid sound, he came to listen for it, it seemed like understanding; he hoped he would hear it last thing before he died, poisoned by her food and this sea of piss). On the third day, he seemed more likely to live. A kind of willingness broke inside him with the dawn. Maybe he could go on. And as though sensing this she ascended with flopping wingbeats into the sun, and sailed to a rocky promontory a kilometer off. There she waited for him.

Nothing but aridity, as far as his own sight reached. But he believed—it made him laugh aloud to find he believed it—that she knew what he hoped, and intended to help him.

But oh God what a dreadful crossing, what sufferings to endure. There was the loneliness of the desert, nearly killing him, and the worse loneliness of having such a companion as this to help him. It was she who sought out the path. It was he who found the waterhole. She sickened, and for the length of a moon he nursed her, he could not have lived now without her, none of these other vermin—mice, snakes—were worth talking to; he fed them to her, and ate what she left. She flew again. They were getting someplace. Then, one bright night of giddy certainty (Was he mad? What possessed him?) he took hold of her in the cave where they hid, and, cooing wordlessly as she did, he trod her like a cock.

Then at the summit of the worst sierra, down the last rubbled pass, there was green land. He could see a haze of evaporating water softening the air, maybe towers in the valley.

Down there (she said, somehow, by signs and gestures and his own words in her coos, she made it anyway clear) there is a realm over which a queen rules. No one has yet won her, though she has looked far for one who could.

He rubbed his hands together. His heart was full. Only the brave (he said) deserve the fair.

He left her there, at the frontier (he guessed) of her native wild. He strode down the pass, looking back now and then, ashamed a little of abandoning her but hoping she understood. Once when he looked back she was gone. Flown.

It was a nice country. Pleasant populace was easily won over by good manners and an honest heart. That's the castle, there, that white building under the feet of whose towers you see a strip of sunset sky. That one. Good luck.

Token resistance at the gates, but he gave better than he got. She would be found, of course, in the topmost chamber, surmounting these endless stairs, past these iron-bound henchmen. (Why always, always so hard? He thought of the boys back home, who had passed on all this.) He reached and broached the last door; he stepped out onto the topmost parapet. It was littered with bones, fetid with pale guano. A vast shabby nest of sticks and nameless stuff.

She alighted just then, in her gracile-clumsy way, and folded up.

Did you guess? she asked.

No, he had not; his heart was black with horror and understanding; he should have guessed, of course, but hadn't. He felt the talons of her attention close upon him, inescapable; he turned away with a cry and stared down the great height of the tower. Should he jump?

If you do, I will fall after you (she said) and catch you up, and bring you back.

He turned to her to say his heart could never be hers. She was, simply and absolutely, not his type.

You could go on, she said softly.

He looked away again, not down this time but out, toward the far lands beyond the fields and farms. He could go on.

What's over there? he asked. Beyond those yellow mountains? What makes that plume of smoke?

I've never gone there. Never that far. We could, she said.

Well hell, he said. For sure I can't go back. Not with— not now.

Come on, she said, and pulled herself to the battlements with grasping talons; she squatted there, lowering herself for him to mount. It could be worse, he thought, and tiptoed through the midden to her; but before he took his seat upon her, he thought with sudden awful grief: *She'll die without me.*

He meant the one he had for so long loved, since boyhood, she for whose sake he had first set out, whoever she was; his type, the key that fit this empty inward keyhole, the bride at the end of this quest, still waiting. And he about to head off in another direction entirely.

You want to drive? she said.

The farms and fields, the malls and highways, mountains and cities, no end in sight that way.

You drive, he said.

Love Toys of the Gods

by Pat Cadigan

Pat Cadigan was born in Schenectady, New York, and now lives in Overland Park, Kansas, with her husband and their son. She is one of the original "cyberpunk" writers whose fiction took the SF world by storm in the early 1980s, and her work has consistently been nominated for the Nebula Award since then. Cadigan has published three story collections: *Patterns* (Ursus), *Home by the Sea* (WSFA Press) and *Dirty Work* (Mark Ziesing) and three novels: *Mindplayers, Synners,* and *Fools* (all Bantam). *Synners* won the Arthur C. Clarke Award for Best Novel. She has just finished a new science fiction novel which will be published by Tor and is currently working on a horror novel. Her most recent story published in *Omni* was "Johnny Come Home" (June 1991).

Equally at ease writing fantasy, science fiction or horror, all Cadigan's writing is sharp and hard-hitting, even her humorous stories, such as the following.

LOVE TOYS OF THE GODS

Pat Cadigan

The night Jimmy-Ray Carver got nailed by the alien, he ran five miles without stopping, all the way to Bill Sharkey's house, and busted in on our card game, screaming and yelling and carrying on like a sackful of crazed weasels. Good sex will do that to a person.

We all just sat and watched while Bill poured three fingers of Wild Turkey and tried to get the glass up to Jimmy-Ray's mouth without losing any, which was interesting enough that we all start laying bets as to whether Jimmy-Ray's gonna get outside of the Turkey or not and if he does, is he gonna puke it right up again on account of being over-excited and all. Shows you what kind of cards we were holding—talk about a cold deck.

Well, eventually Bill gets him sat down on the couch with the glass in his hand and Jimmy-Ray comes back to himself enough to know what he was holding and he starts sipping on it, calming down a lot although the hand holding the glass was shaking pretty hard still. So we all say fuck it and toss in the cards and Bart Vesey collects the pot because he bet that Jimmy-Ray was gonna keep the booze down, and we're all surprised and he ain't. Bart's always had a lot of faith in long shots.

"I'm standin' there in the little woods back of my house," Jimmy-Ray starts saying for about the millionth time, "and all of a sudden, there she is, right over my head and not a sound, swear to Christ not a sound, and then I can't move, I'm frozen there with my head up and then there's this bright light in my eyes and the next thing I know, it's like beam-me-up-Scotty—"

It wasn't like anything you couldn't have read in any supermarket tabloid, but we all sat and listened because Jimmy-Ray's one of us and he needed us to. Only Al Miller looked bored, but that's Al. If he was any more bored, they'd have him down to County Medical on a respirator.

"—what it was, but it's lookin' at me and I'm lookin' at it, I mean, I'm *tryin'* to look at it but that light's all funny and my eyes can't focus, and then I'm feelin' the *goddamnedest* thing, someone touching me—touching me"—Jimmy Ray looks around at all of us, scared-like—"touching me in my *head.*"

Al Miller yawned right in his face but Jimmy-Ray's still freaking too much to pick up on this particular social cue. All Jimmy-Ray knows is, nobody threw a net over him yet so it's okay to go on.

"There's something lookin' through my head like some-body leafin' through a magazine and then it hits on what it was lookin' for all along, I guess and—" He stops to take a drink and he's gotta hold the glass with two hands. "Oh, Jesus, even I don't believe this, but it happened. I *know* it happened." He looks around at all of us again and Bill gives him a pat on the shoulder.

"You go on and say, Jimmy-Ray," Bill says. "You're among friends here."

"Yeah," Jimmy-Ray says, like he's not so goddam sure about *that.* "It was just like when I was down in the little woods. One moment I'm one place and the next moment I'm another and *wham!* like that, I'm in this thing that's like a cross between a hammock and a *trapeze*—"

I'm impressed. I sneak a look at Bart, who's kinda smilin' to himself while he's suckin' on a can of Rolling Rock.

"—and I'm all het up like I'm fifteen years old and I got a free ticket to the fanciest cathouse in the world—"

Het up. Only Jimmy-Ray would have used an expression like that. But that was Jimmy-Ray all over. If he'd been anybody else, he'd have just been calling himself plain old Jim. Grandmother raised him in church; what can you do?

"—I don't even know what it is and I don't even care, like I'm goin' for some kinda world record, look out, it's John Henry the steel-drivin' man—"

Bill makes him take some of the Turkey and winks at the rest of us.

"—and then, oh, Jesus, Jesus, no, I can't tell you this part," Jimmy-Ray pants.

"Now, now, I already told you, you are among friends." Bill pats his shoulder and looks to me. "Right, Fred?"

"Right," I say, and toast him with my own can of Rolling Rock, just because I feel like I should do something right then.

"Damn straight," adds Jack and Bart says, "You betcha," and Al goes, "Uh-huh," through another yawn.

"You don't *got* to tell what you don't want to," Bill goes on, "but if it'll make you feel better, spit it out and don't worry."

Jimmy-Ray's eyes look like a trapped animal's but what he's got to say is too big to hold inside. "It had me," he says hoarsely. "I mean, it had me." He lets his breath out in a rush, shaking his head and staring at the booze like he was gonna see something in it. "And it wasn't against my will, either." Now he looks around at all of us with his chin kinda lifted up, defiant, waiting for someone to call him something. "I said, 'Oh, you want to have me? You have me, go ahead and have me, any old thing you want.' And I guess I know what you-all think that makes me, and maybe I'd think it myself but, son of a bitch, I still don't know what it was, whether it was a woman or a man or both or neither or chocolate frozen yogurt. But I swear to you as I'm sittin' here, it was *the best,* the *goddam best* that I have ever been through. And fellas, I'm *scared.*"

He finishes the Turkey and Bill pours him two more fingers. Jimmy-Ray gulps down half of it and I see Bill take the bottle off the end table and put it out of sight. First aid's one thing, but he's not letting Jimmy-Ray get tanked on the good stuff. If he wants to get hammered now, Bill will point him toward the Rolling Rock in the fridge.

"I'm scared because either I lost my mind and it didn't happen, or it did happen and now I'm a—I'm a—I'm a alien-fucker! Like all those people in them papers in the supermarket. And I don't know what it mighta done to me—aw, hell, what if it laid some eggs inside me and next week they come bustin' out like in that movie—"

Jimmy-Ray goes positively gray at the thought and Bill puts the bottle of Wild Turkey back on the end table. "Now don't go gettin' all hysterical again, JR," he says in a fatherly voice. "There's some things we all know and some things we'll never know, but I can assure you beyond the shadow of a doubt that you ain't in the family way."

Jimmy-Ray blinks at him.

"You ain't pregnant," Bill says patiently. "No eggs, no need to go worryin' that you're gonna belly-out or explode or anything."

"You believe me?" Jimmy-Ray goes bug-eyed again, which makes me think of how we used to think aliens was bug-eyed monsters but the only bug-eyes I ever seen are right here in front of me.

"Well, of *course* I believe you. We all do. Anybody here *not* believe Jimmy-Ray?"

Jimmy-Ray looks at all of us and we're all shaking our heads. "I believe you," Bart says, and I give him thumbs-up and Al gives him a good view of his tonsils with another yawn.

"See?" Bill says. "Told you you were among friends."

"Well," Jimmy-Ray says doubtfully. "Don't think it's like I don't appreciate it or nothin' but . . . *why*? Why do *you* all believe me when I can't hardly believe it myself?"

"Well why do you *think*?" Al says, yawning again. "Hell, do you *really* think you're the first person ever met up with a Unidentified Fuckin' Object?"

"Say *what?*" Jimmy-Ray turns to me, maybe because I'm sitting right next to him on the couch, or maybe because he's married to my second cousin, which makes us legal if distant family.

"Jimmy," I say, "we all believe you because we know you're tellin' the truth. We *know*. Okay?"

"You got to spell it out for him, Fred," Jack says, laughing a little. "We *all* been where you been tonight, guy. Welcome to the Alien-Fuckers Club, glad you could make it. I'd say that calls for a toast."

Bill gives him a look as he takes the Wild Turkey off the end table again. If Jack wants to toast, he can do it with his can; Bill ain't pouring him any of the Turkey, which is what we all know Jack's hoping. Bill starts to say something to Jimmy-Ray, but Jimmy-Ray's looking around at all of us like we've all sprouted two heads and there's horns on both of them.

"You're lyin'," he says, and I can see in those scared, trapped-animal eyes he knows we're not. "You're all lyin' because you think I'm crazy and in a minute, one of you's gonna go say he's gotta call his wife, but really, you'll be callin' County Medical to come throw a net over me, put me in a canvas jacket in the psycho ward—"

Even while he's saying it, I can tell he would prefer this to the other, and why he would is beyond me, but there you have it. "No such of a thing," Jack says, pointing a finger at him. "Come on, pull yourself together. Unless you're not plannin' to go home tonight."

Jimmy-Ray's eyes bugged out *again.* "Oh, sweet Jesus. How the hell am I gonna go home to Karen after this?"

"Well, that's something else we can tell you," Bill says, smiling. "Don't worry, it didn't spoil you for humans. I like women as much as *I* ever did. Maybe even more than I ever did. They ain't aliens, but it's all a matter of acceptin' everyone for what they are and not penalizin' 'em for not bein' what they ain't."

Jimmy-Ray's mouth has dropped open and I can't tell whether it's the alien stuff or Bill's preaching the gospel of tolerance that's got him so shocked. "Nah . . . nah . . . wait a minute here . . ." He looks at Bill and then me and then Jack. "It's a put-on," he says. "It's a joke. Y'all drugged my food and set me up."

"That'd be a neat trick," Bart says. "Tell me, how'd we get into your house and figure what you were eatin' tonight? How'd we get Karen to go along with it? And while we're at it, who'd we set you up with? I sure do want to meet her. Or I would if I hadn't met the alien first."

"Jesus," Jimmy-Ray says and his eyes get so big I'm sure they're gonna just roll right out on the carpet like marbles. "Jesus, you mean to tell me—you mean to *tell* me—"

"Seems like we just *did* tell you," Al says, too bored to live. "Now will you just for chrissakes pull it together here? We all got wild the first time and even the second time, and we had to take Bill's truck out and drive along behind Jack his third and fourth times because he was runnin' up and down the roads and we was afraid he'd get hit by a car. But we all got adjusted and you can, too, if you put your mind right."

"But—but what about your wives?" Jimmy-Ray says, not to Bill who lost Sara in a car wreck nine years ago, but to the rest of us.

"What *about* my wife?" Jack says, a little belligerent. "You want to say something about my wife, you better make it a compliment. And a tasteful one, too."

"How can you do this to them?" Jimmy-Ray says in a little hoarse voice, and then puts a hand to his head like he can't believe he's asking this.

"I'm not doing anything bad to *my* wife," Bart says.

"Nor me," adds Jack. "I love Irene and I respect her."

"But you just told me you're all goin' to this alien—and then you go home? To your wives?" Jimmy-Ray shook his head. "God, what if they *knew*?"

"Who said they don't?" says Al, too bored even to yawn now. "Come on, what do you think this is, 1955?"

"A wife isn't just a part of the furniture, you know," Jack says. "She's a whole person in her own right, and she's entitled to a life of her own besides what she shares with you."

I *almost* bust out laughing at the expression on Jimmy-Ray's face while he's hearing this stuff come out of Jack Foley, who looks like the kind of redneck who might proudly announce that he believes in beating his wife once a week whether she needs it or not. Which just goes to show you that looks don't tell you much.

"Listen here, Jimmy," I say, "we all been through some changes since the alien came." Jimmy-Ray gives me the fish-eye. "Uh, showed up, I mean. They ain't bad changes, either. I know that, even if they ain't the kind of changes your pastor would give his blessing to." I paused, thinking. "Well, actually, *your* pastor would. *Now*. Well, anyway, we're all different. And that's all of us I'm talkin' about, which includes wives."

Jimmy-Ray's blinking and his mouth is opening and closing and he doesn't know whether to shit or go blind. Then he turns green, shoves his glass at me, runs to the bathroom, and pukes like there's no tomorrow.

After a bit, Bill goes to see to him while Jack tells Bart he ought to turn the pot over to him because he'd bet Jimmy-Ray would puke and Bart's arguing that the puking time-limit has expired. Al's too bored to referee and I'm too tired. I go and call Joan and tell her I'll be a little late tonight. Somebody's got to take Jimmy-Ray home and I'm the only one going in that direction.

On the way to Jimmy-Ray's, I keep talking sense to him, quiet and calm, hoping he'll catch some of my mellow and smooth out. He still looks like he's seen a ghost or ten, but at least he's not freaking anymore. That's probably more the Turkey finally kicking in. By the time I leave him off in his front yard, he's bleary enough that I know he'll just go straight to bed and pass out. In the morning, maybe he'll just figure it was some kind of weird dream, which will let him cope okay for a while, until the alien picks him up again. After his second time, I figure, he'll straighten out, understand what a good thing it is we all got going here. Might take a third time, but Jimmy-Ray's young, not even thirty-five, and the younger you are, the faster you adjust.

And that just goes to show you how wrong a person can be. A little over a week later, I get a phone call from Bill right after supper. "Fred, you gotta get out here to my place. It's Jimmy-Ray."

"What happened?" I say. "Alien pick him up again already?"

"Nah. I don't wanna get into it on the phone. Just get your ass out here fast as you can."

I'd have been imagining all kinds of things except I didn't know what to think, so I just get my ass out to Bill's place and there's Jack and Bart and Al and it ain't poker night.

"That goddam Jimmy-Ray," Al is saying, almost showing a little life. "I say we call County Medical and have them send out the guys with the nets. What the fuck, who would argue?"

"What's he done?" I say, getting myself a can of Rolling Rock from the fridge.

"Oh, this is a good one," Bill says. "The little fucker went and talked, is what he done."

"Talked? To who?"

"To anybody and everybody he could get on the phone. He called every paper and TV and radio station in a five hundred mile radius and when they put him off, he called a bunch of those other papers, those fuckin' scandal rags that run all the stories about two-headed babies and guys that eat their own foot. They're comin' out to his place tomorrow to get the whole story and take pictures of the little woods behind his house."

I laugh like hell. "Well, so what? Jimmy-Ray gets his picture in a tabloid next to the story about the latest Elvis sighting. That should pretty much take care of him."

"Sure, it would," Jack says, all grim, "if the FBI weren't comin', too."

I think my chin hits the floor. "Jimmy-Ray called the FBI and they just said, 'Okay, Mr. Carver, we'll be right over'?"

"Not on the first call," Bill says, and lays it out for me. Jimmy-Ray called the FBI ten times a day every day for like three days until they sent a couple agents out. Apparently, that's how the FBI deals with cranks, all the people who call up and claim the KGB is controlling their thoughts with microwaves from space satellites and all that shit—they actually send out a couple of agents to talk to them and give them a story about how they checked on the microwaves and set up a machine to block them, nothing more to worry about, blah, blah, blah. It humors the cranks and gives the agents a chance to decide if they're harmless nutsoids or the kind of flakes who'd think they had to go assassinate the president on orders from space creatures.

So the FBI paid Jimmy-Ray a visit and somehow he got them out in the little woods and they found something—traces of the beam the alien used to pick him up, still sticking to some underbrush or something. Now *that* was a real stunner, because none of us ever saw anything in the way of traces or evidence, but Bart said he thought it was because Jimmy-Ray had spread so much poison around out there, trying to kill all the ticks. Jimmy-Ray was scared shitless he'd get Lyme Disease. The poison must have reacted to the beam somehow, and whatever the reaction was, it was strange enough that the FBI guys took samples back to their lab to get analyzed. Nobody knew exactly what the results were, but the FBI was coming back with a whole lab team.

Jimmy-Ray got back on the horn and called all over to tell everyone about that development, and there was going to be a regular media circus out at Jimmy-Ray's place in the morning.

"Yeah, but still, so what?" I says. "Whatever the FBI lab guys find still ain't gonna prove there was a UFO or a alien, just that Jimmy-Ray put a lotta poison in the little woods. You can't tell me the FBI believes it's anything *like* aliens—"

"Prob'ly they don't," Bill says, "but it's gonna be on the TV and the radio and in the papers and there's plenty others that *will* believe him. Like some of those people on the east coast, including that guy that wrote those books, What's-His-Name. And maybe he'll decide to pay Jimmy-Ray a visit, and Jimmy-Ray'll take him out in the little woods some night. Maybe it'll be exactly the right night. Or the wrong one, I should say. And the guy goes and tells his UFO pals, and then they come out here and Jimmy-Ray takes them out to the little woods. Are you startin' to get the picture?"

Am I ever. "Okay. So what do we do?"

Bill smiles. "Like the man said, I'm glad you asked that question."

Well, that would be the morning I have a dead battery. Finally get the truck started and I get out to Jimmy-Ray's half an hour later than I'd planned, and it's already pretty crazy out there. There's a bunch of reporters from regular papers as well as from those scandal rags and even a couple of TV crews, and the FBI's got them all corralled well back from the house, but then they had to call in some of the Highway Patrol for crowd control because just about everyone and their brother has shown up, too. Jimmy-Ray got serious telephone-itis after the FBI said they were gonna send out a lab team.

I push my way through the crowd and find Bill and the others right up front at the barricades the Hypos put up.

"No action yet," he says. "The lab team's later than you are."

"Couldn't be helped. I had a dead battery."

Bill kind of chuckles. "Not so loud. Everyone'll be saying aliens did it to keep you home."

I look over at the reporters and TV crews. "Anyone talked to them yet?"

Bill shakes his head and then points. Jimmy-Ray is coming out on the front porch with a couple of guys who are FBI for sure, along with the county sheriff, Ed Bailey, who's looking pretty serious. I hear cameras clicking away and there are some videocameras going and people are calling out to Jimmy-Ray. Then Karen comes out and she's obviously at a loss with this circus all over the place, but what can she do?

Then the lab team shows up in a big van and they don't waste no time. Jimmy-Ray and the FBI guys take them right out to the little woods. Bailey starts to tag along but the FBI guys say something to him and he gets a sour look on his face. Then he goes over to where the press is corralled.

"FBI says y'all might as well hold yer water, they gonna be out there awhile takin' samples and lookin' around."

One reporter starts calling to Karen, saying he wants to interview her, and then another one just starts shouting questions at her and she blushes and puts a hand up to hide her face. Karen Carver's a quiet person, no shrinking violet but not much for being the center of a lot of noisy attention, either, and this is something completely beyond her, a real assault on her dignity.

Ten minutes later, the FBI lab team comes back around the house and they look *real* put-out. Jimmy-Ray's running along behind the agents, talking real fast, but they're not listening. One of the lab team is pushing a wheelbarrow full of cans and bottles and he looks the maddest of all. Maybe it's because he got stuck with the heavy work. While the rest of the lab team goes right to their van, he stops right in front of all the reporters with his load.

"Just for your information," he says in a loud voice, and everyone shuts up to listen, "we found this in the wooded area, very clumsily camouflaged under some brush. Just a lot of insecticide and weed-killer and chemicals you can buy in any hardware store, and it's all been splashed around with a liberal hand. Mr. Carver's eagerness to provide evidence of an alien landing is a lot greater than his concern for the health of his trees and the indigenous wildlife."

"Now, wait a *minute*," Jimmy-Ray says, "I don't know how all that got there—"

The guy with the wheelbarrow rolls his eyes and goes on to the van with the rest of the team and they just drive on out. Jimmy-Ray's running around trying to get the FBI guys to stay but they're not having any more of him.

"I been set up!" Jimmy-Ray yells, and then he sees me and Bill and Bart and Jack and Al. "There! There's my friends, they'll tell you!" He runs over to us with this pleading look.

"You got to back me up on this. You *got* to!"

"You're sure that's what you want, Jimmy-Ray?" Bill says.

The Hypos are removing the barricades now and everyone starts milling around, waiting to see if there's going to be any more show. The press is starting to pack it up.

"It's now or never," Jimmy-Ray says and looks at me. "Fred? You'll do it, wontcha? You'll tell 'em I'm not fakin' this?"

I give a sigh and nod and Jimmy-Ray goes running over to the press yelling he's got *corrobation.*

"That's *'corroboration'*!" Al calls after him, but he doesn't hear.

Bill gives me a little shove. "Well, go ahead. Get it over with."

The press doesn't seem too inclined to pay Jimmy-Ray much mind and I'm not so sure they'll pay any attention to me, either, but I give it a try.

"Ladies and gentlemen of the press," I say, "Jimmy-Ray here is telling you the truth. He *has* been set up. Somebody set him up to look like a liar. I know for a fact that Jimmy-Ray has been visited by an alien."

A few of them stop and give me skeptical looks.

"I know, because I been visited, too. Just the way Jimmy-Ray has." I get a few laughs on that and then Bill is standing next to me. "It's a fact," he says. "I met the alien, too." He turns to the sheriff. "And so's Sheriff Bailey. Ain't that right, sheriff?"

"Dammit, Bill," says the sheriff, "if you wanna tell everybody about *your* private life, that's *your* affair, but why'd you have to go spill the beans on me for?"

Jimmy-Ray's mouth is so wide open it might get jammed that way. It occurs to me that's the only way I've seen him lately, and it ain't a good look for him.

"You might as well make a clean breast of it, Ed," Bart says to the sheriff. The press is definitely interested again. A couple of Jimmy-Ray's friends backing him up is one thing, but a sheriff is something else.

"Hey, what I do on my off hours ain't nobody's business but my own," Bailey says. "Just because I'm havin' sex with aliens doesn't mean I'm not in my cruiser ready to roll when somebody needs help. I take my beeper up to the saucer with me." The expressions on all those faces make me glad for Ed that he's retiring at the end of the month.

Jimmy-Ray looks like he's gonna bust something important. "I never told them it was *sex!*" he yells.

"Well, what did you hold out on 'em for?" yawns Al. "That's the best part. Otherwise, they'd just be a bunch of funny-lookin' tourists, even if they *are* from another galaxy."

"Did they say which galaxy?" one of the reporters calls out.

"Andromeda," Al says, boreder than shit. "Where else? It's the closest one, easy trip by space warp."

"Andromedans," says Bart and gives a sniff. "You can have 'em. I like the ones from our own galaxy better. They're all flat-headed, about yea high"—he puts his hand out at waist-level—"so I always got a place to put my beer."

"You don't like the ten-foot-tall ladies?" Jack says.

"I don't know as you can call 'em *ladies,*" Bart says.

"Hey, they're *aliens.* Don't make no difference, you might as well call 'em ladies. They sure *look* like ladies. Great, big, beautiful ladies."

"I wasn't thinkin' of their looks," Bart says, so prim I almost bust out laughing. "I don't like my aliens that aggressive. Could spill the beer."

Then Bill jumps in talkin' about snake-people from Aldebaran and Jimmy-Ray about wets his pants. "It's not like that!" he yells. "It's *not* like that! It's something *beautiful* and *wonderful* and there's no snake-people, there's no flat-top beer-holders, there's—"

"Jimmy-Ray, I think you better come back in the house now and quiet down." Karen's there suddenly, pulling at his arm and kind of wincing at all the reporters.

"*There's no ten-foot-tall ladies!*" Jimmy-Ray screams, and everyone shuts up and looks at him.

"Well, maybe not for *you,*" Jack says, after a long moment. "You got your preferences, I got mine. I don't know what you been foolin' around with, but the ten-foot-tall ladies kinda spoiled me for anything else." He turns back to the reporters who are sticking microphones and little tape recorders in his face. "See, they're big, but they got these little teeny-tiny—"

"Stop it!" Jimmy-Ray sobs, and breaks down crying. This is just too embarrassing for Karen, who lets go of him and moves away. I go over to her and pat her on the shoulder.

"It prob'ly won't last too much longer," I tell her.

She just rolls her eyes and a couple reporters break from the pack and come over. "What about you, Mrs. Carver? Did you know about these aliens?"

"*You leave my wife alone!*" Jimmy-Ray yells, and he runs over, but a chunky guy with a camera steps in front of him to get a picture of Karen.

"Well, of *course* I knew," she says, resigned that she's not gonna get away without having to do her part. "Jimmy-Ray and I don't keep secrets from each other. He knew when I had Elvis's babies, and he was completely understanding. He knew it was a childhood dream of mine, to be the mother of Elvis's children. It only took about six weeks—aliens are so much more advanced than we are—"

Jimmy-Ray has gone positively incoherent and he's either gonna bust a blood vessel in his head or start swinging. Bill and I drag him away kicking and screaming while Karen is still explaining how Elvis was really an alien and had to make like he died when he started to metamorphose into his new appearance, which was when he was getting fat and all.

We take Jimmy-Ray around the other side of the house and let him work it out. It's like watching a giant child have a temper tantrum and I really think he's gone over the brink and we'll never get him back. Maybe we should have just called County Medical in the first place, because it looks like that's where he's gonna end up after all.

But in about fifteen minutes, he's all blown out. He can't think of another bad thing to call me and Bill and everyone else except Karen, and it's just as well because he's starting to lose his voice anyway. Finally, he's just sitting on the ground with his fists on his knees and his face all red and breathing hard. Bill squats down and says, "Okay. Feel better?"

Jimmy-Ray looks at Bill and then at me. "Why?" he croaks. "*Why?*"

"Why?" Bill shakes his head. "Jimmy-Ray, are you *completely* stupid? Why in hell do you think?"

Jimmy-Ray just stares at him.

"You just make me *so mad* sometimes." Bill gets up. "Explain the facts of life to this chucklehead," he says to me. "He's married to *your* cousin."

"*Second* cousin," I say automatically, and kneel down next to Jimmy-Ray. "Look—you had a nice time that night, right? What kinda person kisses and tells? Did you used to do that in high school?"

"Get off it," Jimmy-Ray growls.

"Okay, right," I say, glancing at Bill, "it's not that. Suppose you got someone to believe you. Suppose you got a whole *bunch* of people to believe you, and they all came out here to wait for the alien and the alien picked them up. What do you think would happen?"

"I'd have corrobation," he says defiantly.

" 'Corroboration.' You'd also have crowds. They'd all tell their friends and their friends would tell more friends and pretty soon we'd have the whole damned country comin' here. Now you think on that for a minute. *The whole damned country.* People from New York City. Rock groups, and all their groupies. *Republicans.* Murderers on weekend furloughs. The goddam President and the whole Cabinet, too, and movie stars, not to mention the rest of California. *Geraldo.* How about *that*? You really want to share the alien with *Geraldo*? When your own *wife* goes there, too? What kinda person *are* you?"

Jimmy-Ray just keeps staring at me and I get up, brushing my pants off.

"We got a good thing here," Bill says, "and we *ain't* lettin' *anybody* spoil it. If Geraldo or anyone else wants an alien, let 'em go find one of their own. You got two choices: you pull yourself together and you go back and tell the reporters how you were proud Karen had Elvis's babies or any other crazy thing, the crazier the better. Got it? Or you're cut off. No more alien."

Now, that's the *only* lie we've actually told him because as far as we know, the alien doesn't actually talk to anyone and nobody seems to have any influence on it. It just shows up, beams you aboard, and has a good time with you. And that's not always sex, except for the alien, because it thinks of everything as sex all the time.

Anyway, we figure we got to throw the fear of God into Jimmy-Ray to make sure he behaves. And after a while, he comes around the house and tries a couple of lame stories about lizard-people that can lick their eyebrows. But all the reporters ignore him, maybe because they're all sure that lizard-people don't have eyebrows, or because it's too similar to Bill's snake-people. That's good enough, though, and after everybody leaves, we all go home, too.

Well, the story makes one scandal rag before it dies a
natural death and life goes back to normal. Sometime after
that, we hear Karen Carver's pregnant.

So that's nice, we all say, and think nothing else of it. But
nine months later, we hear she delivers at County Medical and
Jimmy-Ray just runs off and leaves her. Her being my second
cousin and all, I go see her after she gets home, figuring she
must be pretty upset.

"We had a terrible fight right in the delivery room," she
tells me. "I just couldn't believe it, and neither could the doctor
or any of the nurses. They had to make him leave. Then I got
home with the baby and all his clothes and things were gone."

"That's awful," I say. "But some men are like that, Karen.
Can't handle major responsibilities. Maybe he'll straighten
out after a few weeks, though, and want to come back."

"I wouldn't take him," she says. "He's been a complete
mope since that other business a while ago. I think it's just as
well. I got plenty of help with the baby." She brightens up.
"You want to see him?"

"Sure," I say, and she takes me into the baby's room.

Well, do I really have to tell you that then and there I see
why Jimmy-Ray run off like he did? Karen nods at me. "You
want to hold him?" And then without waiting for an answer,
she picks him up and puts him right in my arms. "Don't worry,
he won't break."

Having held three of my own and numerous others of
relatives and friends, I ain't worried about that. I was just took
by surprise for a minute there, because never have I seen a
baby that looked *just like* Elvis. There are lots of real strong
resemblances around here, of course, but no babies that were
ever born *with* the sideburns. Not a single one.

Some Strange Desire

by Ian McDonald

Ian McDonald was born in Manchester, England in 1960 and moved to Northern Ireland in 1965. His short fiction brought him a nomination for the John W. Campbell Award for Best New Writer of 1985, and in 1992 his novel *King of Morning, Queen of Day* won the Philip K. Dick Award. Other books (all published by Bantam Spectra) include *Desolation Road, Out on Blue Six,* and a collection of his short fiction, *Empire Dreams.* His most recent novel is *The Broken Land* (published in England as *Hearts, Hands and Voices*) and a new collection, *Speaking in Tongues,* was published in October.

The following novelette explores the ongoing relationship between an ancient alien race and the humans among which they live here on Earth.

SOME STRANGE DESIRE

Ian McDonald

19 November, 10:30 P.M.

The *hru-tesh* is a beautiful piece of craftsmanship. Mother says he can remember Grandmother taking him, while still very small, to watch Josias Cunningham, Gunsmith by Appointment, of Fleet Street at work on it. In that small shop, in those small hours when the city slept, Josias Cunningham worked away while the spires and domes of Wren's dream of London rose from the ashes of the Great Fire, chasing and filing and boring and inlaying. It was a work of love, I suppose. A masterpiece he could never disclose to another living soul, for it was the work of demons. On the bone-handled stock is a filigreed silver plate on a pivot-pin. Underneath, an inscription: *Diabolus me Fecit.* The Devil Made Me.

He was *ul-goi* of course, Josias Cunningham, Gunsmith by Appointment, of Fleet Street.

After three hundred years, the firing mechanism is still strong and precise. It gives a definite, elegant click as I draw back the bolt and lock it.

Lights are burning in the apartment across the street. The white BMW sits rain-spattered under its private cone of yellow light. Have you ever known anyone who drives a white BMW to do anything or be anyone of any significance? I cannot say that I have, either. I blow on my fingers. I cannot let them become chilled. I cannot let their grip on the *hru-tesh* slacken and weaken. Hurry up and go about your business, *goi,* so I can go about mine and get back into the dry and the warm. Cold rain finds me in my bolt-hole on the roof, penetrates my quilted jacket like needles. None so cold as the needle I have waiting for you, *goi.* I touch the thermos flask beside me, for luck, for reassurance, for the blessing of the *hahndahvi.*

Come on, *goi,* when are you going to finish what you are doing and go out to collect the day's takings from your boys? Voices are raised in the lighted apartment across the yellow-lit cobbled street. Male voices. I cannot make out the words, only the voices.

Even on my rooftop across the street, the blow is almost palpable. And then the weeping. A door slams. I uncap the thermos, shake a tiny sliver of ice into the breech of the *hru-tesh.* The street door opens. He is dressed in expensive leather sports gear. In the dark I cannot read the labels. He turns to swear one last time at the youth at the top of the stairs.

I let a drop of saliva fall from my tongue onto the needle of ice resting in the chamber. Slide the breech shut. Move from my cover. Take aim, double-handed, over the fire-escape rail.

Coptic crosses and peace medallions catch the yellow street light as he bends to unlock the car door. The silver filigree-work of the *hru-tesh* crafted by the three-hundred-year-dead hand of Josias Cunningham, Gunsmith by Appointment, glitters in that same light. I squeeze the trigger.

There is only the faintest *tok.*

He starts, stands up, clasps hand to neck. Puzzlement on his meatlike face. Puzzlement under that so-cool baseball cap at that ideologically correct angle. And it hits him. He keels straight over against the car. His head rests at a quizzical angle on the rain-wet metal. Complete motor paralysis.

I am already halfway down the fire escape. Flat shoes. No heels. I have it all planned. As I had thought, bundling him into the passenger seat is the hardest part of the operation. I think I may have broken a finger wresting the keys from him. It will be academic, soon enough. As I drive up through Bethnal Green and Hackney to Epping Forest I pass at least twenty other white BMWs. I sample his CD selection, then scan across the AM wavebands until I find some anonymous Benelux station playing hits from the forties. Childhood tunes stay with you all your life. I chat to him as we drive along. It is a rather one-sided conversation. But I do not think he would have been much of a conversationalist anyway. It is really coming down, the wipers are on high speed by the time we arrive at the car park. I shall get very wet. Another crime against you, *goi.*

It is wonderful how much can be expressed by eyes alone. Anger, incomprehension, helplessness. And, as I pull the syringe out of my belt-pouch, *terror.* I tap the cylinder a couple of times. I can tell from his eyes he has never seen so much in one needle before. He may consider himself honored. We have our own discreet sources, but we, like you, pay a price. I squat over him. He will take the image of who I am into the dark with him. Such is my intention.

"Hear these words: you do not touch us, you do not harass us, you do not try to recruit us or bully us into your stable. We are *tesh,* we are older and more powerful than you could possibly imagine. We have been surviving for centuries. Centuries."

He cannot even flinch from the needle.

I find a sheltered spot among the bushes and crushed flat lager cans, away from the steamed-up hatchbacks, and go into *tletchen.* I strip. I dress in the denims and shell-suit top I brought in my backpack. I stuff the rainsoaked clothes in around the *hru-tesh.* I go to the cardphone half a mile down the road and call a minicab to pick me up at the pub nearby and take me back to Shantallow Mews. The driver is pleased at the generosity of the tip. It is easy to be generous with the money of people who have no further use for it.

The *hru-tesh* goes back to its place under the hall floorboards. Rest there for a long time, beautiful device. The unused needles go into the kitchen sink to melt and run and lose themselves in the sewers of London town. The soaked clothes go into the machine, the jacket will need dry cleaning. I make tea for my sister, bring it to him on the Harrods tray with the shelduck on it.

The only light in the room is from the portable television at the foot of the bed. The remote control has slipped from his hand. His fingers rest near the "mute" button. Late-night/early morning horror. Vampires, werewolves, Freddies. A little saliva has leaked from his lips onto the pillow. So peaceful. On the pale blue screen, blood is drunk, limbs dismembered, bodies chain-sawn apart. I want that peace to last a little longer before I wake him. By the light of the screen I move around the room setting the watches and wards, the little shrines and votaries to the Five Lords of the *tesh* that keep spiritual watch around my sister. Père Teakbois the Balancer, Tulashwayo Who Discriminates, Filé Legbé Prince of the Changing Ways, Jean Tombibié with his bulging eyes and hands crossed over replete belly, Saint Semillia of the Mercies: the five *hahndahvi*. I trim wicks, tap ash from long curls of burned incense, pour small libations of beer and urine. I may not believe that *hahndahvi* are the literal embodiments of the character of the universe, I have lived long enough among the *goi* to know the universe is characterless, faceless. But I do believe power resides in symbol and ritual.

He is awake. The brightness in his eyes is only the reflection of the television screen. Awake now, he seems a thing of horror himself. Shrunken, shriveled, transparent skin drawn taut over bird bones, fingers quivering spastically as they grip the edge of the duvet. Trapped in that final *tletchen,* too weak to complete the transformation. His breasts are slack and withered like the dugs of old bitches.

"I've made tea, but it's probably cold now." I pour a cup, milk and sugar it, hold it steady as he lifts it to his lips. The tea is cold, but he seems glad of it.

"You were out." His voice is a grotesque whisper.

"Business." He understands. Our clients, both *ul-goi* and *goi,* are never *business.*

"That pimp?"

"He won't trouble you again. I can promise that."

"This isn't forty years ago. They've got computers, genetic fingerprinting."

"The people in the car park, if any of them even noticed, will tell them it was a woman got out of the car. The taxi driver will swear he drove a man."

"Still . . ."

I take his hand in mine, modulate my pheromone patterns to convey calm, assurance, necessity. It was more than just a pimp harassing us to join his stable, more than him breaking into this apartment, terrorizing my sick sister, overturning the furniture, desecrating the shrines of the *hahndahvi.* It was *security, tesh* security, which is more powerful and paranoid than any *goi* conception of the word, for it has its roots in ten thousand years of secrecy.

I offer him a Penguin biscuit. He shakes his head. Too weak. Too tired. I pull the stand from its position behind the headboard close by the side of the mattress. From the fridge in the kitchen I take the next-to-last bag of blood. As I run a line in, he says,

"There was a call for you. I couldn't get to it. Sorry. It's on the answering machine."

I am back in the kitchen, filling a basin with water. I test the temperature with my elbow.

"Vinyl Lionel?"

I fetch the natural sponge I bought from the almost-all-night chemist around the corner, whip the water to froth with Johnson's baby-bath.

"A new one," my sister Cassiopia says.

I pull back the duvet. The smell of the sickroom, the terrible smell of prolonged, engrained sickness, is overpowering. As the blood, my blood that I pumped out of myself into plastic bags yesterday, runs into him, drip by drip, I wash my sister's body. Gently. Lovingly. With the soft natural sponge and the gentle baby-bath; neck and arms and sagging, flat breasts, the small triangle of pubic hair and the tiny, wrinkled penis and testicles, smaller even than a child's, and the shriveled labia.

15–16 November

Only four days. It seems like a small forever, since the afternoon Cassiopia came back from the pitch at Somerville Road with twenty pounds in his pocket.

"He insisted on paying. One of the lace-G-string-and-stocking brigade. Took me back to his place. Why do they always have posters of racing cyclists on their walls?"

Though we do not do it for money—genetic material is the price we ask for our services—cash in hand is never refused. I had taken the twenty down to the off-license for a bottle of Californian Chardonnay and a sweet-and-sour pork while Cassiopia changed for the evening client, an *ul-goi* who liked to tie our wrists to the ceiling hooks while he slipped rubber bands around our breasts, more and more and more of them, tighter and tighter and tighter. Thank God once every six weeks seemed to satisfy him. Vinyl Lionel had Word he was Something in the Foreign Office. Whatever, he had taste in tailoring. We made sure he paid for his game with the rubber bands.

When I returned Cassiopia had *tletched*. He is very beautiful as a woman. When he *tletches,* it is like a flower blossoming. Yet there was a subtle change in the atmosphere, something in his personal aroma that smelled not right.

"It hurts," he said. "Here. Here. Here. And here . . ." He touched breasts, loins, neck and on the final *here,* pressed fingers into belly in the way that says *deep within, everywhere.*

Of course, you never think it can be you. Your lover. Your partner. Your sibling. I gave him two paracetamol and a cup of corner-store Chardonnay to wash them down with.

He scratched all night. I could not sleep for his scratching, scratching, scratching. In the shower he was covered in yellow crusted spots. The sting of hot water made him wince. Even then I pretended not to know. I convinced myself he had picked up some venereal bug from one of the *goi*. Despite the fact that our immune systems make us almost invulnerable to *goi* infections. Such was my self-deception, I even bought some under-the-counter antibiotics from the Almost-All-Night Pharmacy.

You can imagine the smell of sickness. It is not hard, even for your limited senses. Imagine, then, a whole street, a whole town, terminally sick, dying at once. That is what I smelled when I came home after an afternoon with a first-timer who had passed furtive notes—*what are you into . . . I'm into . . . I got a place . . .* —under the partitions of the cubicles in the gents' toilets.

I found him lying on the carpet, hands opening and closing spastically into tight, futile fists. He had failed halfway in *tletchen,* caught between like something half-melted and twisted by flame. I cleaned thin, sour, vomited-up coffee and slimmer's soup from his clothes. Over and over and over and over and over and over, he whispered, *Oh my God oh my God oh my God oh my god.* I got him into bed and a fistful of Valium down him, then sat by his side in the room that was filling with the perfume of poisoned earth, looking at everything and seeing only the shadow my thoughts cast as they circled beneath my skull.

We have a word for it in our language. *Jhash.* There is no direct translation into your languages. But you know it. You know it very well. It haunts your pubs and clubs and Saturday-night scores. It is the unspoken sermon behind every mint-scented condom machine on the toilet wall. Like ours, yours is a little word too. When I was small and ran in gray flannel shorts wild and heedless over the bombsites of Hackney Marshes, my grandmother, who was keeper of the mysteries, taught me that *jhash* was the price Père Teakbois the Balancer with his plumb-bob in his hand demanded of the *tesh* in return for their talents. I think that was the point at which my long, slow slide from faith began: Grandmother had been a gifted spinner of tales and his graphic descriptions of the terrible, enduring agony of *jhash* left me nightmarish and seriously doubting the goodness of a god who would deliberately balance the good gifts he had given us with such dreadfulness.

The bombsites have given way to the towerblocks of the post-war dream and those in turn to the dereliction and disillusionment of monetarist dogma and I no longer need faith for now I have biology. It is not the will of Père Teakbois, Père Teakbois himself is no more than the product of ten thousand years of institutionalized paranoia: *jhash* is a catastrophic failure of the endocrinal, hormonal and immune systems brought on by the biological mayhem of *tletchen.*

It can take you down into the dark in a single night. It can endure for weeks. None are immune.

Let me tell you the true test of caring. We may be different species, you and I, but we both understand the cold panic that overcomes us when we first realize that we are going to die. We understand that there is an end, an absolute end, when this selfness will stop and never be again. And it terrifies us. Horrifies us. Paralyzes us, in the warmth of our beds, in the dark of the night with our loved ones beside us. The end. No appeal, no repeal, no exceptions.

You are *goi* and I am *tesh* and both love and life are different things between us but this we both understand, that when we contemplate the death of the one we love and it strikes that same paralyzing, cold panic into us as if it were we ourselves, that is caring. That is love. Isn't it?

20 November, 9:15 P.M.

Vinyl Lionel's Law: Everyone is either someone's pimp or someone's prostitute.

By that definition, Vinyl Lionel is our pimp, though he would be quite scandalized to think that the word could be applied to himself.

Vinyl Lionel subscribes to the roller-and-tray school of cosmetics and wears a studded leather collar. Studs, in one form or another, characterize Vinyl Lionel's personal style. Studded wristbands, studded peak to his black leather SS cap, studded motorbike boots pulled up over his zip-up PVC one-piece with studded thighs and shoulders.

I remember PVC from the Swinging Sixties. You sweated like shit in those boots and raincoats. Vinyl Lionel maintains they are trying to remix the Sixties for the Nineties. Vinyl Lionel should know about the Sixties. He has an old-age pensioner's free bus pass, but he won't show it to anyone. If the Nineties are anything like the Sixties, it will be that whatever is happening is always happening somewhere else. My memory of the Swinging Sixties is that they may have been swinging in the next street or the party next door, but never swinging in your street, at your party.

Strangefella's is the kind of place where advertising

copywriters and the editors of those instantly disposable street culture magazines like to convince people they party all night when in fact they are at home, in bed, exhausted by their workloads, every night by ten-thirty. If the Nineties are swinging, it is somewhere else than Strangefella's. Vinyl Lionel has a customary pitch as far as the architecture will permit from the AV show and the white boys with the deeply serious haircuts doing things to record decks. He is always pleased to see me. The pleasure is mutual. When he has a couple of gin slings down him he can be a delightfully effervescent conversationalist.

"Darling heart, you're looking especially radiant to-night!" He kisses me, on the cheek, not the mouth-to-mouth soul kiss of *tesh* meeting. He calls for cocktails. "Your mother is well, dismal suburbia notwithstanding?"

I reply that business is booming, and tell him about the pimp.

"I heard about that on *News at Ten*. That was you? A gangland killing, they said, made to look like an overdose." He takes a Turkish from his silver cigarette case, taps it once, twice, three times. "That was bit of a bloody risk, wasn't it, dear heart?"

"He'd broken in. Credit him with some intelligence, he could have worked out something was going on."

"Still, Orion darling, you could have left him to us. It's our job to look after you, and yours to provide us with what we want. You people have a vicious streak a mile wide. One of your less endearing traits. Smoke?" I take the proffered cheroot.

"So, this new client."

Vinyl Lionel examines his chrome-polished nails. "Well, there's not a lot to say about him. Nice enough boy. You wouldn't think to look at him, but then you never do, do you? Fat Willy recruited him, you know, the usual way." He moistens a finger in his Singapore sling, draws a yin-yang symbol on the marble tabletop.

"How much does he know?"

"The bare minimum. He'll talk the leg off you, dear heart. One of those confessional types. Well, fiddle-dee-dee, if that isn't him now . . ." Vinyl Lionel waves flamboyantly, trying to attract the attention of the lost boy by the door, fidgeting and conspicuous in a chain-store gent's-ready-made suit. "Oh God, I told him don't dress up, Strangefella's isn't that kind of place, and what does he do? Well, don't blame me if the gorillas bounce him."

"Nerves, Lionel," I say. "You were as bad the first time."

"Bitch," says Vinyl Lionel. He resents any overt re-minder of his fall from youth and beauty while we remain changeless, ageless, ever-young. He beckons the young man between the tables and the smokes and the back-beat and the bass. "I'll bet you fifty he drives a Ford."

One bet I won't be taking, Lionel. A Ford Sierra, metallic gray, F-registration, the odd rust spot. Something to do with metallic finishes, I always think. Garfield crucified upside-down on the back window. Open the glove compartment and cassettes fall out. Home bootlegs, all of them, apart from the mandatory copy of *Graceland*. Nothing more recent than three years ago.

He is nervous. I can smell it over his Heathrow Duty-Free aftershave. Nerves, and something I cannot quite place, but seems familiar. I do not much like being driven by someone who is so nervous. Gaily lit buses swing past headed down across the river South London way; girls in smogmasks, denim cut-offs over cycling shorts and ski-goggles weave past on clunking ATBs like the outriders of some totalitarian, body-fascist invasion. I light up a cheroot Vinyl Lionel gave me as a keepsake as we surge and stop, surge and stop along Shaftesbury Avenue. Lionel, the outrageous old *ul-goi,* was right. This one seems to want to talk but is afraid of me. I weave pheromones, draw him into a chemical web of confidence. On New Oxford Street, he opens.

"I cannot believe this happening," he says. "It's incredible; that something so, so, *huge,* could have been secret for so long."

"It has several thousand years of pedigree as a working relationship," I say. "As long there have been *tesh,* there have been *ul-goi.* And our mutual need for secrecy from the *goi.*"

"Goi?"

"Humans." I wave a lace-gloved hand at the rain-wet people huddling along Holborn. "Those. The ignorant mass."

"And *tesh?*"

I draw a circle on the misted-up quarter-light, bisect it with a curving S-shape. Yin and yang. Male and female in one. From time before time the symbol of the *tesh.*

"And *ul-goi?*"

"Those who can only achieve sexual satisfaction with a *tesh.*"

The word seems to release him. He closes his eyes for a reckless moment, sighs. "It's funny. No, it's not funny, it's tragic, it's frightening. It's only recently I've found where it started. When I was a kid I read this comic, the *Eagle* or the *Lion* or the *Victor.* There was one story, one scene, where this skindiver is trying to find out who's been sabotaging North Sea drilling rigs and the bad guys catch him and tie him to the leg of the rig until his air runs out. That was where it started for me, with the guy in the rubber suit tied and helpless, with death inevitable. It was such an anticlimax when he got rescued in the next issue. I used to fantasize about wetsuits. I must have been Jacques Cousteau's number one fan." He laughs. Beneath folding umbrellas, girls in Sixties-revival PVC raincoats and Gerry-Anderson-puppet hairdos dart between the slowly grinding cars, giggling and swearing at the drivers.

"You don't know what it is at that age. But it was a major motivation in my childhood: tight clothing. Superheroes, of course, were a real turn-on. I remember one, where the Mighty Thor was being turned into a tree. Jesus! I nearly creamed myself. I was addicted to downhill skiing. If there was ever anything in the Sunday color supplements about downhill skiing, or ballet, I would cut it out, sneak it up to my room and stare at it under the sheets by the light from my electric blanket switch.

"Jane Fonda was, like, the answer to my prayers. I used to borrow my sister's leotard and tights and dress up, just to feel that head-to-toeness. Sometimes . . . sometimes, when the evenings were dark, I'd pass on late-night shopping with the family so I could dress up, nip over the back fence onto our local sports field and walk about. Just walk about. It was good, but it wasn't enough. There was something in there, in my head, that wanted something more but couldn't tell me what it was.

"When I was about seventeen I discovered sex shops. The number of times I would just walk past because I never had the nerve to push that door and go in. Then one day I decided it couldn't be any harder going in than just walking past. It was like Wonderland. I spent the fifty pounds I'd been saving in one pig-out. There was one magazine, *Mr. S.M.* . . . I'd never seen anything like it before, I didn't know people could do that sort of thing to each other. Then, after I'd read them all twenty, fifty, a hundred times, I realized it wasn't doing it anymore. I bought new mags, but they were the same: there were things going on in my head that were far, far more exciting than what was going on in those photographs. In my best fantasies, there were things like no one had ever thought of before."

"This happens," I say. They all think they are the only ones. They start so differently, men and women, back among the sand castles and Dinky toys and Cindy dolls of childhood; they think there cannot be anyone else like them. But already they are being drawn toward us, and each other. They realize that what excites frenzies of passion in others leaves them cold and uncomprehending, and everything falls apart: friends, lovers, jobs, careers, hopes, dreams, everything except the search for that something that will fulfill the fantasy in their heads. Can anyone be as tormented, as depraved, as they? I do not disillusion them: fantasies and confessions, and the small absolutions and justifications I can offer; these are treasures held close to the heart. Tell me your story, then, *ul-goi* boy in your best suit, and I will listen, for, though it is a story I have heard ten thousand times before, it is a story that deserves to be heard. You have had the courage that so many lack, the courage to reach for what you truly want.

For the homosexual, it is the image in the mirror.

For the transvestite, it is the flight from ugliness to imagined true beauty.

For the sado-masochist, it is the two-edged embrace of guilt.

For the bondage enthusiast, it is the relieved plummet from the burden of being adult into the helplessness of childhood.

For the rubber fetishist, it is the return to the total comforting enclosure of the womb.

For the *ul-goi,* it is the frustration of desiring to be what they *are* and what they *are not* simultaneously.

Where have all the fluorescent re-spray Volkswagen Beetles started to come from?

What is he saying now? About some 0898 Sexline he used to dial called "Cycle Club Lust"; how he sat hanging on the line running up obscene bills waiting for the payoff that never came. How Telecom regulations compel them to use words like "penis" and "buttocks" and "breasts." How can you get off on words like that? he says.

And I sense it again. A scent . . . Almost totally masked by my own pheromone patterns; that certain uncertainty. I know it. I know it . . . . Tower cranes decked out with aircraft warning lights like Christmas decorations move through the upper air. Towers of London. Close to home now. I show him a place to park the car where it will be fairly safe. In this area, you do not buy car stereos, you merely rent them from the local pub. On the street, with his coat collar turned up against the drizzle, he looks desperately vulnerable and uncertain. The merest waft of pheromones is enough to firm that wavering resolution. Gentle musks carry him through the front door, past the rooms where we cater for the particular tastes of our *goi* clients, up the stairs and along the landing past Cassiopia's room, up another flight of stairs to the room at the top. The room where the *ul-goi* go.

18 November

On the third day of the *jhash,* I went to see Mother, a forty-five-minute train journey past red-brick palazzo-style hypermarkets under Heathrow's sound-footprint.

When the great wave of early-Fifties slum clearance swept the old East End out into the satellite New Towns, it swept Mother and his little empire with it. Three years after the bombing stopped, the Blitz really began, he says. After three hundred years of metropolis, he felt a change of environment would do him good. He is quite the born-again suburbanite; he cannot imagine why we choose to remain in the city. With his two sisters, our aunts, he runs a discreet and lucrative brothel from a detached house on a large estate. The deviations of suburbia differ from, but are no less deviations than, the deviations of the city, and are equally exploitable.

As Mother opened the door to me an elderly man in a saggy black latex suit wandered down from upstairs, saw me, apologized and vanished into the back bedroom.

"It's all right dear, he's part of the family," Mother shouted up. "Really, you know, I should stop charging him. He's been coming twenty years, boy and man. Every Tuesday, same thing. Dresses up in the rubber suit and has your Aunt Ursa sit on his face. Happily married; he's invited us to his silver wedding anniversary party; it's a nice thought but I don't think it's really us, do you?"

To the eye they were three fortysomething slightly-but-not-too-tarty women, the kind you see pushing shopping trolleys around palazzo-style hypermarkets, or in hatchbacks arriving at yoga classes in the local leisure center rather than the kind that congregate at the farthest table in bars to drink vodka and laugh boorishly.

My mother was born the same year that Charles II was restored to the monarchy.

We kissed on the mouth, exchanging chemical identifications, tongue to tongue. I made no attempt to mask my feelings; anxiety has a flavor that cannot be concealed.

"Love, what is it? Is it that pimp again? Is he giving bother?" He sniffed deeply. "No. It's Cassiopia, isn't it? Something's happened to him. The Law? Darling, we've High Court judges in our pockets. No, something else. Worse. Oh no. Oh dear God no."

Chemical communication is surer and less ambiguous than verbal. Within minutes my aunts, smelling the alarm on the air, had cut short their appointments with their clients and congregated in the back room where no non-*tesh* was ever permitted. In the deep wing-chair drawn close to the gas heater sat my grandmother, seven hundred years old and almost totally submerged into the dark, mind wandering interminably and with death the only hope of release from the labyrinth of his vast rememberings. His fingers moved in his lap like the legs of stricken spiders. We spoke in our own language, sharp-edged whispers beneath the eyes of the *hahndahvi* in their five Cardinal Points up on the picture rail.

Jhash. It was made to be whispered, that word.

I suggested medical assistance. There were prominent doctors among the *ul-goi*. Sexual inclinations do not discriminate. What with the advances *goi* medicine had made, and the finest doctors in the country, surely something . . .

"It must be concern for your sister has temporarily clouded your judgment," whispered Aunt Lyra, "otherwise I cannot imagine you could be so stupid as to consider delivering one of us into the hands of the *goi*."

My mother hushed him with a touch to his arm.

"He could have put it a bit more subtly, love, but he's right. It would be no problem to recruit an *ul-goi* doctor, but doctors don't work in isolation. They rely upon a massive edifice of researchers, technicians, laboratories, consultants: how long do you think it would be before some *goi* discovered the truth about Cassiopia?"

"You would let my sister, your daughter die, rather than compromise security?"

"Do not ask me to answer questions like that. Listen up. One of our regulars here is a *ul-goi* lawyer. Just to make conversation I asked him once what our legal position was. This is what he told me: we may think and talk and look like humans, but we are not human. And, as non-humans, we are therefore the same as animals—less than animals; most animals enjoy some protection under the law, but not us. They could do what they liked to us, they could strip us of all our possessions, jail us indefinitely, use us to experiment on, gas us, hunt us down one by one for sport, burn us in the street, and in the eyes of the law it would be no different from killing rats. We are not human, we are not under the protection of the law.

To compromise our secrecy is to threaten us all."

"He is dying and I want to know what to do."

"You know what to do." The voice startled me. It was like the voice of an old, corroded mechanism returning to life after long inactivity. "You know what to do," repeated my grandmother, stepping through a moment of lucidity into this last decade of the millennium. "Can I have taught you so badly, or is it you were such poor pupils? Père Teakbois the Balancer demanded *jhash* of us in return for our enormously long lives, but Saint Semillia of the Mercies bargained a ransom price. Blood. The life is in the blood; that life may buy back a life."

Of course I knew the story. I even understood the biological principle behind the spurious theology. A massive blood transfusion might stimulate the disrupted immune system into regenerating itself, in a similar sense to the way our bodies rebuild themselves by using *goi* sex cells as a template. I had known the answer to *jhash* for as long as I had known of *jhash* itself: why had I refused to accept it and looked instead for, yes, ludicrous, yes, dangerous alternatives that could not possibly work?

Because Saint Semillia of the Mercies sells his dispensations dear.

Mother had given me a shoeboxful of equipment, most of it obsolete stuff from the last century when the last case of *jhash* had occurred. She did not tell me the outcome. Either way, I was not certain I wanted to know. In the house on Shantallow Mews I ran a line into my arm and watched the *Six O'clock News* while I pumped out two plastic bags. Internecine warfare in the Tory party. Some of the faces I knew, intimately. The blood seemed to revive Cassiopia but I knew it could only be temporary. I could never supply enough: after only two pints I was weak and trembling. All I could do was hold the sickness at bay. I took the icon of Saint Semillia of the Mercies down from the wall, asked it what I should do. His silence told me nothing I did not already know myself. *Out there. They are few, they are not perfect, but they exist, and you must find them.* I *tletched,* dressed in black leotard, black tights, black mini, black heels, wrapped it all under a duster coat and went down to the Cardboard Cities.

What is it your philosophers teach? That we live in the best of all possible worlds? Tell that to the damned souls of the cardboard cities in the tunnels under your railway stations and underpasses. *Tesh* have no such illusions. It has never been a tenet of our faith that the world should be a good place. Merely survivable.

Cloaked in a nimbus of hormonal *awe,* I went down. You would smell the piss and the beer and the smoke and the dampness and something faint and semi-perceived you cannot quite recognize. To me that thing you cannot recognize is what is communicated most strongly to me. It is despair. Derelicts, burned out like the hulls of Falklands' warships, waved hallucinatory greetings to me as I swirled past, coat billowing in the warm wet wind that blew across the wastelands. Eyes moved in cardboard shelters, cardboard coffins, heads turned, angered by the violation of their degradation by one who manifestly did not share it. When it is all you possess, you treasure even degradation. Figures gathered around smudge fires, red-eyed from the smoke, handing round hand-rolled cigarettes. Where someone had scraped enough money for batteries there was dance music from boom boxes. They would not trouble me. My pheromones made me a shadowy, godlike figure moving on the edge of the darkness.

Where should I go? I had asked.

Where no one will be missed, my mother had replied.

I went to the viaduct arches, the motorway flyovers, the shop doorways, the all-nite burger-shops, the parking lots and playgrounds. I went down into the tunnels under the stations. Trains ground overhead, carrying the double-breasted suit men and cellphone women back to suburbs ending in "ing" or "wich," to executive ghettos with names like Elmwood Grove and Manor Grange. The tunnels boomed and rang, drops of condensation fell sparkling in the electric light from stalactites seeping from the expansion joints in the roof. I paused at the junction of two tunnels. Something in the air, a few vagrant lipid molecules carried in the air currents beneath the station.

How will I know them? I had asked.

You will know them, my mother had said.

The trail of pheromones was fickle, more absent than present. It required the utmost exercise of my senses to follow it. It led me down clattering concrete stairways and ramps, under striplights and dead incandescent bulbs, down, underground. As I was drawn deeper, I dissolved my aura of *awe* and wove a new spell: *allure.* Certain now. Certain. The lost children in their cribs barely acknowledged my presence, the air smelled of shit and *ganja.*

She had found a sheltered corner under a vent that carried warmth and the smell of frying food from some far distant point of the concourse. An outsize Aran sweater—much grimed and stretched—was pulled down over her hunched-up knees. She had swaddled herself in plastic refuse sacks, pulled flattened cardboard boxes that had held washing machines and CD midi-systems in around her.

I enveloped her in a shroud of pheromones. I tried to imagine what she might see, the tall woman in the long coat, more vision than reality, demon, angel, standing over her like judgment. How could she know it was my pheromones, and not her own free will, that made her suddenly want more than anything, anything she had ever wanted in her life, to bury her face between my nylon-smooth thighs? I knelt down, took her chin in my hand. She looked into my eyes, tried to lick my fingers. Her face was filthy. I bent toward her and she opened her mouth to me. She ran her tongue around the inside of my lips; whimpering, she tried to ram it down my throat.

And I was certain. Truth is in the molecules. I had tasted it.

I extended a hand and she took it with luminous glee. She would have done anything, anything for me, anything, if I would only take her away from these tunnels and the stink of piss and desperation, back to my apartment: I could do whatever I wanted, anything.

The corridors shook to the iron tread of a train.

She loved me. Loved me.

With a cry, I snatched my hand from the touch of her fingers, turned, walked away, coat flapping behind me, heels ringing like shots. Faster. Faster. I broke into a run. Her calls pursued me through the tunnels, *come back come back, I love you, why did you go, I love you . . . .*

I rode the underground into the take-away-curry-and-tins-of-lager hours. *We are not human,* my mother told me from every poster and advertisement, *we cannot afford the luxuries of human morality.* Saint Semillia of the Mercies smiled upon me. I rode the trains until the lights went out, one by one, in the stations behind me, and came home at last to Shantallow Mews.

The house looked and smelled normal. There was nothing to see. From the outside. He had broken in through a rear window and trashed a path through the rooms where we entertained the *goi.* Finding the locked door, he had kicked his way into Cassiopia's room.

The pimp had done a thorough and professional job of terror. Empty glasses and cups of cold tea shattered, a half-completed jigsaw of the Royal Family a thousand die-cut pieces scattered across the floor, magazines torn in two, the radio-cassette smashed in by a heel. Shredded cassette tape hung in swaths from the lights and stirred in the draft from the open door where I stood. The metal stand by the bedside was overturned; the blood, my blood, was splashed and daubed across the walls.

Cassiopia was in the corner by the window, shivering and dangerously pale from shock. Under the duvet he clutched the icons of the five *hahndahvi* and a kitchen knife. Bruises purpled down the side of his face, he flinched from my gentlest touch.

"He said he'd be back," my sister whispered. "He said unless we worked for him, he'd be back again. And again. And again. Until we got wise."

I made him comfortable on the sofa, cleaned the blood from the walls, made good the damage. Then I went to the never-quite-forgotten place under the floorboards and unearthed the *hru-tesh*.

Saint Semillia, the price of your mercies!

20 November, 10:30 P.M.

But for the insistence of my perfumes urging him through the door at the top of the stairs, I think he would run in terror from what he is about to do. Often they do. But they are always drawn back to this door, by the sign of the yin-yang drawn in spilled vodka on a table top, by addresses on matchbooks or slipped under toilet partitions. They come back because nothing else can satisfy them.

The *hahndahvi* placed at their five cardinal points about the room fascinate him. He turns the icon of Filé Legbé over and over in his hands.

"This is old," he says.

"Early medieval," I say, offering him a drink from the cocktail bar. He takes a tequila in one nervous swallow. "The *hahndahvi*. The Five Lords of the *tesh*. We have our own private religion; a kind of urban witchcraft, you could call it.

Our own gods and demons and magics. They've taken a bit of a theological bashing with the advent of molecular biology, when we realized that we weren't the demonic lovers, the incubi and succubi of medieval legend. Just a variant of humanity. A subspecies. Two chromosomes separate me from you." As I am talking, he is undressing. He looks for a wardrobe where he can hang his smart suit and shirt and jazz-colored silk tie. I slide open one of the mirror-robes at the end of the room. His fastidiousness is cute. I pour him another tequila so that he will not be selfconscious in his nakedness and guide him to the Lloyd-loom chair at the opposite side of the room. As I seat him I smell it again, that uncertain something, masked and musked in a cocktail of his own sweat, aftershave and José Cuervo. Familiar.

He sips his drink, small, tight, fearful sips, as I strip down to my underwear. I slowly peel off panties, stockings, suspenders, kick them away. His penis comes up hard, sudden, taking him by surprise. The glass falls to the floor. The tequila spreads across the carpet. He begins to masturbate slowly, ecstatically. Standing naked before him, I slip into *tletchen*. I feel the familiar warmth behind my eyes as waves of endocrines and hormones surge out through my body. I will them into every part of me, every empty space, every cell, every molecule of me. I am on fire, burning up from inside with chemical fire.

"Do you know anything about mitosis and meiosis?" I ask him as the hormones burn through me, changing me. *Moses supposes mitosis are roses. Moses supposes erroneously.* "The old legend was that incubi and succubi visited humans to steal sexual fluids. Sperm, eggs. It's true, insofar as we need haploid cells to self-impregnate every cell in our bodies and, in a sense, continually give birth to ourselves. That's how we live five, six, seven hundred years, world events permitting. Though, of course, our reproductive rate is very very low." I have found over the years that many of them find the talking as exciting as the physical act. It is the thrill of abandoning themselves to the implacably alien. As I speak my breasts, so full and beautiful, dwindle and contract to flat nipples; the pads of flesh on my hips and ass are redistributed to shoulders and belly; muscles contract my pelvis; my entire body profile changes from wide-hipped narrow-shouldered hourglass femininity to broad-shouldered, flat-chested narrow-waisted triangular masculinity. My genitals swell and contract and jut and fold themselves into new configurations. It excited me enormously, that first time when Mother guided me into *tletchen,* the ebb and swell of my genitals. Now what I sense is an incompleteness, a loss, when I change from female to male. But I can see what a shock of excitement it is to my client.

I come to him, let him savor my new masculinity. He runs his fingers over my flat chest, twists my flat nipples between thumb and finger, caresses my buttocks, thighs, genitals. As he thrills to me, I continue, my voice an octave lower.

"We're essentially an urban phenomenon. We were there in the cities of the Nile and Indus, of Mesopotamia, of Classical Greece and Rome—some lesser members of their respective pantheons are *tesh* in disguise. We need a large population to draw genetic material from without becoming too obvious—in rural communities we have rather too high a profile for our liking. Hence the medieval legends, when the country was almost entirely rural, which died out with urbanization when we could become anonymous in the cities. My particular family came with the Norman invasion; but we're comparative new kids on the block; the branch we bred into one hundred and fifty years back up in Edinburgh has been here since the end of the Ice Age."

There are tears in his eyes. Pressed close within his embrace, I smell it again. Intimate. Familiar.

Too familiar.

I know what it is, and where I have smelled it before. But I am not finished with him yet. I step backward, out of the reach of his imploring fingers and summon up the *tletchen* energy again. Contours, profiles, genders melt and run in the heat of my hormonal fire. My body, my identity, my teshness, my Orion-ness dissolve into a multiplicity of possible genders. I blossom out of genderlessness into full hermaphroditism. Male and female, yin and yang in one. He is sobbing now, milking his penis in long, slow, joyous strokes. He is close now to complete sexual satisfaction for the first time in his life. I let him touch me, explore the mystery of my two-in-oneness. He stands, presses his body to mine, shuddering, moaning; long keening, dying moans. Exposed. Truly naked. From every pore of his body, every gland and mucous membrane and erogenous tissue, it pours out. The room whirls with his giddy perfume, the storm of chemicals is overpowering. *Yes! Yes! Yes!*

I look into his eyes.

"Do you know how we get our names?" I tell him. "We have public, *goi,* names, but among ourselves we use our *tesh* names. We are named after whatever constellation is in the ascendant on the night of our birth. My name is Orion. My sister is Cassiopia." I tell him, because I want him to know. I owe him at least a name. I open my mouth to kiss him, he opens to receive me. Thin ropes of drool stretch and break. I taste him. And he is right. It is the work of moment for my saliva glands to work the chemical changes. A drop of toxin falls from my tongue onto his. It runs like chain lighting from neuron to neuron. Even as the thought to react, the awareness that he may have been betrayed, is upon him, it locks him into rigidity.

He is easy to lift. In hermaphrodite gender we have the benefit of the musculature of both sexes, and the hormonal

violence of *tletchen* gives us a supernatural strength. I carry
him down the stairs and along the little landing into Cassiopia's
room. I can feel his heart beating against my shoulder. He fits
comfortably into the bedside chair.

Cassiopia is suspended in a fever dream between sleep
and waking; muttering, crying out, twitching, eyeballs rolled
up in his head, crazy with hallucinations. I fetch the equipment
from the Reebok box under the bed, run a line into Cassiopia's
right arm, and let the blue, burned, poison drip from his arm
into a basin on the floor.

Only his eyes can move. He sees the needle I have for
him. Have I said elsewhere it is remarkable how much can be
expressed by the eyes alone? Say a thing once, and you are sure
to have to say it again, soon. He does not flinch as I run a line
into his right arm and connect him to Cassiopia. As I pump his
blood along the old rubber tubes, I tell him the tale my
grandmother told me, of Père Teakbois's bargain and the price
of St. Semillia's mercy. At the very end, he deserves to know.
And at the very end, I think he does begin to understand. Vinyl
Lionel's Law. Everyone is someone's pimp, someone's prostitute. Everyone is user or used. Down in the tunnels, she had
loved me. You had desired me. She had not loved me of her
own free will. You did. I made her love me. I did not make you
desire me. Understand, *goi,* why I could kill the pimp without
a moment's moral uncertainty, why now it is your blood
pulsing down the rubber tube. We were both the used, she and
I. You and he, the users. Believe me, *goi* boy, I bear you no
malice. I do what I do because an older, harder mercy
demands it.

When the last drop is gone, I close the tubes. Cassiopia
has lapsed into a quiet and tranquil sleep. Already the *jhash*
pallor is gone from his skin, he is warm to my kiss.

I look at the boy, the rigor of my neurotoxins glazed over
now with the serenity of death. When you went to those clubs

and bars and made those contacts, did they never tell you the unwritten law of the user?

Every prostitute has his price.

In *tesh,* the words for *love* and *passion* are antonyms. It is not so different, I think, with you.

Virus Dreams

by Scott Baker

Scott Baker was born in the American midwest but has been living in Paris, France with his wife for over a decade. He has published several novels including *Dhampire* and *Webs*. He has recently sold an untitled dark fantasy to Tor, finished a science fiction novella, and is working on a novel about African magic in Paris. He is notorious for his strange and disturbing stories, particularly "The Lurking Duck" (*Omni,* December 1983), about a psychotic girl and her mechanical killer duck. The novelette was nominated for the World Fantasy Award; the full novella version was recently published for the first time in the anthology *Foundations of Fear* edited by David G. Hartwell (Tor). "Still Life With Scorpion" won the World Fantasy Award for best short story in 1985.

The following is a science fiction novella about computers, cults, and sexuality which displays Baker's skill at making weird ideas believable.

VIRUS DREAMS

Scott Baker

The fight with Claire had kept him up until four in the morning, and Kamutef's secretary had insisted he be ready by seven. The traffic south out of Paris was just crawling along. Mark Gyoko soon fell asleep in the overheated stretch limousine's back seat.

He dreamed it was his birthday and Claire had invited him to a Chinese restaurant in Belleville with her fashion and advertising friends, none of whom he recognized. The restaurant, a strawberry blond Swedish girl told him excitedly, was being financed by the Chinese mafia's biggest heroin importer. It was perfect for his birthday dinner, she said, because disfigured as his disease had left him, none of them could normally risk being seen with him. But this restaurant was popular just because it was so disreputable, so they didn't have to worry.

Inside, the restaurant was a big, square room with maroon tiles on the floor and no furniture. It was filled with Chinese men wearing white linen monks' robes. They were all crowded together in a tight, murmuring mass around something in the center. Mark could see only their straight, heavy black hair, the dark sheen of the backs of their necks, and sometimes a bit of an ear or a cheek, but no faces. The blond girl told him they were holding a funeral and the body was laid out so the mourners could pay their respects.

Claire took his arm. We have to circulate, there's nothing to see, she whispered. They began to promenade with stately dignity around the packed Chinese, as if leading off an embassy ball. Claire's friends followed at one-meter intervals.

Suddenly, one of the Chinese noticed Mark. His mouth fell open and he stared at Mark in shock. His teeth were rotten, yellow-green stubs, and Mark realized he wasn't Chinese at all, but French, wearing an extravagantly cut white linen suit and a silly white velvet beret. A few other westerners in white suits were scattered here and there among the packed Chinese.

The Frenchman plucked at his neighbor's sleeve and pointed at Mark. The Chinese looked as shocked as the Frenchman. He said something incomprehensible to the others, and then the murmuring stopped and all the mourners were turning toward Mark like sunflowers to the sun and fixing him with their dull, black, empty eyes. When Uncle Toshi was drunk he sometimes muttered about how the Chinese were their hereditary enemies.

We have to leave, Claire whispered, plucking insistently at Mark's sleeve, but he shook her off and asked the Frenchman with the bad teeth what he was staring at.

The man said that they were all amazed at how much he resembled someone. Because of his disease.

Someone Chinese? Mark asked, because he didn't dare ask how everyone knew he was diseased when it wasn't supposed to show on the outside yet.

Of course.

Who?

The Frenchman said something to an elderly Chinese woman. She linked her arm through Mark's and they began promenading again, but instead of circling around the outside of the room they were spiraling in toward its center, the packed

Chinese parting before them. The whole thing was as perfectly choreographed as a dance sequence from a Busby Berkeley movie. Claire and her friends followed, still frantically enthusing and networking in overbright chipmunk voices.

In the center of the room was a low, pink-veined marble pedestal, surrounded by a ring of waist-high planters like the window boxes on Mark's balcony, but lacquered white and filled with gleaming black sand. Some boxes had odd-shaped rocks in them. One held a sickly cactus plant bristling with long gray spines, and another had an old XT motherboard, with a missing 8088 chip, half-buried in the sand. All the memory chips were painted a livid pinkish-gray. The effect was somewhere between a Kabuki theater and the flower shop by the Pont Neuf with all the stunted cacti out front. The old woman was wearing an embroidered gray silk kimono. She looked Japanese, exactly like the grandmother he had never met in the photograph hanging on his father's living room wall.

A big tarnished silver dome with a knob on top, the kind used in carveries to keep the meat hot when they wheel it around, was posed on top of the pedestal. Mark's grandmother clapped her hands. Everybody, even the Chinese, started singing "Happy Birthday."

Mark lifted the silver dome, revealing a fossilized human pelvis, lovingly polished so it shone like tobacco-stained ivory. Pick it up, Mark's grandmother told him sharply, taking the silver dome and handing it ceremoniously to Claire. Mark cradled the fossilized bone in his arms, rocking it like a baby, and that was when he knew that this was his own funeral and he was dead.

The knowledge came as a great relief. He wouldn't be a burden to Claire anymore.

April Fool! *Poisson d'avril!* all the mourners shouted, and he nodded back at them, grinning to let them know he appreciated the joke. His grandmother held the tray steady while he climbed up onto it and tucked his legs in under him. Claire put a candy-apple red 80486SX chip in his mouth, which was more than he deserved, and covered him with the silver dome.

When Mark awoke, the sun was noon-high. They were somewhere in the country, turning off a one-lane road in through a gate in a low stone wall. The countryside was hilly, green, dotted with black and white cattle. In the distance, on the highest hill, Mark could see a slate-roofed chateau surrounded by agricultural buildings.

The limousine wound its way toward the chateau, occasionally pausing to let cattle cross the road.

Mark leaned forward, tapped on the glass. "Mr. Kamutef breeds cattle?"

"Yes," the driver answered. "He is very proud of his herds."

Mark slouched back in his seat, took the letter out of his coat pocket again.

Dear Mr. Gyoko,
    It has come to my attention that you might be available for some programming work. Your skills and technical ability have been most highly recommended to me, and I

Of course he was available. A year ago, before one of his co-workers and supposed friends had spliced a virus into the beta-test version of his latest theatrical animation toolkit, he had been living the good life with his lovely French wife in Santa Cruz as one of the few pre-Nintendo video game designers still making big money, mainly because he and the company he had worked for had known when to switch to computer-generated graphics for television before diversifying off into interactive multi-media. Now he was an unemployed expatriate in Paris, living off what his wife brought in from the job father had given her her with the family perfume company, while he tried to make a living as a freelance programmer whom nobody trusted to touch a program.

The driver pulled up in front of the chateau. It was bigger than Mark had thought—easily the size of some of the larger *chateaux de la Loire,* not just some nineteenth-century bourgeois's pretentious manor house.

Mark had no idea what this Khalid Kamutef wanted—all he had been able to find out was that he was the CEO of some vague Egyptian industrial cartel, and so presumably Egyptian and rich. Now he also knew Kamutef had a chateau and raised cows. He hoped Kamutef spoke English so they wouldn't be forced to communicate in Mark's execrable French.

He also hoped the job would turn out to be not only something he was competent to do, but something he could accept.

A striking but harsh-faced Mediterranean-looking woman met him at the door. She was in her late thirties or early forties, wearing a short-skirted but severely tailored gray silk suit. As she led him across a marble floor through a waiting room decorated in overly ornate Louis the Somebody frumpery—chairs with squat gilt legs, stylized yawning lions' heads and dolphins, all that stuff—he saw she herself had great legs.

She opened a massive wooden door.

"Mr. Kamutef is waiting for you. Go right in."

The office was paneled in the same dark wood as the door. There was another door in the wall behind his desk. The only light came from a window looking out on a fenced-in pasture with more cows. Kamutef was a dark, unhealthy-looking man of about sixty with a beaklike nose and thick silver hair. He was seated behind a polished mahogany desk that was bare except for a few unobtrusive buttons set into the wood within easy reach of his right hand, and an oversized book bound in white leather like that hagiography of Elvis that Mark's Aunt Anabelle was so proud of, the one the Elvis look-alike in the white satin suit had personally delivered to her door in a white Cadillac.

"Mr. Kamutef? I'm Mark Gyoko."

"Sit down." He gestured to a leather chair in front of his desk. He had a soft, dry voice, a faint public school British accent. "I understand you are looking for work."

"Possibly. It depends on the work."

"We are looking for someone who can program an interactive simulation for us—a game of sorts. We don't need any viruses."

Shit. "What's that supposed to mean?"

"Correct me if I'm wrong. This time last year you were employed at Electronic Art Realities as their top programmer. Then one of your programs was released with a virus in it."

He paused. Mark nodded.

"The virus wasn't just tacked on to the program, but integrated into the code. Whenever it found a program containing the signature code of one of your co-workers, it corrupted all the data files. It started by destroying six months' work on Electronic Art Realities' own mainframe, then almost made the jump into the main Disney network before it was discovered. You claimed you had nothing to do with it, that it was your co-worker himself—"

"Bob Schenk." Kamutef had to have known all this before asking him to come down, so whatever the job was, he wanted Mark to do it anyway. This was just to soften him up, drive home to him how much he needed to do whatever it was they wanted him for.

"—who spliced it into your program. You also claimed he did it not only because he was jealous of you and wanted your job, but to cover up a dangerous bug in his last two programs. Electronic Art Realities stated that no one else in the company was good enough to do that and get it past you, so you had to have done it yourself. Is that correct?"

Mark felt himself starting to lose control, choked his anger back. He needed a job, almost any job, even if Kamutef was a complete asshole.

"That was what they said."

"And you denied it?"

"Yes." Mark shrugged. "They didn't believe me. I showed them the bugs in Bob's programs, but it didn't make any difference."

"You didn't deny that you could have created the virus if you'd wanted to."

"A lot of people could. The point is, I didn't." He fixed Kamutef with a stare. "I'm not going to write programs like that for you or for anyone else."

"Because that would be tantamount to an admission of guilt?"

It was hard to keep the anger hidden behind his face where it couldn't get out and hurt him. He might have been able to convince Knoffler if he had just been able to keep his temper down. If he hadn't started yelling that Knoffler was an asshole for even thinking he could have done something like that after all the years they'd known each other, so Knoffler could either apologize or fire him then and there.

Think about Claire, he told himself. Don't let this asshole get to you, he doesn't mean anything to you except maybe a job and if he's too fucked you don't want that anyway. No matter how bad you need the money.

He took a long deep breath, let it out slowly, forced his hands to unclench. Kept his voice calm, level, sincere as he said, "No. Because I don't approve of it and I never have."

"Even so, you have not had a real programming job since. Electronic Art Realities sued you for a lot more money than you had, so you had to leave the United States in a hurry. You have been translating computer manuals from English into French, and doing a fairly mediocre job of it, because even with your wife's help your French isn't good enough."

"Look, Mr. Kamutef, if you're trying to convince me that you've researched my financial situation and you know I need the work, fine, I believe you. I still won't write you any viruses or crack into anybody's system and trash it. But if you want me to do that other job you mentioned, can we just talk about it and skip all this stuff?"

"All right. The job involves using some material we will furnish you to create a—let's call it an animated interactive game, like the one you did for the U.S. Army, only with three-hundred sixty-degree full-body virtual reality."

"Wait a second. Full-body VR?"

"Yes."

"Nobody's ever done that. It'd cost millions of dollars—hundreds of millions—to develop the hardware alone."

"It has already been developed. What we need is a programmer to make it work for us."

"You've already got hardware and software like that and you're trying to recruit someone like *me* to use it for you? That doesn't make sense."

"The person we had intended to have do the programming isn't available. We're working under a strict time limit, so we don't have the time to train anybody else."

"You'll have to train me to use the system anyway. So why me?"

"The game is extremely complex. We need someone with extensive experience in both procedural and object-oriented paradigms who can program in Fortran, Prolog, Smalltalk 93, C, and APL, who is competent with case tools, game theory, high-definition 3D, interactive virtual space expert systems and neural nets, and who can create something aesthetically satisfying without violating certain absolutely inflexible parameters. There aren't many people like that available on a rush basis."

"No, I guess not." The way Kamutef had reeled off the list of skills they needed made it clear that it was just that, a list he had memorized, not something he understood himself. The confusion of languages and paradigms meant they needed to integrate work from a lot of different programmers working in ignorance of one another. And APL usually meant the U.S. military: guided missiles, air control, weapons systems. It was beautifully compact, but not many people outside the DOD used it because you had to be comfortable with reverse Polish notation. Mark was the only programmer he knew doing animation and VR who had ever done a lot of work with APL, so it made sense they needed him as much as he needed the work. All the stuff about EAR had just been to soften him up, make sure he didn't refuse or hold out for more money.

Maybe they needed him a lot more than he needed them. The only reason Mark had learned APL was because of EAR's defense contract. Which Kamutef knew about, even though it was supposed to have been secret—and if Kamutef was using equipment you had to program in APL, he was using DOD equipment. But there wasn't any legal way an Egyptian company could get classified DOD equipment unless they were a CIA front, and probably not even then. So it had to be stolen.

Which meant that whatever was going on was big enough to be scary. Like cracking the Israeli defense system, and programming it to destroy Tel Aviv. Real scary.

Kamutef seemed to be waiting for him to say something. "Why do you need so many different languages?"

Kamutef pushed one of the buttons set into his desk, asked a question in a language that didn't sound like Arabic or anything else Mark recognized. Another voice replied in the same language.

He turned back to Mark. "There are modules already written in all five. You can write the rest in whatever language seems best to you."

"What kind of simulation did you have in mind?"

"Here." Kamutef pushed the white leather-bound book across the desk to him. "Look at this."

Mark opened it. On the first page he saw:

Thy mother is the Great Wild Cow, living in Nekheb,
The White Crown, the Royal Headdress,
With the two tall feathers,
With the two pendulous breasts.
She will suckle thee,
She will not wean thee.

The Great Wild Cow with feathers and breasts. Great. If this was the kind of material they needed a programmer for, he hated to think what the inner workings of the company had to be like.

He started flipping through the book.

It started with a comic-book style picture of an exaggeratedly powerfully built version of Kamutef, white-haired but much younger, a sort of Arnold Schwarzenegger muscular superman in ancient Egyptian costume, complete with headdress and fake beard. He was standing on the crest of a hill, surrounded by a herd of cattle. Mark skipped ahead, found a picture of the Kamutef muscleman having graphic sex with a manacled voluptuous blond woman with Grace Kelly's face. He flipped ahead a few more pages. A woman who looked exactly like Marilyn Monroe in *The Misfits* except for the short horns sprouting from her temples was performing fellatio on a minotaur with the same body builder's physique as the

Kamutef in the other pictures.

This was what he'd been sitting there letting Kamutef insult him for? The top secret project they were using stolen DOD equipment for?

Shit. There was no way something this off-the-wall could be a cover-up for anything serious. Kamutef had to be off his head. It would be just a matter of time before they brought in the men in the white coats.

So much for the project that would re-establish his reputation while rescuing him from financial disaster. Mark's disappointment was so intense he could taste it.

But just because Kamutef was insane didn't mean he wasn't dangerous. The best thing would be to pretend to take it all very seriously and respectfully while making it clear they'd be better off hiring someone else.

Kamutef's face was bland and unreadable. "What is this supposed to be?" Mark asked.

"Take your time. Look through it in sequence."

"I'm not interested. I don't know what you're looking for, but whatever it is, it isn't me."

So much for subtly convincing Kamutef that yes, it was a great project, just not right for him.

"Look through it first. Then I'll tell you where you come in."

Mark shrugged, flipped forward again, saw a bull mounting a cow with Jayne Mansfield's face, platinum blond hair and pendulous human breasts instead of udders. The cow was tied up rodeo-style, only with ridiculous red velvet ropes like in movie theaters.

Mark went back to the beginning. Apart from bizarre fragments of archaic verse inserted at random, it was a bondage and bestiality comic book with a glorified Kamutef as a protagonist. Except, Mark realized after a few more pages, that it was quite a bit stranger than that.

The book started with Kamutef roping and tying up cows and having sex with them. Only, as soon as he tied them up, they began to take on the characteristics of a number of famous American movie stars—mainly Grace Kelly, Marilyn Monroe, and Jayne Mansfield, though there were a few others—all from the same period and all of them now dead. As the cows became cow-woman hybrids, Kamutef took on bull-like characteristics, until he was either a sort of minotaur with a bull's head, or a bull with a man's head.

Halfway through the book, the barriers separating human and animal broke down altogether, so that Kamutef and the cow-women could have any combination of bovine and human characteristics, no matter how ridiculous or implausible.

The final sequence of images, drawn in a somewhat different style, showed the three principal actresses, completely human except for large, cow-like ears and short curving horns. They were all breast-feeding identical infants that looked like miniaturized Kamutefs. The book ended with the lines:

Hail to thee, Great One
He who came forth from the Heavenly Cow.
He who has been reborn as the Bull of His Mother.

"Well?" Kamutef asked.

"You really want my opinion?"

"Of course." He sounded vaguely amused.

"It's an S&M and bestiality comic book. It must have been printed in Thailand or someplace like that because anybody who tried to sell it here would get arrested."

"Even in France, Mr. Gyoko?"

"Especially in France. They take the late Princess Grace very seriously here. As I'm sure you know."

"It was never meant to be distributed, and, with the possible exception of yourself, nobody who might be offended will ever see it. Do you personally find it morally objectionable?"

Time to backpedal. "Well, all the women in it are dead, so it would be hard to hurt their feelings. And it's none of my business what you want to fantasize about. But I don't feel comfortable with the attitude toward women. And I don't approve of cruelty to animals."

Kamutef was just sitting there, still looking faintly amused. Like an avuncular vulture. Mark shrugged. "You asked."

"True. However, there's no real cruelty involved compared with, say, a bullfight, or even one of your American rodeos. So it isn't really S&M. Nor is it bestiality, because the subject isn't really sex with animals. The cattle are all symbolic figures, avatars of the Egyptian Goddess Hathor. The book is a symbolic portrayal of the union—the *hierogamos,* if you will—of one of Hathor's worshipers with Hathor Herself. With the godhead. The actresses are her human manifestations."

"Marilyn Monroe?"

"And the others. The quintessence of a certain kind of womanly beauty."

"With you as Hathor's worshiper."

"Yes.

"You want me to be frank?" He'd put up with Kamutef as long as he could. It was time to get out.

"Please." Kamutef's smile had gone from avuncular to paternal.

"Well, that strikes me as a crock of shit. That kind of ancient Egyptian religion's been dead for thousands years."

Kamutef shrugged. "You can think of us as a silly secret society like your Freemasons. Or just another group of Middle Eastern fanatics, if you prefer."

"Middle Eastern fanatics haven't been getting very good press lately."

"Those are Muslim fanatics, Mr. Gyoko. We're a little more conservative. We prefer to keep out of the public eye."

"If you say so. So the job you're offering me is to program this for a VR simulation?"

"Something based on this. I called it an interactive game earlier, but it might be more appropriate for you to think of it as a ritual."

"You're serious?"

"Deadly serious."

"If you're such a top-secret religious group, why are you telling me all this?"

"None of our people has the combination of programming knowledge and artistic talents we need. We don't have the time to train them."

"Look, after the research you did on me, you must know I'm an atheist. Not the kind of person to trust with your sacred mysteries."

"Especially since the whole project seems insane to you?"

Mark hesitated, then decided, fuck it, if he thinks you don't take it too seriously he won't be tempted to do anything drastic to keep you from revealing his deep dark secrets.

"Since you mention it, yes."

"My only other option would be to use followers of some other religion. You, at least, are neutral."

"I don't have any"—he hesitated—"call it feel—for your project."

Kamutef's face showed real amusement for the first time. "What you are trying to tell me is that cows in bondage don't turn you on? And that you're not really the man we need to re-create the—shall we say, ecstatic joy?—involved in a full-body simulation of sexual intercourse with Hathor of the Munificent Udders?"

"Exactly."

"All the better. You are not being hired to portray your personal obsessions, but to do a specific task. You are being hired as an artist, a craftsman—like the ones who built the pyramids in ancient Egypt. They were not expected to be members of the priesthood."

"Weren't they also killed after they finished, to keep them from betraying the location of the Pharaoh's body? Since you insist on the parallel."

"We have no intention of telling you where any bodies are buried, Mr. Gyoko. You can deposit your contract with your lawyer in Paris, with whatever other legal safeguards you'd like, so long as they don't involve revealing the nature of the project. But before you make up your mind one way or another, you might be interested in what we're prepared to offer you."

"Go ahead."

"First of all, if you accept the job, we're prepared to pay all the remaining damages the court awarded your former employer. All the arrangements will be made for you. You will not have to deal with them at all, and you'll be able to go back to the States."

"Wait a second. You said, if I accept the job? Does that mean whether or not I complete it?"

"Yes. In addition, you will be paid twenty thousand dollars a month and another one hundred fifty thousand dollars upon successful completion. Enough to go back to California and start over."

If Kamutef could pay that kind of money it might be worth going along with him even though he was crazy and just hope to get paid before Kamutef started foaming at the mouth and was relieved of his functions. Unless the whole pornographic comic book and esoteric religion bit really was a cover-up for getting him to reprogram the Israeli defense network or whatever. But then why would Kamutef be acting so weird about it? It didn't make sense either way.

"Would I be working for you, personally, or for the company?"

"For the company."

Then again, maybe he owned the company, and nobody could relieve him of his functions. "Assume I agree. What happens next?"

"You must keep it secret, even from your wife, and live here until the project has been completed. Your wife will have to stay behind in Paris. And you must remain chaste for as long as the project takes."

"For religious reasons?"

"Exactly."

"That would never hold up in a court of law."

"Your contract will state that the project can be terminated at any time before completion, in which case you will receive your initial fee plus whatever monthly salary has been accrued up to that point."

"How long do you expect it to take?"

"Based on what I have been told, it should take you about three months. But you must have it completed within six months at the outside."

"Three months is an awfully short time for something like you're asking me to do, but it's a long time to remain chaste. Six months is still too short, and it'd be a lot worse."

"Are you trying to bargain with me?" Kamutef's voice was suddenly hard. "Your wife is moving out on you as it is. For financial reasons. You are being more than generously paid for your inconvenience."

That evening Mark called Claire at her father's house in Neuilly from the suite they'd given him above Kamutef's office, with a view out over the fields and hills. There were no towns or villages in sight, no lights at all in the darkening landscape. The sky was perfectly clear, full of more stars than he had seen in years.

"Claire?"

"What do you want?"

"I've found a job. A real job, this time. Programming on a rush project for this Egyptian company with a whole lot of money. It's going to pay me enough to take care of our debts back in the U.S.—"

"Your debts."

"My debts, then. Plus it'll give us something to live on and a bonus that'll pay our way back home."

"Three quarters of a million dollars?"

"Better than that. They're going to pay off everybody I owe in the States, and set things up so we can go back. Plus, I'm going to be getting twenty thousand dollars a month while I'm working for them, and a hundred-fifty-thousand dollar bonus when I complete the project."

"That sounds like complete bullshit. April Fools, right?"

"That's what they're offering me."

"To do what?"

"I'm not allowed to tell you. And I know that sounds like more bullshit, but I can't help it. Maître Saintonge will have a copy of the contract by this evening if you want to check it out. You could meet me there, look it over with the two of us, listen to what he says for yourself."

"I don't believe you. I'm sick of this whole thing. All your promises that never work out."

"Claire, listen. I want you to move back in. I'm not going to be there at all. They need me on site, at this chateau they own. But they just deposited the first twenty thousand—that's dollars, not francs—in our account, so all our overdrafts are covered."

"What do you care if I move back in or not if you're not going to be there?"

"I just do. After I see Maître Saintonge I won't be back

until July or maybe September. I have to stay here until the project's finished. If you want to stay with your father that's fine, but the apartment's going to be empty and the money's going to be deposited in our account every month, with an automatic transfer from the bank to pay the rent. You can use as much of the rest as you want to. When I'm done and I've got the hundred fifty thousand dollars we can talk about the future, OK?"

"You always pretend the money's the whole problem. If you could just get enough everything would be perfect again. But it wouldn't be."

"I didn't say everything would be perfect. It's just that I can't do anything worth shit for either one of us in Paris. I'm stuck in a hole here, and all I can do is dig myself deeper. But if we go back to California, start over again.... Maybe I could find a way to make it work again. Better this time, not just the same as before."

She didn't say anything for a moment. When she did her voice was different. "You really expect this to work? This isn't just more of your optimistic it's-all-going-to-work-out-in-the-end-so-don't-worry bullshit?"

"I don't know. How can I? It looks real but like you said, it's hard to believe. You said you needed to be alone to think about things. All I'm asking you is to wait until this either works out or doesn't before you make any final decisions. OK? Why don't we talk about all this then?"

Still, he was almost ashamed that what had really clinched it all was when Kamutef's technician Ali—at least that's what he'd told Mark to call him, though something about the way he said it made Mark sure it wasn't his real name—had demonstrated how to use the Cray, a preproduction room-temperature superconductor model that wasn't supposed to be released until next year, and then only to selected U.S. clients like the Defense Department. Again. It came with not only all the voice recognition, image grab, and VR equipment he had ever heard of, plus a lot he hadn't had any idea existed, but also with some astonishing neural-net front ends for the operating system, and with multilingual compilers that learned his programming style as he went along and would allow him to do things that might otherwise have taken years, and get them exactly right the first time. After being limited to what he could do with a pitiable second-hand South Korean 50 mega-hertz 486DX2, it was like getting out of jail to work on decent equipment again.

The fact that they really had the equipment and really wanted him to work on the project Kamutef had hired him for just made the whole thing crazier. He couldn't think of any alternative explanation that wasn't even weirder than what Kamutef had told him. Which made it no less scary, but scary exciting: proof positive that the world was not only stranger than he knew, but stranger than he could ever know, in ways that would directly affect the rest of his life. The trap he had been in, his whole life closing in around him, had been open all along in ways he would never have been able to guess but that had been there anyway.

He never actually saw the Cray itself, of course, just the terminals and peripherals: room-temperature superconductors still needed temperatures closer to Antarctic winters than to anything he could have survived at. He did his work in a huge converted salon on the ground floor, with a gigantic gilt-framed mirror over a black marble fireplace big enough to roast an ox whole inside, and a baroque painted ceiling showing angels and cherubs congratulating what he supposed was the chateau's original owner. The VR set-up was like nothing he had ever seen, a cross between a wetsuit and a sheer, multilayer whole-body nylon woven out of fiber-optic, piezoelectric, and a dozen other kinds of hi-tech strands. The headmask was surprisingly light and comfortable, with bulging eyepieces that projected images directly onto his retinas, and breathing equipment to let him remain submerged in the sensory deprivation tank next to the terminal. It was filled with some heavy tasteless and odorless white fluid at body temperature and looked like a huge vat of greasy milk. There was a thoroughly modern bathroom attached to the salon in what he supposed must have originally been a walk-in closet where he could wash the tank fluid off.

When Ali had first shown him the VR suit it had looked far too small, despite Ali's assurance that it would stretch to fit him. He'd thought that, sheer though they were, all the layers would make it horribly constricting, but a moment after he put it on he couldn't feel it at all. He almost panicked the first time he slipped the mask on over his head and groped his way blind into the tank, let go of the side and floated there weightless, trying to relax in the total darkness—he had never been in a sensory deprivation tank before—but then suddenly he was standing in the middle of an emerald-green jungle. There was a moment's dizziness, his semicircular canals telling him he was floating on his back while his other senses indicated he was standing up, but then that passed and the illusion was complete.

Looking down on himself, he saw that he was wearing combat fatigues and jungle boots and had some sort of automatic weapon slung over his shoulder. Everything was incredibly detailed, sharper, if anything, than in real life. He could even feel the gun's weight, and when he tried spinning around, he could feel it lift a little from the centrifugal force. If he concentrated hard enough on the gun it felt impossibly light, just as his whole body felt impossibly light, and with enough work he could break the illusion down into at least some of its component sensations: vibrations, warmer and cooler spots, tinglings, what must have been contractions in

the VR suit's fibers but felt like his own muscle contractions
. . . yet even so he could actually feel himself turning as he
spun, feel the heavy, moist, hot breeze on his face, his tight
boots and the ground beneath his feet. Whenever he concentrated on any one sensation it fled and he realized how faint
and incomplete it really was, but all the other sensations
seemed real, like things you're aware of in the back of your
mind while you're focusing intensely on something else.

But faint though the sensations were, spinning around
too long made him dizzy again. Maybe that was because he
was spinning around in the tank. He couldn't feel his real
body . . . . No, that wasn't right, because when he reached up
to touch his nose he could feel it, even if it wasn't exactly *his*
nose.

The sensation seemed as attenuated as everything else—
maybe there was something in the white fluid to deaden
sensation—but when he closed his eyes and pushed harder he
could feel a different nose, his own nose. Like pushing in a
nose-shaped balloon to find a real nose just inside it. The
system was somehow mixing the sensations it simulated with
those he was feeling naturally.

He was still poking his nose when the guerrillas started
firing at him out of the forest. All he felt when the first bullet
hit him in the right shoulder was a brief sting, like a pin-prick,
followed by a dull ache, but at the same time he could see the
wound spurting blood, feel it running hot and wet down the
arm hanging awkward and useless at his side. He tried to hide
behind a tree, but another unseen sniper opened up on him
from the left.

A bullet gouged a hole out of the tree in front of him. He
tried to touch the hole with his right hand, but his arm remained
stubbornly at his side. He strained, concentrated; for an instant
he felt the arm moving, but all his other senses told him it was
just hanging there immobile. Like the phantom limbs ampu-

tees still feel where their missing arms or legs used to be.

More bullets hit him in the chest and legs and he fell, lay sprawled and paralyzed. There was little or no real pain, but he could feel the convulsive spasms as his failing heart tried to keep blood flowing through his body, the hot wind on his exposed entrails. He heard footsteps approaching, and then there was a pinprick pain just behind his left ear and he was floating blind back in the sensory isolation tank.

By the time Ali helped him out of the tank he was hooked. It didn't really make any difference what Kamutef wanted to do with his simulated ritual, since there was no way it could do anybody real harm anyway: the VR set-up was the most incredible toy he had ever encountered. He could already tell that he would be able to bring the new skills he was learning to bear on his own projects. The hardest part was always imagining what you wanted a program to do, visualizing the final result clearly before you got bogged down in translating it into code. Even without Kamutef's equipment he would be able to revolutionize the field—and when the technology *did* trickle down to the public he would be able to use it immediately, while everyone else was just beginning to explore its possibilities.

Once Ali demonstrated how to use the system to reproduce the salon around him—simulating climbing back out of the tank to find himself back in the reality he had just left, with only the fact that he was no longer dressed in the VR suit but wearing jeans and a nondescript blue shirt to remind him that it wasn't real—Mark found he could see everything the mask's eyepieces re-created for him with no perceptible distortion, just the faintest hint of a blue-white aura on the fringe of his perceptual vision. The only way he could feel he had the suit on was by touching himself, concentrating on filtering out the illusion until his fingers felt the suit's fabric—and then he still couldn't distinguish between the part that might be coming from the suit simulating feeling itself and the part he was feeling with his own skin. The sole exception was his crotch, where the suit's VR fabric gave way to a ski-slope—bright built-in nylon athletic supporter. When Ali finally left Mark tried touching himself there. It felt just like touching himself wearing a wetsuit.

By the end of the first week he had settled into a comfortable routine. He got up around four in the afternoon, had breakfast in the dining room, then spent an hour or so wandering around the fields or surrounding woods. He almost never saw Kamutef. Except for the kitchen staff, Kamutef's assistant in her tailored suits, Ali, and the French-looking peasants complete with regulation berets whom he occasionally saw working out in the fields, he rarely saw anyone at all.

When it got dark he came back in and got down to work. He'd always done his best work late at night, in such classical hacker style it sometimes embarrassed him, living on peanut-butter-and-whatever sandwiches when he was home, on whatever the vending machines had when he was at the office. At EAR the machines were filled with raw vegetables and vitamin-enriched protein bars; here the kitchen staff left him little care packages of American-style sandwiches and fresh vegetables.

It only took a few days to master the unfamiliar versions of the programs he was going to be using, since the Cray's neural net-driven interface enabled it to adapt them to him at the same time he was learning to use their new features; a few more days to realize he could create a functional virtual terminal inside the VR tank. The Cray had less trouble learning to translate finger twitches into characters typed on a keyboard, sweeping movements into mouse strokes if he closed his hand as though he had a mouse in it or into scrawls on a blackboard when he held his fingers as if gripping a piece of chalk than he did remembering which gesture to use, and before he had had time to perfect his gestures the Cray had already learned to take the variations into account.

Working in the virtual office was exhilarating, as if gravity suddenly no longer had any hold on him and he could soar, fly if he really wanted to. After a twelve-hour day he would emerge from the tank as fresh as when he went into it, with none of the usual backaches and eyestrain and sour taste from too much vending-machine coffee.

He'd tried simulating the coffee as well, but though he could feel the cup hot in his hand, even the warmth of the vapor as it rose to tickle his nose, it was completely odorless and, when he tried to drink it, tasteless. He still felt the need to drink something while working, so he stocked the simulation with bottles of Evian. Since he never usually drank mineral water the difference between the almost tasteless original and the tasteless fake didn't bother him.

It took a little longer to feel comfortable enough with the virtual office so he could forget it wasn't really there and just use it instead of playing with it.

For a while he concentrated on working out algorithms and drawing up flow-charts, recoding the jumble of different programs and paradigms into modules that fit together despite their divergent origins and that could process the data Kamutef provided once he had worked out ways to translate it into objects they could access.

The data. Kamutef had all the late actresses' publicly available films, still photos, interviews—even Princess Grace's book about flowers—plus stuff that could only have come directly from the studios or private collectors—outtakes from Grace Kelly films, some of the rejected photos from Marilyn Monroe's first nude pictorial for *Playboy*—as well as items of more dubious origin, like lots of out-of-focus pornographic black and white footage of a woman who might have been

Jayne Mansfield at what seemed to be a black mass. Mark seemed to remember having read that she had been involved with an L.A. Satanist with a name like a South American country, Sandinista or Salvador or something.

There were also hundreds of photos and kilometers of footage taken through keyholes or with telephoto lenses of the actresses getting dressed, in their baths, making love (including some of Marilyn Monroe with a man who might have been JFK), and a vast number of porn films featuring women resembling the actresses. Not to mention hundreds of photos in which Grace Kelly's head had been more or less successfully spliced to some far more voluptuous woman's body.

It took Mark awhile to realize that despite this profusion of licit and illicit detail, there was no mention anywhere of their deaths. Even the documents put together after they'd died had all been carefully censored.

Kamutef, curiously, was represented only by a few photographs of his head, obviously taken at least twenty years ago, though there was a complete set of measurements and data for the muscular body he was supposed to have. But that made things easier: it would have been hard to work from accurate photos of the old man, digitalized images of his sunken chest, his no-doubt shriveled genitalia. This was a lot less intimate.

There was also a vast database on the habits—especially the mating habits—of cows. The eighteen cows in the "game" were not only all distinct individuals with specific characteristics, personality traits, and detailed, carefully enumerated and elaborately justified (though in Mark's opinion, totally specious nonetheless) resemblances to one or more of the screen goddesses—as defined by photographs, film footage, X-rays, measurements, and the like—but were, in fact, the same eighteen cows grazing in the fenced-off pasture beneath his window. The data on them was updated continually, presumably by Ali while Mark slept.

As for the job itself... it seemed not only insane but fairly slimy, but he had to admit that if what was involved wasn't a religious ritual, it didn't make any sense at all. As a ritual, it seemed only an order of magnitude or two more nonsensical than most other religious rituals. His father's side—the Japanese side—of his family were all good stolid Catholics, and had been since the Jesuits converted them in the nineteenth century, but some of his mother's cousins were members of one of those Alabama white trash churches where the congregation slung live rattlesnakes back and forth during worship services to give God a chance to demonstrate how much He loved them by saving them from snakebite. Mark had been taken to a service where three people got bitten once when he was a kid, and you couldn't get much crazier than that.

The scenario began with a sort of rodeo-orgy. Old Dynasty superman Kamutef had to subdue each of the eighteen cows before having sex with them, and then—through the precise way in which the cows were bound, the odd arrangements of highly specific twists and knots, accompanied by English translations of hymns to Hathor and a variety of even sillier invocations—he would trigger off their metamorphoses into hybrids and, eventually, into all but completely human women.

As the cows underwent their transformations into the various actresses, the hybrids would coalesce into one another, until six cows and a number of hybrids with features from other actresses would have collapsed into each of the three women's final forms.

Kamutef would then impregnate all three and watch over and protect them from attacks by other Egyptian gods and demons—all of which had to be warded off with the appropriate ritual words and gestures—until they gave birth to three identical infants, all smaller versions of Kamutef himself, thus marking the successful completion of the game . . .

. . . though not, perhaps, of the ritual, since the final sequence showed the three dwarf Kamutefs facing one another in the same ritualized stance the king-sized Kamutef had adopted whenever faced with attack from one of the other gods or demons.

In any case, since the point of departure was always the same, everything was completely deterministic, with no need to code for chaos factors. If the voice analyzer registered the right words and tones of voice while input from the gloves and suit verified that the right knots had been tied and the right sexual acts performed, then specific metamorphoses in the cows or hybrids had to take place. The problems came from the system's built-in feedback, since the transformations triggered off corresponding metamorphoses in the Kamutef figure, which in turn produced further transformations in the female figures. All of these took place at specified rates, and the player—the person performing the ritual—had to pace his actions to the evolution of their rhythms or see everything go out of control.

Ritual chastity proved no problem. Not only were there no women at the chateau—with the exception of Kamutef's assistant, who was more forbidding than tempting despite her short skirts and great legs—but Mark had always tended to put all of himself into his work anyway. Even when things with Claire had been at their best there had been long periods of total abstinence while he was working on a project, followed by an orgy of sensuality and luxurious living as he made up for lost time. Besides which, his sex life with Claire had been disastrous since he had lost his job, and his self-confidence with it.

At first Mark had been afraid that all the sexual material would keep him in a constant state of frustrated arousal, but in fact he had never felt less like a sexual being. Possibly because he had always been attracted to women like Claire: slim, athletic and fashionable, even a bit androgynous, rather than blatantly bovine.

He caught himself. That was Kamutef's mindset, not his: distasteful and reductive, but at the same time proof he had successfully internalized the project, now had it bubbling away on the back burner. Before, he would have seen Kamutef's screen goddesses as somewhat over-voluptuous symbols of the fifties (except for the original Grace Kelly, of course, but the specifications for the ritual put her ice-queen's head on a Sophia Loren body). He would even have found them attractive, if not exactly to his taste. The same kind of thing had happened when he was working on educational games for kids: though he hadn't believed her at the time, Claire had been right when she complained he'd regressed to an eight-year-old's sense of humor. When this project was over, he would let the whole thing drop again the same way, go back to normal.

Mark still wondered how much of his reaction Kamutef would have been able to predict, and whether it had been one reason they'd picked him.

Two weeks later Kamutef's assistant was waiting for him when he returned from his walk. Kamutef wanted to see him immediately.

The office was even darker than before. Kamutef had him sit down, asked him a few general questions—how was the work going, was he having any trouble with the programs and equipment, did he have everything he needed, that sort of thing—before passing the cream-colored cordless phone on his desk over to him.

"All the arrangements with Electronic Art Realities have been made. I want you to telephone them and get confirmation for yourself."

Mark hesitated, then dialed EAR's number in California. A young woman with a generic receptionist's voice he didn't recognize answered the phone.

"Can I speak to Mr. Knoffler, please?"

"I'll see if he's come in yet. Who should I say is calling?"

"Mark Gyoko, from France."

"Just a moment please." She put him on hold. The same blandly anonymous New Age music as when he had been working there.

"Hello, Mark?" Knoffler's voice was bright, impersonal. It was hard to believe he had once thought the man was his friend.

"Hello, Dave. Uhh—I'm calling to find out if . . ."

"If we got the money."

"Yes."

"We did."

"Does that mean everything's settled between us?"

"Legally, yes. You don't get your old job back, and we're still ready to sue your ass off if you use any work you did on our time to compete with us, but other than that we're willing to let bygones be bygones."

"That's very kind of you," Mark said sarcastically.

"We think it is. Are you planning on coming back to the States any time soon?"

"I was thinking of moving back, yes, in three or four months. Unless you've got some objection?"

"None whatsoever. I've got to go; would you like to speak to Bob?"

"Not just now, no."

"Call me when you get back to California. Nice talking to you, Mark."

He hung up.

Mark called Maître Saintonge in Paris, confirmed that that end of the deal was being fulfilled as well.

"Satisfied?" Kamutef asked.

"Yes. Thank you." He hesitated. "Would it be OK if I called Claire this evening and told her?"

"If you want. You *do* realize that any call you make from here will be monitored?"

"I suppose so. I hadn't thought about it."

She wasn't at the apartment when he called, so he left a message on the answering machine and tried her parents' house, but she wasn't there either. Her father seemed a little too happy to announce that he didn't know where she was since she had so many friends that kept her *so* active that he sometimes scarcely saw her for weeks at a time . . . . Mark took an equal pleasure in asking him to tell her he'd had confirmation that all their legal problems in the States had been solved and they'd be able to leave France for good soon.

Three weeks later Mark had the first sequences ready. He'd started out with the purely visual aspects of the various metamorphoses and the simplest types of copulation, where the protagonists were either entirely human or entirely bovine, or one copulating with the other but without any hybridization, then tried to work out the metamorphoses for the hybrid forms and combinations required without anything getting too ridiculous.

Though all sense of the ridiculous had quickly faded. He'd expected that as time went on the project would come to seem more and more ludicrous but the exact opposite was true. Perhaps because of the obsessional thoroughness of the material supplied him, or because of the obsessional way he always worked—dusk to dawn with only a few short breaks—it had all come to seem deadly serious.

Especially when, lying floating in the tank but looking down Godlike on his preliminary efforts from above, he realized that what he was coming up with was not only pitiably unconvincing—worse than the first Hanna-Barbera cartoons despite the perfection of the 3-D modeling, as jerky and unconvincing as his first Commodore 64 games, back in prehistory—but utterly repellent.

The images, the acts were not neutral. He was not neutral. He'd been hired for his neutrality; intellectually he knew that the content of the simulation was none of his business—he was enough of a child of the sixties and seventies that he honestly believed that if somebody wanted to spend a fortune on a pornographic video game for their private amusement they had a perfect right to do so, so long as nobody got hurt in the process—but he still found the images unendurable.

He tried to tell himself it was because he was a perfectionist, but when he discovered that every improvement made the simulation that much harder to tolerate he had to admit that it was their content he found so disturbing, and that his attempts to convince himself anything different had just been lying to himself.

But he couldn't figure out why it sickened him so. The whole thing was as abstract as *Fantasia,* as conventional as a rodeo, and, as Kamutef had pointed out, none of the cows was shown actually suffering physical pain. And they weren't even real cows.

It might have been the degrading view of women implicit in the subjugation of the cow-woman hybrids, except that was too much of a moral abstraction; it didn't *feel* like it was what was behind his visceral revulsion, no matter how much he might agree in principle.

As the weeks dragged on, working on the sequences got harder and harder. Screening old Marilyn Monroe comedies or looking out the window at the cows grazing on the hillsides, he found himself shuddering. Even the basic algorithms revolted him.

But he had some great ideas for a sixth-generation CAD program that would work on available VR equipment. All he needed to do was code it. Whenever he found himself unable to concentrate on the project any longer he would lean back in his chair or alter it into a couch, think about how the program was going to work, how he was going to set up a company to market it back in California. If he could just get the right backing it would bring in a fortune.

Enough to buy himself his own Cray by the time they came on the market.

He was floating up by the ceiling, one of the cherubs looking down on the Kamutef minotaur wrestling with an almost human Jayne Mansfield—if you ignored the horns, tail, many-nippled breasts and the gigantic tongue hanging out of a mouth too small to contain it—while he tried to think of a way to get the tongue in and out of her mouth that wouldn't be too grotesque, given that the protocol demanded the tongue be full-sized bovine and her face standard human at this point—when the scene cut off and he found himself floating blind in the tank.

Kamutef's assistant was waiting for him when he climbed out, dressed as usual in one of her severely tailored suits, navy blue this time.

"What is it?" He grabbed a terrycloth robe he had put by the tank the first day but never used, feeling ridiculous in his sheer stretchsuit with its orange jockstrap.

"Mr. Kamutef would like to see you."

"Tell him I'll be there as soon as I shower and get dressed."

It had been a month or more since he had last seen Kamutef. The change was shocking. Where before the Egyptian had been slim and wizened, but graceful, he was now hesitant and emaciated, as if he had used up ten years during the last month.

His voice, however, remained as dry and precise as ever. "I showed what you've come up with to my computer people. They tell me you haven't made any progress."

"That's not true. I've solved all the theoretical problems, integrated all the techniques and paradigms into a functioning object-oriented whole—"

"You had that done a month ago. I've seen the results you've come up with. They're pitiful. Worse than anything you did at Electronic Art Realities. Certainly not the work their top programmer was capable of. Or that we hired you for."

"These things take time, that's all."

"Do you want me to show you, say, the work you did for that amusement park in Nevada the year you joined Electronic Art Realities, so we can compare them? You did that job in two months. Or that Australian film two years ago? Or, for that matter, even your ill-fated toolbox, minus the virus?"

"No."

"You have a saying in English, about the carrot and the stick. You're familiar with it?"

Mark nodded.

"We'll start with the carrot first. I've decided to increase what you get if you succeed in completing this project within the deadline by another fifty thousand dollars. Making your total reward for successful completion two hundred thousand dollars."

With that he could really put together his start-up, come up with something to show potential investors. "And the stick?"

"If you fail, my company will take you to court the same way that Electronic Art Realities did. We will claim you sabotaged our computer system. We will claim we took you on because we had faith in you, because we believed you were innocent, but that you were unable to resist your sick need to destroy our system with a Trojan-horse program, which we luckily discovered before it was activated. After that, you won't ever be able to get a job anywhere in the computer industry again. Not even translating manuals."

"Look, I know I'm behind schedule, and I'm sorry. But I've got this great idea for a VR CAD program that could make you a lot of money instead—"

"I'm not interested in a CAD program." Kamutef leaned forward, his voice trembling with a suppressed rage that was all the more terrifying because it was the first time he had ever let any real feeling show. His breath was foul, like some animal that had died and been left to rot. "Just this. Nothing else, no matter how cute an idea you think it is."

He's not just old, he's sick, Mark realized. Really sick, dying. That's what this is all about, giving him back his lost youth.

Fuck, I'm supposed to save his life.

"Mr. Kamutef, the problem isn't that I don't want to do it. I'm trying as hard as I can. I just can't get any further."

"What do you mean, you can't? Why not?"

"I don't know why not! I just can't, that's all."

"Explain." He was calm again, poised, in perfect control. "What's stopping you?"

"Something, I don't know . . . . Look, I don't particularly like this idea of yours—OK?—but that's none of my business. You've got a perfect right to do what you want, I don't have any problems with that—"

"Then what *do* you have a problem with?"

"It makes me sick to my stomach! I hate it and I can't concentrate, I can't do anything. Just fiddle with details."

"Ah." Kamutef smiled, pushed a button on his desk, leaned back. "That, I can deal with."

"What do you mean?"

The door behind Kamutef slid open, revealing an elevator. Two huge, dark-skinned, hard-faced men who could have served as models for the muscleman in the program except that they were wearing Cerruti suits stepped out of it. Mark had never seen either of them before.

Everything was suddenly a whole lot scarier. The fact that it was like something out of a low-budget spy movie just made it worse. Mark started to push himself up out of the chair but there was nowhere to go, unless he wanted to cower back against the wall.

Kamutef said something incomprehensible to them as they came around the desk. One of them patted Mark lightly on the shoulder, gestured toward the elevator.

"Go with them, please," Kamutef told Mark.

"Go where? What is this?"

"They're going to help you overcome your resistance."

"What do you mean, help me overcome my resistance?" He could hear the hysterical shrillness in his voice but couldn't do anything about it. He pictured Middle Eastern terrorists torturing people with lighted cigarettes, cattle prods. Remembered pictures he had seen in the streets, Iranians trying to get him to sign petitions against the regime by showing him photos of mutilated, burned victims. That was all done for religious reasons, too.

Kamutef sighed. "Mark, you're being childish. Just go with them."

"No! Not unless—"

Kamutef said something else in that language Mark didn't understand. They took him by the arms, firmly but without violence, dragged him effortlessly towards the elevator. There was nothing he could do.

"Look, I'll go, you don't need to—"

"They don't speak English or French," Kamutef said behind him. "But there is nothing to be afraid of. I promise you

you will not be harmed."

"Shit," Mark said, because there wasn't anything he could say that would do any good, but he still had to say something.

The elevator was barely large enough for the three of them. As soon as they were inside, the door closed and the floor dropped out from under them. There were no buttons to push, so Kamutef had to be controlling it from his desk. A minute or more passed before the sudden sensation of weight told Mark that they were decelerating rapidly.

Fuck, they had to be at least ten stories underground, maybe more.

The door opened onto a huge, dimly lit rectangular corridor carved out of yellowish limestone. Closely-packed vertical columns of incised hieroglyphics covered the walls.

One of the oversized Egyptians tapped Mark on the shoulder again, motioned. Mark stepped out of the elevator, the two men behind him. The door closed.

The corridor stretched away as far as he could see in both directions. It was perhaps ten meters high and three wide, lit at long intervals by concealed lights, and the hieroglyphics covered not only the walls but the ceiling as well. The air was chill but dry, stale-smelling, and Mark shivered, hunched his shoulders against the pressure of all the millions of tons of rock he could feel overhead, pressing down on him.

I can't believe this, he thought numbly. Things like this don't really exist.

He hoped that they weren't planning on using some traditional ancient Egyptian form of persuasion on him. The Pharaohs had never gotten particularly good press for their kindness to captives and slaves.

The two men turned right, led him down the corridor, which almost immediately intersected another corridor. Each corner had been carved into a rounded column topped with a capital in the form of a bulbous blue flower. The columns were covered with painted red, blue and green bas-reliefs. The corridor itself seemed exactly like the one they were following except that the hieroglyphics were different.

A few hundred meters past the intersection the corridor forked. The two soldiers—Mark realized that he had been thinking of them as soldiers for some time—took the right fork, then turned left into another corridor, followed it until it, in turn, forked, took the right-hand fork this time, turned again . . .

The sheer, impossible scale of the whole thing was numbing. They had to have gone at least a couple of kilometers by now, somewhere far beyond the chateau's walls and outbuildings, out under the hills. Any farther and they'd need a golf cart.

The project he was working on was so trivial in comparison that, in one way at least, he should have felt reassured: it was no longer hard to believe that they were really going to pay him what they'd offered for something whose only use was for some silly ritual. And he didn't need to worry about the program's pornographic content further besmirching his already-sullied reputation: these people could obviously keep a secret.

Which was what was worrying him. They'd shown him too much to risk letting him talk about it, and they had no reason to trust him to keep quiet. He'd been joking—half-joking, anyway—the first day, when he had mentioned the slaves who were killed to keep the tombs they'd dug and the passages leading to the Pharaohs' pyramid burial chambers secret, but it no longer seemed remotely funny. For people who could construct something like this and keep it secret, disposing of an out-of-work foreigner everyone would rather see gone anyway would be no problem whatsoever.

People disappear every day anyway and a lot of them

never turn up, as that provincial woman the French government had tried to prove had gotten rid of her husband's body with a chainsaw had stated complacently at her trial.

They continued on through the maze of deserted tunnels, following no logic or pattern Mark could detect. Maybe the hieroglyphics included street signs. At intervals the walls were broken by massive but incongruously normal-looking wooden doors flanked by pharaonic figures carved in bas-relief. He was so far underground that there had to be layer on layer of intermediate levels above him. A huge stacked maze of underground tunnels, like some gigantic subterranean termite mound. In California none of it would have survived ten years, but France wasn't on any major fault lines he knew about.

Finally they stopped in front of a door flanked by two winged bulls. One of the soldiers got an oversized but otherwise normal key-ring out of his pocket, unlocked the door and pushed it open, flipped a standard cream-colored plastic light switch on, and waved Mark inside.

The room was circular, vaulted, perhaps fifteen meters high, its ceiling painted gold. Mark couldn't see where the light was coming from. The chamber was dominated by the huge pink-granite statue in its center of a seated bare-breasted woman with a triangular, almost catlike face and the ears of a cow. She was depicted wearing a reed headdress from which two stylized horns protruded, supporting a golden sphere surmounted by two equally stylized feathers.

"Hathor?" Mark asked, but they just led him around to the front of the statue. A walnut-brown leather armchair, incongruously like the one in Kamutef's office, had been set there on the bare stone floor.

One of the soldiers put his hands on Mark's shoulders, pressed down. The motion was impersonal, more a way of indicating that Mark should sit down in the absence of a common language than an overt show of force, but Mark didn't even consider resisting.

The soldier strapped Mark into place with some leather bands that came out of concealed recesses in the chair. So the chair wasn't as much of a duplicate of the chair in Kamutef's office as it seemed. Unless that chair could be used for strapping people in too. This whole setup—he didn't know what else to call it—seemed to be organized that way, based on concealment, like those Russian dolls with a whole series of littler dolls hidden inside: religious rituals hidden in pornographic video games, Egyptian temples disguised as French chateaux, some sort of bizarre religious organization doing business as a multinational corporation . . .

If the video game masked a religious ritual, then what did the ritual itself mask?

When Mark was securely strapped in place, comfortable enough but unable to move, the second soldier came back into view carrying a scepter carved from some light-colored wood. Its head was a stylized flower surmounted by a ring of carved feathers that curved outward like more petals. The flower and feathers were varnished a shiny red.

The soldier stood in front of Mark, eyes closed in concentration. He opened them and touched Mark on the forehead with the tip of the scepter, then withdrew it and closed his eyes again, murmuring quietly to himself. With his eyes still closed, he reached out with the scepter and touched Mark, first over the heart, and then on the crotch. He pulled the scepter away and paused again, utterly immobile, concentrating.

Not a soldier, Mark realized. A priest. They're both priests.

The priest opened his eyes and went around behind Mark. Mark could hear him doing what sounded like opening a door, though he hadn't seen any doors before they strapped him in.

A moment later both priests returned, carrying crudely tanned black and white cowhide robes with the hair still on them. They draped the stiff robes over Mark, adjusting them with the impersonal efficiency of flight stewards making an old lady comfortable. The robes stank of urine.

They disappeared back around the statue. Mark heard the massive door to the corridor close behind them, the sound of the key turning in the lock.

He was alone with the statue of Hathor, with nothing to do but look up at it. He kept waiting for the priests to return and do whatever it was they were going to do to him to overcome his resistance, but nothing happened.

Maybe they thought the sheer awesomeness of what they'd shown him down here would be enough to show him how insignificant his resistance really was? Thousands of man-hours had to have gone into digging out the corridors and carving the hieroglyphics alone. Even if the job had been done with modern power tools, which he doubted. The statue had to weigh at least as much as the Obelisk at the Place de la Concorde, and Napoleon had had his whole army to drag that back for him. The sheer effort involved in transporting the statue from Egypt and getting it down to this level in secret— if it hadn't been carved directly out of a vein of granite below the chateau—was unbelievable. For all he knew the country-side for miles around was honeycombed with corridors leading to thousands of identical chambers.

At least the chair was comfortable, and the robes kept him warm despite their stench. Eventually he feel asleep.

He dreamed it was night and he was staring up between the huge cylindrical pillars and massive rectangular stone architraves of a ruined temple at the full moon, shining silver in the darkness.

217

He didn't know how long he stared at the moon, but when he finally looked away he saw that he was sitting in front of his bedroom window at the chateau. His bed, the armoires with his clothes in them, everything was in its proper place, as if the entire bedroom's contents had been transported undisturbed to the vast, open spaces in one of the ruined temples of Karnak.

The floor under the chair in which he sat, comfortably wrapped against the chill night air in his hide blankets, was made up of massive blocks of pale stone worn smooth with the feet of a thousand generations, but the wall in front of him was still papered in the same silver-gray wallpaper with the delicate white fleur de lys design, and the window still looked out on the cows in the pasture below, only the pasture too was now inside the ruined temple.

Suddenly he saw a naked man among them. Kamutef, but powerfully-built, so young he must have been still adolescent, though his silver hair gleamed in the moonlight.

Kamutef stood there on the crest of the hill, regal and silent, arms upraised. Mark saw that what he had taken for Kamutef's hair was a silver-horned crown. Kamutef waited, and the cows came to him, circled slowly around him, spiraling in until he was lost in a tight-packed rotating mass of gleaming horns and dark, dull bovine backs.

Then, as one, all the cows raised their heads and turned to stare up at Mark, their huge dark eyes glinting wetly at him in the moonlit darkness.

When Mark awoke, he was floating comfortably with the other cherubs in the clouds painted on the ceiling, looking down on an endless action loop in which Kamutef wrestled a cow with four long, beautiful human legs in sheer stockings and high heels to the ground again and again.

He didn't remember having programmed the loop, but it was a smooth piece of work despite the ludicrous subject matter. Good craftsmanship.

And that was all it was. It didn't bother him any more than any other animated sequence.

He watched the scene a little longer, trying to find the revulsion it would have caused him before, but it was gone, with nothing in its place. No relief, no pleasure, nothing. Total indifference.

Which meant that whatever the two priests had done to him had been successful.

If there'd ever been any priests in the first place. He'd started out in the tank and it would be easy enough to program a sequence where Kamutef's assistant came and got him, after which the two priests dragged him down into a subterranean labyrinth. Even if Ali hadn't known enough to do it himself before Mark showed up, the Cray had learned enough of Mark's programming techniques so that anyone moderately competent could use them for a straightforward simulation: four people, two of whom looked like comic-book goons and one of whom was already in the system, a bare elevator, some empty corridors with the only difference between them the hieroglyphics on the walls, a single room that he had seen from what was essentially a single point of view.

Except for the stench of sickness on Kamutef's breath, the urine with which the cowhide blankets had been tanned. There were no odors in the tank.

But all they'd had to do was dump a few strong-smelling molecules into the air supply and let suggestion do the rest. Mix in some gas to render him hyper-suggestible while they were at it. That was probably what the DOD had been working on all along, an ultrasophisticated brainwashing system.

He redefined his point of view to put him at the Cray's console, called up data, looking for things he should have been able to access but couldn't, contradictions or patterns that felt wrong, but everything matched up perfectly. He hadn't really expected to find anything: the security subsystems would have learned his programming techniques at the same time as the rest of the system.

Whether or not the subterranean labyrinth was real, they had perfect deniability: he didn't know where the chateau was, he had been working on a project that sounded like the product of a deranged mind, and even if he found someone who'd believe the rest of his story, there was no way he could prove the episode under the castle hadn't been a simulation. It sounded a lot more convincing, even to him.

A drug-induced state of hyper-suggestibility was also a more plausible explanation for how they'd changed the way he felt than weird rites involving giant idols and Egyptian body-builder priests. Already, it was getting harder to distinguish between what had really happened or been simulated and the dream he had awakened from in the tank. But the real question wasn't whether what had happened was real; the real question was how he felt about the fact that they'd brainwashed him. It didn't make any difference how.

He pictured himself trying to tell Claire about it, the way she would laugh at him. Her contemptuous disbelief. And then, once she realized he was sincere and wasn't trying to bullshit her, the way her anger and scorn would give way to pity. She would be so kind, so loving, as she locked him out of her life forever.

With that he started to get angry. He didn't particularly want to feel revolted by his work, and the new life they were offering him meant enough that he could live with the fact they'd brainwashed him, whether he hated it or not. All he could do was adapt. And if they could change his attitudes like that, then at least they wouldn't have to do anything more drastic, like killing him. All they'd have to do to keep him quiet was manipulate him so he didn't *want* to talk about them.

Unless that was something else they'd manipulated him

into believing. But even so, it made sense. And there was nothing he could do to change things anyway.

What he couldn't accept was that they'd put him in a situation where he had no choice but to lie to Claire, where he could never share what had happened, what he felt about it, with her. He was doing it so they could start over again together; that wasn't all of it, maybe, but it was the most important thing—and it was already fucked up: he couldn't even choose whether or not to tell her, because if he told the truth he would lose her for good. She might even decide he was crazy enough to have programmed the virus in his toolbox himself.

And if he couldn't convince Claire, when she loved him or at least used to and she already knew he had been hired for a secret project by people who were willing to pay unreasonably huge amounts of money, then who could he convince? The people who read those supermarket tabloids that always ran stories about Elvis's bimonthly reincarnations and women whose unborn children were stolen from their wombs by Satanic saucer people?

Perfect deniability. They could do whatever they wanted to do to him, turn him into a gibbering idiot, and there was nothing he could do to stop them, because he was no threat to Kamutef and never could be. But even so, he wasn't going to tell them how much the program could be improved with a few odors, selected pheromones. It wasn't much, but it was all he could do: deny them some of what he could have done for them, fulfill their definition of the project and nothing more.

Mark tensed his hand to call the mouse to it, clicked the action loop off and stared down at his body floating loose-limbed in the tank, just below the milky surface, at the perfectly pressed, pristine white terrycloth robe hanging just where it always hung, then clicked that off too and was back in his body.

Maybe there'd been drugs in the fluid all along, soaking in through his pores to be picked up by his capillaries and pumped into his brain, and the longer he spent in the tank the more suggestible he became. For all he knew the concentration kept building up in his body, like arsenic, and he would spend the rest of his life happy to do whatever people told him to do.

He groped around until he found the short ladder, grabbed a rung and pulled himself over to it, climbed out of the tank.

When he took the mask off everything looked the same as in the simulation. The early morning sun was shining brightly in through the window. He stared out at the cows for a long time, remembering the watching intelligence in their eyes as they'd turned as one to stare up at him. But that had just been the dream; they were just cows. Steaks on the hoof, as his Uncle Toshi would have put it.

It was bad enough being manipulated from outside without letting his unconscious distort things even further.

He showered, dressed slowly, went downstairs and knocked on the door to Kamutef's office. There was no response. He knocked again, louder, tried the door. It was locked.

"Are you looking for Mr. Kamutef?" His assistant, wearing loose burgundy slacks and a peach-colored blouse for a change.

"Yes."

"He had to return to Cairo. He'll be back next week."

"Did he leave a message for me?"

"No."

"Would anyone mind if I called my wife?"

"I'm afraid that won't be possible for the moment. Possibly when Mr. Kamutef returns."

Of course they wouldn't let him call Claire. He might as well ask for a guided tour of the labyrinth.

Nobody seemed to be watching him, nobody tried to stop him when he went for his walk, but there was nowhere he could go anyway. He had some vague idea that he could discover something—loose piles of stones from excavations, maybe, or air vents, he wasn't sure what—that would corroborate or repudiate the labyrinth's existence.

He didn't find anything. Even if the tunnels were real, they might have been dug when the chateau was built, all evidence of their existence effaced by the centuries.

Leaving him with no other option but to keep on doing what he had been hired to do, never let himself forget just how powerful and fanatical his employers were, and just hope he could come up with something that would satisfy them.

But the programming went well that night. As soon as he started he not only found himself caught up in the programming problems the metamorphoses and hybrid copulations posed, but he could see where his earlier efforts had gone wrong. Instead of starting with two separate classes of objects for the cows and actresses he should have started with the hybrids, and considered the others just extreme transformations of them. Once he had figured that out he started writing tight, elegant code.

It felt good to be programming again, feeling it flowing almost effortlessly up and through and out of him.

About five in the morning he paused for a sandwich and ran a chunk of rewritten code to see if any new bugs had worked their way into it.

The transformation of a cow's udders into a pair of voluptuous human breasts was a fascinating technical problem and nothing more.

He stopped, suddenly reminded of what that meant, trying to make himself feel something that just wasn't there, then gave up and went back to programming. He wrote code furiously until noon, then went directly to his bedroom and passed out.

The dream began where it had left off. All the cows were staring up at him, their huge, beautiful, liquid eyes glinting silver now in the moonlight, and as the wind brought their scent to him he felt the first faint stirrings of desire.

The next night he started weaving the way the cows had looked at him into the program, as part of their reaction to the Kamutef figure. When he finally collapsed back into bed, utterly exhausted from the strain of sixteen hours of uninter- rupted concentration, even if it had all been spent floating in the tank, he fell back into the dream. But this time he was no longer a spectator, watching from his window as Kamutef stood there in his silver-horned crown. Now he was the one standing with his arms upraised as the cows crowded in closer and closer around him, their odor rich and exciting like nothing he had ever known before.

Awakening, he saw how he could weave what he had dreamed into the program again. And when, after three nights of furious activity and three days spent looping over and over again through the dream, he finally managed to recode the sequence from Kamutef's POV, the dream led him further, constantly taking him deeper into the program, until he was little more than a vehicle for the dream, an interface through which it translated itself into code.

All he held back was the odor, the excitement of their scent, though every night it was more thrilling, more compel- ling.

Occasionally, when he was eating or leaning back in his simulated chair with his eyes closed, trying to picture the next step, he would wonder about what was happening to him, where the dreams were coming from and what Kamutef had done to make him dream them, but the abstract idea of what had been done to him was more frightening than anything he really felt. He wasn't even scared anymore. Like a Kamikaze pilot, too wrapped up in getting his plane perfectly lined up with the target to worry about what would happen when it hit.

By the time Mark finally saw Kamutef again three weeks later, looking old and feeble and sick as his assistant helped him hobble down the hall, he was too caught up in the decision trees for the sequences of gestures and incantations to ward off Horus to do more than nod distractedly before forgetting about him completely again.

He no longer went for walks. When he left the chateau, it was only to stand watching the cows, trying to see the women immanent in them. Sometimes he glimpsed one for a fraction of a second before she disappeared again, leaving behind a sort of resonance, a richness that filled everything around him with unseen light.

He knew, when he thought about it, that any psychiatrist would diagnose him as clinically insane, but the knowledge was distant, irrelevant.

It was only after Kamutef finally asked to see him again that Mark realized a month had passed since he had been taken down to the labyrinth. Curiously, it was easier to accept it as real now than when he had first awakened.

Kamutef's hands were trembling on his desk. He was sicker, a wasted old man whose body was shaking itself to death.

"Are you making progress?" His voice now had the same trembling quaver in it as his body.

Mark nodded. "It's coming along."

"How long until you finish?"

"A month for the alpha-test version, another month to get the bugs out. Say two months."

"You have to finish before then." Kamutef was trying to sound commanding, but only managed to seem desperate.

"When?"

225

"One more month. No longer."

"You said six months. I've got three left."

"Circumstances have changed."

"What circumstances?" Challenging him to say it.

"I'm dying."

What happened when Kamutef died and the program hadn't saved him? Unless it was supposed to assure some kind of spiritual rebirth or reincarnation, and even then . . . How would the others decide whether or not it had been successful?

What would they do to him if they didn't think it had been?

"You're sure?" he finally asked.

"Yes."

"This . . . ritual is that important to you?"

"Yes."

"But if it's some kind of last rites—" Mark paused, waiting to see what Kamutef would say. When he saw that Kamutef wasn't going to say anything he went on, "I mean, you must have had some other way to do it before. Without computers."

"Your program is only part of the complete ritual, which was begun over a year ago. It is too late to go back and start over again."

"If you know anything about computer companies, you know that software is never quite ready when it's supposed to be. There are always a couple of major bugs nobody expected."

"You had a reputation for getting your programs in under schedule. That was one reason we hired you."

Mark fell silent again, thinking about the dream, all the things remaining to be translated into code.

"Well?"

"Maybe I can do it in a month. If everything goes right. But I can't promise you anything."

"If you don't—"

Mark cut him off. "Look, Mr. Kamutef, it won't do you any good to threaten me. Or make me a bigger offer, either, though if you want to, go ahead. You already made sure I'm working at top speed with whatever you did to me downstairs." He gestured at the door behind the desk. "I don't suppose you want to tell me anything about that?"

"No."

"Then just let me get back to work."

Kamutef stared at Mark, finally nodded. "You said you will have a version in a month?"

"*About* a month. A preliminary version."

"But the program will work? Despite whatever minor bugs may be left in it?"

Mark shrugged. "I hope so. I won't know until I run it."

"What if you cut down on the quality of the animation? Simplify it?"

"It's too late for that. I'd have to rewrite too much code. It would be easier to simplify the rules a little—"

"No."

"—but if you want, what I can do is concentrate on getting all the sequences done and leave fine-tuning the animation for last."

"How much time will that save?"

"It depends. A lot, if there are some major problems with the animation quality. Almost none, if I get everything right the first time. But if I skimp on the animation now it'll take me a couple extra weeks to get it right in the end."

"That's not important. Do it that way."

Mark was grateful when Kamutef let him go. Memories of the previous day's dream were waiting, looping through his head whenever he let his attention wander, demanding he translate them into code so he could go on to the next step.

He did as quick and dirty a job on the verisimilitude as the dream would let him while he focused on linking the ritual sequences of subjugation, copulation, defense and metamorphosis into a coherent whole. At the end he was working twenty hours a day, pausing only to sleep long enough to dream, or to stand among the cows, run his hand over their flanks and stare into their eyes.

Though his dreams were all sexual now, ecstatic multiple copulations with the herd in their bovine or hybrid forms, he felt no sexual desire for the physical animals. Or for anyone or anything else, for that matter. But when he slept, the dreams were more demanding. He was a conduit through which the dreams were being channeled, were channeling themselves, and whenever something slowed or blocked their realization, the pressure built up inside him, the dreams intensifying until they were unbearable, looping through him faster and faster. He was experiencing them from multiple points of view now, as a spectator, as Kamutef, the women, and even the cows, though much of what he felt and knew when he was dreaming vanished when he awakened, leaving only the need to get the ritual right.

And Hathor was there in the dream. Looking up from the pasture, the cows circling him in disciplined array, he could see the Goddess staring down at him from his bedroom window. When he copulated with the cattle and women, forced the cattle into human form, embodied the Goddess in her hybrid avatars, he knew he was drawing Her ever closer, he felt the awe and the mystery of Her, Her refusal to be commanded.

With the Cray's ability to suggest solutions based on his own programming techniques, it took him only three more weeks to get the first version done. He ran through it a final time, then defined his POV back in his body, got out of the tank and called Kamutef.

This time Kamutef came to see him. He was in a wheel-chair, pushed around by one of the priests who had taken Mark down into the underground labyrinth. But the priest could have been programmed into a simulation; his physical existence proved nothing.

"It's finished?"

"Pretty much. There are still a few bugs."

"What kind of bugs?"

"There are places where the program doesn't always respond to the prayers and incantations the way it should."

"Are you sure you have the prayers and incantations right?"

"Yes."

"What else?"

"The animation is uneven. Most of the sequences are perfect, but some of the ones at the end are very bad. And there's something wrong with the feedback between the metamorphoses. You ... the character representing you keeps getting forced back into human form, I'm not sure why."

"Perhaps the ritual is more demanding than you realized."

"Perhaps."

"No other problems?"

"No."

"Run it for me."

"On the screen, or do you want to get in the tank?"

"The screen, this time."

Mark sat down, called up the program. It felt strange, seeing it reduced to the screen's two-dimensional world. And he had been living his dream, embodying it for months, but now, with Kamutef watching him manipulate the Kamutef figure on the screen, he suddenly felt like a voyeur.

"There!" Kamutef jabbed a skeletal finger at the screen.

Mark halted the program.

"Go back a little . . . . Stop. Right here."

On the screen an almost completely bovine cow was trying to gore the Kamutef figure, which was twisting adroitly out of the path of her horns.

"She shouldn't miss him completely. Her left horn should graze his chest and draw blood."

It felt right. Mark nodded. "OK."

"I will try it tomorrow night," Kamutef told Mark after seeing the results of his next two days' almost uninterrupted work. "Alone. I'll let you know what I think of your work when I'm done. If it's satisfactory you can return to Paris tomorrow."

"There's still a lot of minor stuff to clean up—"

"If it's minor my people can take care of it."

Kamutef's priest wheeled him out again. Mark went back to the final sequences.

He had been working on the animation quality for more than twenty-four hours straight and the full moon was already shining in through his window by the time he finally staggered up the stairs to his room, lay down fully dressed on his bed and fell asleep.

He stood on the crest of his hill, naked except for the horned crown of polished silver and his long black beard of plaited reeds, the endless coils of velvet red rope looped over his shoulder. His herd milled around him, full moon gleaming off long curved horns, dark smooth muscular flanks. The night air was rich with the excitement of their scent.

He raised his arms and let out an enormous bellowing roar that shook the very earth beneath him. The cows froze, then slowly lifted their massive heads and stared up at him.

The Goddess gazed out at him through their eyes and he exulted in Her scrutiny, gloried in it.

He raised his arms again and the herd came to him, fascinated, spiraling slowly and inexorably in on him, a flower curling in around its center for the night, until they were packed so tightly around him that a lesser man would have been crushed by their massive flanks, gored by their horns as they drowned him in their hot, feverish adoration.

Slipping a coil of rope from his shoulder, he took the first cow by the horns, wrestled her to the ground despite the press of the others, subdued and bound and mounted her. He left her tied there as he rose from her and took another cow. This time he felt the Goddess in her, the sudden thrust of her horns that drew blood from his side, the first subtle transformations by which She tried to conceal Herself from him. But he was too strong for Her, and though She panicked the herd and sent them fleeing, he pursued them at his leisure and took them one by one, his strength and desire burning ever brighter, limitless and insatiable as he pursued the Goddess incarnate in their many bodies through the multiplicity of forms and aspects in which She tried to elude him. Udders into breasts, hooves into feet and hands, primeval bestiality into human voluptuousness and beauty, sophisticated seduction. But he refused to be taken in by the temptations and traps She set for him, matched Her metamorphoses with transformations of his own, the multiplicity of Her aspects with his insatiable desire to unite himself with Her in Her final, threefold splendor.

Crocodile-headed Sekmet, falcon-headed Horus, the mummy that was Ptah lay in wait for him, but he knew Them, knew the chants and gestures to ward Them off. The Goddess made a final attempt to escape him into a world of fluctuating color and depth, flickering in and out of two-dimensionality, where time ran forward and backward in bizarre, jerky halts and starts. She tried to trap him there, in two-dimensional loops, but he followed her back to reality, inescapable, until at last they met and fused in a final all-consuming hierogamos that burned away his former flesh, his old self, leaving only ashes behind as he was caught up and lost in the infinitely self-replicating algorithm of the Goddess's radiance, as joined in their embrace they mounted higher, ever higher into the arched blue vault of the sky, the starry womb from which he would be reborn—

The telephone ringing on his bedside table woke him. He groped for it but he was tangled up in the sheets, and when he tried to extricate himself he fell out of bed and knocked the table over.

The receiver was lying near his head. He worked his arm free, grabbed it.

"Mr. Gyoko?" Kamutef's assistant's clipped, unfriendly voice.

"Yes." His mouth was full of acid bile, like after a night of drinking until you vomit everything up, only to start in again as soon as your dry heaves die down.

"Mr. Kamutef has asked me to inform you that he is completely satisfied with your work as it is and that you have fulfilled the terms of your contract. A car will take you back to Paris as soon as you are ready."

"But the animation—"

"Is perfectly satisfactory, and no longer your concern." She hung up before he could think of an answer.

Which was just as well, because where the algorithms and the code they had spawned had been growing and prolif-erating and developing in the back of his mind every waking moment for the last months, there was now just a dead emptiness, like the hollow ache after a tooth has been pulled. Even the dream that had inhabited him for so long was breaking up into disconnected images and fragments, fading.

Mark wriggled clumsily out of the tangle of sticky sheets and rumpled clothing, stood up. When he took a breath the stench from his body was so disgusting it almost made him gag. Like that old man who had spent every day coughing and nodding out in the reading room of the public library where Mark had worked after school back in Monterey. His clothes had always looked neatly pressed but he must not have washed for years.

Mark staggered into the bathroom. In the mirror he looked as old as he felt, gray-skinned, grizzled and haggard.

There was a six-inch hairline scar on the right side of his chest that hadn't been there yesterday.

Fuck it. The whole thing was over, done with. He didn't want to even think about it.

He shaved, took a scalding hot shower, dressed. His reflection still looked more like a poorly embalmed corpse than a hi-tech boy wonder back on his feet again after a few momentary reverses, but a couple nights' real sleep in his own bed would take care of that.

The same driver who had brought him from Paris was waiting in the stretch limousine. As Mark got into in the back seat he found himself picturing some sort of James Bond ending for the whole episode: the space behind the glass partition filling up with yellow gas, his dead body returned to the chateau, taken down into the yellow-lit tunnels and ripped open up with jeweled knives, his viscera removed and his brain dragged out of his nose with hooks as the priests prepared him for a traditional mummification—

He lost interest and opened the window, breathed in fresh morning air with the promise of heat ahead. None of that was real anymore, if it had ever been. Life was back to business as usual during alterations.

Mark knocked, waited, knocked again, then let himself in. There were fresh tulips in a vase on the living room table, some books piled on the floor next to the armchair. Claire was obviously living there. When he opened the closet, he saw new dresses, purses, shoes.

As he was closing the closet he noticed a neatly-pressed man's linen suit hanging on the far end. He supposed that meant that as a good American husband he should check out the bathroom for intruding brands of toothpaste, a man's razor with blond hairs caught in it or a bottle of unfamiliar after-shave. The whole thing followed by a passionate confronta-tion leading to a final break-up or tearful reconciliation. Or he could do the gallant thing, drag his suitcases back down the five fights of stairs and park himself in a café, keep phoning until she got back, then tell her he would be home in a few hours, leave her enough time to get everything back in order so they could both pretend nothing had ever happened.

Fuck it.

He left the suitcases unopened in the center of the floor, checked his bank accounts by minitel and found out he had $268,000 in his dollar account and about 20,000 francs in his franc account. Not only had Kamutef paid him in full, but Claire had been saving most of what he earned. Combined with the fact she hadn't changed the locks, he supposed that meant something positive.

Anyway, the suit in the closet made not telling her about what had happened OK. They'd both have secrets they weren't sharing, and that put everything back in equilibrium, balanced it and made it workable.

Kamutef's people weren't going to try to disappear him or do anything else, not after having paid him in full and left records all over the place. He could forget about that sort of thing.

All he had to worry about now was picking up the rest of his life and getting started over again. Beginning with Claire.

I don't want to just pounce on her when she gets back, he decided. I should give her some warning. Time to prepare, even if I don't go the whole nine yards and pretend I haven't been home yet.

There was a florist's across the street. He bought a dozen red roses and carried them upstairs, left them in a vase on the boarded-up fireplace's marble mantle with a note saying he would be back around eight and he would like to take her out to dinner. Then he went out to kill a couple of hours.

He decided to take in a movie at one of the sleazy neighborhood theaters, ended up with a choice between a slasher film, a martial arts film, and an old Italian western.

He chose the western but left halfway through. He told himself he was leaving because the film was bad, but the real problem was that all the cattle in it were hideously ugly steers—far too scrawny, and empty-eyed, without a trace of that intelligence he had come to recognize in Kamutef's cows.

No more westerns for a while. But the way the whole episode in the chateau was fading, blurring, he'd get over it all soon enough.

And when he got home that evening and found Claire waiting for him with champagne, slim and pert and lovely in a new dress that he didn't remember seeing in the closet a few hours earlier he felt that maybe everything really was OK after all and they could make a fresh start together that would really mean something.

In September, two months later, a few miles after they'd turned off Highway One into Carmel Valley, where Mark had rented an immense house that was easily big enough to double as his office even after he got things off the ground and needed space for a few employees, they passed a clump of mud-colored cows grazing in a sun-scorched pasture by the side of the road. Mark just glanced at them, his mind on other things, when a gust of wind carried their odor in through the open window to him, and then suddenly algorithms were exploding like fiery pinwheels out of some place in the back of his mind, a fractal forest growing with incredible speed, filling his thoughts and spreading out to encompass the world as the algorithms took root and proliferated, sending out synesthetic shoots and runners of code, flowering into fractal modules that shot out new seeds that germinated and matured and reproduced instantly.

Mark continued driving the new station wagon sedately past the crystallizing vineyards and golf courses and old age homes and shopping centers as the program surged back into him. As it took on structure he saw how he could give it a sort of twist, like twisting the end of a kaleidoscope around, and make the code fall into object modules he could use to program the new Sun workstation back at the house. He would have to do without the tank, but he could already see that the whole VR set-up was just a crutch he didn't need anymore, the kind of useless bells and whistles that only ignorant technophiles like Kamutef thought they needed.

"Mark," Claire said, "you've got that far-off look again. Where are you?"

"Just some programming ideas." Looking at her he knew that all the photos and footage had been just more of Kamutef's fetishism, as unnecessary as the VR: the real Goddess was there looking out at him through Claire's eyes, speaking to him with her voice, immanent in every movement of her slim body.

She brushed her hair back from her forehead and he automatically broke the gesture down into its component movements, translated them into tight, elegant code.

"Mark, I want to do things different this time. I don't want to make the same mistakes all over again."

"What do you mean?"

"I'm not sure, not all the way yet anyway, but— I think I want to have a baby. Children, a home that isn't just a place to work and sleep. Something *solid,* not just riding the crest of the wave one day at a time, and everything's wonderful as long as you don't go under, but when you do, there isn't anything left. That's what happened last time. Why it all fell apart so fast."

Mark nodded. "Children." Everything about Claire, the catch in her voice, the way she was frowning as she tried to find the right words, the words themselves—everything was generating code so fast he couldn't even follow it. He let his eyes close for an instant, just a blink, but he almost lost himself completely before he managed to make himself open them again, barely in time to negotiate the curve up the hill after the MidValley Shopping Center.

"Are you all right?" Claire asked, and even her concern was instantaneously translated into such tight, beautiful, elegant code that he almost lost track of what it meant. It was so hard to drive, listen, concentrate on anything outside the program.

Like some sort of disease, a cancer that had taken root in him and was devouring all of him from within—his mind, his body, his love for Claire—to feed its runaway growth.

"Is it because I said I wanted a baby?" Claire asked, and as her question, the worry in her eyes crystallized into code, he saw himself as the baby in her arms, the Bull of his Mother, and the last of his apprehension dropped away.

"I was just thinking. You're right. I want to have a baby too. As soon as we can."

His fingers twitched on the steering wheel, longing for his keyboard. He forced himself to grip the wheel tighter, wait just a little longer, until they got to the house and he could get to the workstation.

He watched Claire out of the corner of his eye as he drove, integrating her every gesture and expression, the gentle rise and fall of her chest as she breathed, the way the wind from the open window played with her hair, until at last they turned off the road into their driveway and he didn't have to worry about keeping his mind on driving anymore.

Just a little longer.

A Cartographic Analysis of the Dream State

by Pat Murphy

Pat Murphy lives San Francisco, California, and works at the Exploratorium, a type of hands-on science museum. She has written four novels, including *The Shadow Hunter,* the Nebula Award-winning *The Falling Woman* (Tor), and *The City, Not Long After* (Bantam). Her stories have appeared in most of the major genre magazines. "Rachel in Love" won the Theodore Sturgeon Award for Short Fiction as well as the Nebula Award in 1987; her novella "Bones" won the World Fantasy Award in 1991. Many of her short stories are collected in *Points of Departure* (Bantam). Her story "Peter" was published in *Omni* in February 1991.

The following novelette is about an exploratory mission to Mars. It combines hard science with the language of dreams.

A CARTOGRAPHIC ANALYSIS OF
THE DREAM STATE

Pat Murphy

I have a snapshot. One of the researchers at Endurance Station took it. It shows the four women of the second Trans-Polar Mapping Expedition, standing beside a SnoCat. Over our heads, Tibetan prayer flags fly from the SnoCat's cab, their colors brilliant against the salmon-colored Martian sky.

Four women wearing bulky parkas over our lycra compression suits: Nan, Yukiko, Maria, and me. I stand at the end of the line of women—half a step away from the others. Nan, Yukiko, and Maria are smiling. My expression is hidden by the glare of sunlight on the faceplate of my helmet.

We wave and pose. Historic photos of the first expedition across the Martian polar ice. Photos for our children. For our grandchildren. Photos for the time when we are history. Frozen smiles, with the frozen wastes behind us.

My name is Sita. I'm a cartographer with a talent for interpreting the shades and squiggles that the computer produces from satellite photos and sonic recordings. I take ambiguous data and produce a map, drawing hard boundaries where suggestions of lines once existed, interpreting one set of smudges as meaningless noise and another as irregularities in the landscape.

The map, as everyone knows, is not the territory. A map is a representation, subject to the misinterpretations and confusions of the mapmaker. A map can show you how to get from here to there. But that only helps if you know where you're going.

When I went on the Trans-Polar Expedition, I was looking for something. Like most people who are searching, I didn't really know exactly what I was looking for. But I was looking, and looking hard.

Long ago, mapmakers drew dragons at the edges of maps, in the unknown lands that were still unexplored. Today, there are fewer dragons. But you can still find them, if you know where to look.

Beneath the ice and snow of the Martian polar cap are lands that have been hidden for hundreds of thousands of years. Before the seismic studies of the Trans-Polar Expedition, no one knew the shape of those hidden lands. We mapped lands that no one had ever seen, learning the secrets of Mars.

"We leave in one month," Maria Calida said. She leaned on her desk, studying me with intense blue eyes. I had never spoken with her before, though I had heard her lecture on the findings of the first Trans-Polar Expedition. That expedition had turned back because of unseasonable storms. They lost one SnoCat in a crevasse, and Maria herself was responsible for the rescue of the two expedition members from that vehicle. You know all this, I'm sure. Everyone does.

When Maria interviewed me, she looked just as she did in the videos of the first expedition, except that her hair had a few more streaks of gray and her face had a few more lines around the eyes. "This expedition has been in the planning for three years now," she said. "And last month, Janice Katura, our cartographer, snapped her Achilles tendon playing racketball. Three months recovery time, minimum. I found a replacement: Dita Rachlin. Then Dita broke her leg in a climbing accident. Multiple fracture." Maria leaned back, scowling—not at me, but at some vague point behind my head. "Both Janice and Dita recommended I talk to you."

I nodded. Dita had warned me that Maria would scowl, but had advised me not to take it personally.

"What's your experience on long expeditions?"

I took a deep breath. "I was cartographer on a mining survey trip across Hellas Basin. One month in two Rovers and a jumping truck. We mapped the landforms under the sand, searching for mineral deposits."

"A picnic in the park, compared to this one. No polar experience?" Her scowl deepened when I shook my head.

"Look," I said. "You've seen my résumé and you know my background. And I'm sure Dita and Janice told you that I have considerable experience interpreting both satellite data and sonic recordings. I've been checking over your route, and I'd like to show you a few things I've found. Do you mind?"

"Go ahead."

"I'll need to access the central data base." I pulled my chair up to the work station beside her desk and tapped an access code into the keyboard. A map of the polar cap appeared on the screen. "I've been wondering about this patch." My fingers traced a line on the map. "I know that you've been using this map series, drawn up last year. The cartographer in charge of the project interpreted this area as an ice plain—hard-packed. But look here." I tapped on the keyboard again and called up a satellite photo mosaic of the same area. There were faint shadows, gray smudges on the white surface. "I suspect that region is actually a thin crust over loose snow. Similar to the patch where you lost that

SnoCat on your first expedition. I'd recommend that you reroute to skirt this region altogether."

She studied the screen. "You're suggesting a significantly longer route. Why should I trust your interpretation?"

I shrugged. "If I'm wrong, you lose a day's time to a detour. But if I'm right and you don't detour, you risk the success of the expedition. And I did a little more checking." I called up another satellite photo mosaic. "This series was taken a decade ago. The shadows in that area have shifted—see here? If they're crevasses, that's a further indication of an unstable substrate." I glanced at her face. She was still frowning. "If you'd like, I can check the rest of the route."

Maria nodded thoughtfully. "Dita told me you were good."

"I am."

She continued to study my face. "But you're young. And you've no experience in polar conditions. What makes you think you can handle this?"

I hesitated. She had already talked to my colleagues; I had received all the highest recommendations. There was not much new that I could say. If you can make her laugh, you're home free, Dita had said.

"My father tells me that my great-grandfather used to guide expeditions in remote regions of the Himalayas to search for yeti. He never found a yeti, but he was quite popular as a guide. He never lost an expedition. And he didn't have the advantage of satellite photography. I figure it's in the blood."

She cracked a smile. "Yeti, eh? You never know what you might find up there." She nodded thoughtfully. "Why don't you take another look at those maps," she said. "Let's talk again tomorrow."

I returned Maria's smile, guessing in that moment that I'd be asked to join the expedition.

* * *

243

One of the technicians must have climbed the low ridge near Endurance station to take this photo: a long shot of our two SnoCats heading away from the station across a plain of ice. Here and there, the treads of SnoCats from the station had scraped away the top layer of ice, revealing the red dust deposited by last summer's storms. Our SnoCats are bright yellow against the glittering white and dull red surface. One SnoCat tows the living module, the box in which we would live for the next few months. The other tows the jumping truck, the clumsy vehicle that we needed to make seismic recordings.

I rode in the second SnoCat with Nan. Our vehicle towed the living module. Maria and Yukiko led the way in the SnoCat that towed the jumping truck.

The wind was blowing—the steady gale characterizes spring weather at the North Pole. In the relative warmth of spring (when the temperature rises to a balmy 144 Kelvin), the carbon dioxide that froze during the winter chill returns to the atmosphere and rushes south. In the low atmospheric pressure of Mars, the wind has little force, but it was strong enough to carry tiny ice crystals aloft and send them skittering across our windshield.

Nan drove, operating the vehicle with confidence that came from experience. She had been a researcher at Endurance Station for the past three summers. On the expedition, her primary responsibility was equipment maintenance.

"I'll let you take a turn later," Nan said. "Sightsee while you can. The scenery here is nothing compared to what we'll see a few days in, but it's still pretty spectacular."

I stared through the windshield. Sunlight glittered on the plain of ice. This was a forbidding world of light and shadow: the relentless glare of the sun; whirlwinds of ice particles; the black shadow of the SnoCat, following us across the ice.

In the distance, massive cliffs rose from the plain. Shaped by the winds, the cliffs spiraled outward from the North Pole itself. The cliffs, like all the ice of the polar cap, contained the history of Mars. The ice had formed, layer by layer, over millions of years. Each winter, a layer of ice crystallized on the surface; each summer, dust storms covered the ice with reddish brown grit. Looking at the cliff was looking back in time: a thin layer of ice indicated a balmy winter thousands of years ago; a thick layer of dust indicated a time of intense volcanic activity or dust storms. These cliffs, recent by planetary standards, had formed over the last hundred thousand years or so. Looking at them across the plain, I felt very young.

A sudden gust of wind flung ice crystals at the windshield and made me flinch. The SnoCat rocked as it crossed a series of ripples in the ice. "You got to watch out for those," Nan said. "*Sastrugi,* they call them. The wind makes them." She glanced at me. "So what do you think of the scenery?"

"It's so empty," I said. "I'd seen photos, but I hadn't realized . . ."

"You can't realize how empty it is until you get here," Nan said. "You can look at all the pictures you want, but it's hard to take a picture of all this nothing and make it look as empty as it really is. A picture has a frame—it's bounded, contained. But this . . ." She took a hand off the wheel and waved it at the window. "This just goes on and on. Can't escape it. Can't get used to it, either. Every time I come back, it takes me by surprise."

"Why'd you decide to come back?"

"I like it here," Nan said. "There's time to think. Things are so much simpler than in the colonies. Just a few people and a whole lot of nothing." She grinned, wrestling the wheel of the SnoCat to steer around an outcropping of ice.

I turned in my seat and stared out the back window. I could just see the bright blue dome of Endurance Station dwindling in the distance. "The station's almost out of sight," I said.

"Goodbye, Endurance Station," Nan said cheerfully. "Hello, Nothing."

My father gave me the flags that flew from the back of the SnoCat. He painted them himself, using UV-resistant ink on ripstop nylon. Every time they flapped, they sent up a prayer: *Ohm mani padme ohm.* Literally translated, it means "the jewel in the lotus." Basically, it's a prayer for enlightenment. My father was doing his best to help me in my search.

The story about my great-grandfather was true, by the way. My father came to Mars from India, where he had earned his engineering degree. But his family had come from Tibet, refugees from the Chinese occupation.

When I was growing up, he told me stories that his father had told him—tales of mountains covered with snow, rushing rivers that ran beneath blue skies. Fantastic stories. After all, everyone knew that the proper color for the sky was pale pink with a beautiful green sun. My father's stories were filled with unlikely creatures like elephants and rhinoceros and yeti. In my memories, the yeti that lived in the snowy reaches of the Himalayas was at least as plausible as the elephant that lived in the heat of India.

I have a photo of the expedition's first camp. I took it myself. To take the photo, I skied away half a mile away from camp just before sunset. I told the others that I wanted to go out to get a little exercise. In truth I wanted to go out alone because the idea of going out alone frightened me.

When I was a child, I would sit awake in the darkness of my room. I was afraid of the dark, but at the same time I was eager for a confrontation. I dared the unknown things that lived in the darkness to come and get me. They never did.

I skied out on the ice plain, defying the emptiness. In the photo that I took, the sun is setting and its light paints the salmon-colored sky with vivid streaks of green and blue. In the wash of light, the horizontal streaks that mark the cliff are the color of dried blood. The living module is at the foot of the cliff. The windows are points of light, like distant stars.

I started back toward camp before the sun was down. The temperature was already dropping—carbon dioxide frost was forming on the surface of the ice, a carpet of diamonds that I crushed beneath my skis. The wind had let up.

I wasn't cold—the exertion of skiing kept me warm—but I was aware of the chill air around me. There was a relentless quality to the cold at the pole. It had always been cold there; it would always be cold. I knew I was only a tiny spot of warmth, a temporary anomaly.

I hailed the living module on my suit radio. "I'm on my way in," I told Yukiko.

"Roger," Yukiko confirmed. "Dinner will be ready when you get here."

Then there was only static and the rasp of my own breath. The ice plain was empty and I was aware that I was alone. Lonely, very lonely, and the living module seemed far away.

I made good time, slowing only when I encountered a patch of *sastrugi*. It would be easy to turn an ankle on the rough snow, so I slowed my pace, working my way between the bumps and valleys.

I was halfway to the living module when I caught a glimpse of a shadow moving away from me. I turned to get a better look, but the landscape was still: white mounds and ridges dusted with white. I skied in the direction that I thought I had seen the movement, but stopped. The sun was almost down; the mounds cast long shadows across the plain.

The movement, I was certain, was a trick of the light. Out

there on the snow fields, a smudge of frost on the faceplate of a pressure suit could become a moving shadow in the distance. A vagrant breeze could lift a swirl of ice crystals and create a ghost dancing across the plain. The shadow of a hummock could take on substance and solidity, a dark creature that crouched on the glittering snow.

I did not linger to chase phantoms. I continued back to camp. But I felt a little colder, and once or twice I stopped to look back over my shoulder, checking the barren landscape for movement.

I reached the living module, stepped through the airlock, and left my skis and compression suit in the equipment alcove. The living space was warm and fragrant with curry. I heard laughter as I entered. Yukiko was stirring the pot; Nan was repairing a strap on her parka. Maria was apart from the others, typing her notes from the day's journey into the computer.

"Did you find them?" Yukiko called to me.

"Find who?" I asked.

Nan and Yukiko were both grinning at me. "Maria said you might be looking for the abominable snowman."

"Abominable snowperson," Maria corrected firmly, looking up from the computer screen. "They never caught one, so they don't know if it was male. Better yet: abominable snowape. Abominable snowghost. Abominable goosechase. An excuse to tromp around in the mountains."

"Sounds good to me," Nan said.

Maria nodded, smiling. "You have a point there."

"Curry's ready," Yukiko called.

"We'd better eat it quick. It smells good enough to attract a herd of abominable snowthings," Nan said.

I followed them to the table. They were just teasing, I knew that. But the laughter made me edgy. I did not want to joke about the yeti. I did not mention the shadow I had seen out on the ice. It had been a trick of the light, I told myself. Nothing more.

* * *

Nan was wrong about one thing: the smell of curry, no matter how good, would not attract the yeti. Yeti don't eat curry. The yeti feed on dreams. That is always what has sustained them. They come from our minds and our hearts to fill the emptiness of a barren world, and they feed on our dreams.

I dreamed vividly that first night. You could blame it on the curry or on the excitement of the expedition, but the moving shadow—that phantom I had declined to chase—could have been equally to blame.

I dreamed of the yeti. Squat, broad-faced beasts with clever hands and fur as warm and shaggy as a child's dream of Mama Bear. The yeti had the enormous dark eyes of nocturnal creatures. In my dreams, they wandered a strange landscape, through twisting canyons and up the steep slope of an ancient volcano. I followed them as best I could, but they were swift and elusive, ducking into the shadows and vanishing.

I woke feeling bewildered. For the first few hours of the day, as we broke camp and began traveling parallel to the cliff face, I was preoccupied, thinking about the impossible beasts of the dream. As Nan drove, I found myself watching for moving shadows in the snow.

Another snapshot—not a very good one. Maria must have taken it. I am skiing away from the camera on the stubby skis that work well on the ice. On my back, I carry a clumsy pack of equipment: geophones designed to listen to the rumblings of the ice; bright flags to mark the locations of the geophones. My parka is a blur of red against the ice.

It is still early in the day, and the plain is dusted with carbon dioxide frost. Behind me is a pair of dull white tracks, where my skis have crushed the glittering crystals.

That was the morning we took a seismic reflection profile, giving me my first glimpse beneath the ice. Early in the morning, before the carbon dioxide frost had vaporized in the sunlight, Yukiko, Nan, and I set out on skis to place the geophones.

Yukiko and Nan skied parallel to the cliff—Yukiko heading westward and Nan eastward. I followed a straight line south, away from the cliff, steering by the sun. Every thirty meters, each skier anchored a geophone.

I worked quickly, applying the heat stick that I carried at my belt to the ice at my feet. The ice vanished beneath the warm metal of the heat stick; water vapor swirled away, having made the transition from solid to gas without passing through a liquid stage. I made a neat square hole, just the size of the packet of electronics and listening equipment, then pressed the stick point-first into the ice, making two deep holes for the geophone's sensors. I placed the listening device neatly in place and planted a flag to mark the spot.

Over the suit radio, I could hear Nan and Yukiko chatting and joking. Nan was teasing Yukiko about her music—lately, Yukiko had been listening to an opera by the hottest young Jamaican composer. Nan said that it was just noise and Yukiko accused Nan of having an ear for music that was exactly as well-developed as the geophones we were planting in the ice. "They listen," Yukiko said, "but they don't really hear."

I skied on, stopping occasionally to place another geophone, laying out a neat line of the listening devices. As I worked, one part of my mind noted the landscape, searching for clues that would tell me about the lands beneath the ice. That bulge where the ice had cracked, revealing the reddish dust below; that upthrust section—too small to be called a cliff, but the beginnings of a cliff—these betrayed the secret movements of Mars, activity deep inside the ice or in the rocks beneath it.

With another part of my mind, I kept watch for shadows, alert for movements in the snow. It made no sense to watch for moving shadows and I knew that, but the landscape of ice and wind did not seem to demand rationality. This was the landscape of dreams, an empty place, waiting to be filled.

Nan was singing one of Yukiko's favorite songs from the Jamaican opera—butchering the tune—and Yukiko was laughing. I knew that they felt the emptiness too—they were struggling to fill the silence with noise of their own making. Nan finished the song with a yodeling cry. "What do you think, Sita?" Nan called. "What do you think?"

"I think you'd better stick to fixing equipment. You don't have a career as a singer."

"Ah, don't listen to her, Nan. She just doesn't understand modern music."

I paid no attention to their conversation after that. It faded, becoming inconsequential background noise. I studied the features of the ice plain and noted shadows where yeti might hide. It was a joke, a game I was playing with myself. I did not really think that there were yeti living on the plain. But I did watch for them.

I returned along a route parallel to my original course. In the distance, I could see the jumping truck and Maria's small, brightly clad figure beside it.

As I skied closer, I could feel a steady humming through my skis and boots. The rotating flywheel in the heart of the truck had reached its optimum speed. A massive piston extended downward from the base of the truck, lifting the body of the heavy vehicle high off the ice. As I watched, the truck began to move on the piston, dropping downward, but stopping just short of contact with the ice. The piston transmitted the downward force to the ice and the plain jerked, moving visibly beneath the truck. The truck rose, then fell again, in a regular rhythm that would gradually slow as the flywheel expended its energy and spun to a stop.

Each time the piston slammed the ground, sound waves spread, traveling through the layers of ice and snow to echo from the lands that lay buried in eternal winter. The array of geophones that we had painstakingly arranged picked up the echoes. From the echoes, the computer and I would draw a map of the mountains and valleys and canyons where no human being had ever walked.

Maria waved. I lifted a hand and waved back, like a castaway signaling a passing ship, like a friend departing for a distant land.

Another snapshot. The photo is muddy, the colors are off. Nan took the picture, using my camera. She took it about a week after we began making seismic reflection readings. It is night inside the living module, and the artificial lighting gives the scene a blue cast, making human faces look gray and unnatural. Maria and Yukiko are sitting at the small table that served as kitchen counter, dining table, and card table. There's a deck of playing cards on the table and Maria is looking up, as if asking Nan to come join them. Behind Maria, you can see my head: dark hair cut short to fit under a helmet.

"Why don't you come and play cards?" Maria called to me.

"Maybe tomorrow." I sat at the desk, examining the results of that day's seismic reflection profile on the computer screen. I was working with data from the sonic recordings, using the computer to draw a preliminary map of the land beneath the snow. I always found a sort of comfort in mapmaking. I take vague data and I produce something clear and precise. Maps are black and white portraits of a world that exists in shades of gray.

"Oh, join us for one hand," Nan urged me. "This is our last one tonight."

"Not just now," I said.

The others had been playing poker for the past hour, a cheerful game in which Nan made all the noise and Yukiko quietly raked in most of the money. Maria played carefully. The caution that made her a good expedition leader made her a bad poker player.

I clicked for enlargement of the center section of the map I had just drawn. A pattern of contour lines pressed close together, indicating a steep slope, rising from a smooth plain. Possibly a *moberg*, a volcano that had erupted beneath the ice, taking on a characteristic, steep-sided shape. I shifted the view back to the plain, searching for indications that it might be of volcanic origin.

"How's it going?" The game had broken up; Maria was looking over my shoulder at the map. She eased herself into the chair at my elbow.

"There's evidence that we're coming up over a moberg. You see right here?" I clicked back to the section of the map that showed the steep slope. "With luck, we'll find out for sure tomorrow."

Maria nodded, but she seemed distracted. "You know," she said, "you really ought to relax now and then. Take time out for a game of cards. Or a conversation."

I leaned back in my chair, studying Maria's face. The older woman looked concerned. "I'm fine," I said. "It's just ..." I stopped and waved a hand at the computer screen. "This is the first time anyone's seen this. I can't stop now."

Maria reached over and patted my shoulder. "I understand. But you have to relax sometimes. This last week, you've been at the computer every free moment."

I studied the screen, avoiding Maria's eyes.

"I really do understand," Maria said. "But you can't

spend every free moment analyzing data. And when you're not at the computer, you seem preoccupied. Are you worried about something?"

I shook my head, a quick dismissive movement. "I'm fine." I knew by Maria's expression that she did not agree. Maria watched my face for a moment, as if waiting for me to say something more.

Maria frowned. "I really think you're working too hard. You need to have a little fun."

"I am having fun."

"Humor me. Take a little more time off. Go to bed now. We'll be up early tomorrow."

I nodded reluctantly. "All right."

Maria patted my shoulder as she headed off to bed. I switched the computer off, and the plains and mountains of the secret lands faded to black.

As I lay in my sleeping bag in the living module, I considered the map of the land beneath the ice. Maria didn't understand—not really. She understood the intellectual curiosity, but that was all.

In my dreams, I strolled along the rough rock of the volcanic plain, stared up at the steep slope of the moberg. At night, I explored the secret lands and followed the yeti.

Placing the geophones had become routine, a ritual. Yukiko, Nan, and I worked together smoothly. Nan and Yukiko talked as they worked; I kept watch for moving shadows.

A sunny afternoon, with few shadows to be seen. I had finished anchoring a geophone and was scanning the horizon, waiting for the others. In the distance, I saw a line of darkness. A crack in the surface, maybe a meter across.

"There's a crevasse in the distance," I said to the others over the radio. "I'm going to go take a look."

As I slowly skied closer, I realized that I had misjudged the size, an easy thing to do when the landscape offered nothing for comparison. The dark line was a crevasse at least four meters wide.

"This thing is big enough to swallow a SnoCat whole," I said.

"Just what we need." Maria's voice crackled through her helmet.

I stopped several meters from the edge, wary of the ice underfoot. Here and there, bridges of water ice extended across the gap. As the weather had warmed, much of the snow and ice that had covered the gap in the winter had melted. In the spring thaw, the ice could be treacherous, ready to give way and drop a skier or a SnoCat into a hidden chasm.

I studied the gap in the ice. On the far wall, I counted ten layers of summer dust and winter snow, piled one on top of the other. The near edge hid the deeper layers from view. Beyond the crack, I noticed that the ice plain tilted downward. In the distance, it sloped up again, making an enormous depression.

"The ice on the other side shows some evidence of subsidence," I said. "I wonder what's going on underneath."

"We'll know soon enough," Maria said sensibly. "All you have to do is finish setting the geophones and you won't need to speculate."

"I'll place the last one here," I said. I anchored the geophone in the ice at my feet and headed back. The wind helped me along, pushing from behind and hurrying me back to camp.

Not a photo this time: a computer printout of a map, an abstraction of lines and shading. Here is the side of the *moberg,* a blocky, square-sided mountain that towers above the plain. And here—this shadow right here—that's the crevasse. The crack cuts through the ice, extending 400 meters beneath the surface, to meet the side of the moberg. On the southern side of the moberg, the ice had pulled away from the mountain, creating a bergschrund, a gap between ice and rock.

If you squint at the map, you can see something else, right here. A slight shift in shading. Some would dismiss it as insignificant. But it wasn't insignificant, not at all. That shift in shading marked an entrance to the hidden lands beneath the ice.

"We need to have a little fun," I said, using Maria's own words against her. "We can take the time off for a climb." I tapped my finger on the line that marked the crevasse on the map. "Besides, it's not so far to the underlying rock. This may be our only chance to gather some actual rock samples."

Maria frowned. "I'm not sure. What do you think, Nan?"

Nan eyed the map. "I skied out and took a look at the crevasse. It doesn't look like a difficult climb. We could rappel straight down; nothing tricky about it."

"We're right on schedule," Yukiko said. "We can spare the time." She didn't care about the climb, I knew, but she was supporting Nan.

Maria nodded reluctantly, and I rejoiced. Maria and Nan kept talking about safety procedures and gear, but I barely listened. We were going down, and that was all that mattered.

Snapshot: Nan and I—laden with ropes, climbing gear, and extra tanks of air—stand beside the crevasse. The sun is behind us, and the light reflects from the snow, a wash of bright light. Our faces are underexposed, lost in the darkness.

I had been scrambling up and down canyon walls since I was big enough to snap a carbiner into a harness and cling to a rope. I volunteered to be the lead climber, the first to back over the lip of the crevasse and rappel down the smooth wall of ice.

The red nylon straps of the climbing harness crisscrossed over my compression suit. The rope wrapped around my waist, weaving through a set of three interlocked carbiners, oval metal rings through which rope slid smoothly. In my right hand, I held the free end.

"This'll be a stroll in the park," I said over my radio. The climbing harness and rope supported me so that my feet were against the ice wall. By letting the rope slide slowly through my right gloved hand, I controlled the rate of my descent as I walked downward. The ice creepers strapped to my boots scored the ice, providing just enough traction to keep my feet from slipping. "No problem at all."

At the top, the climbing rope was anchored to a SnoCat—we had not trusted the ice for an anchor. At the other end—I did not know for sure what lay at the other end. According to the computer's map, the crevasse descended 300 meters before it reached the stone of the moberg.

Light from above reflected from the crevasse's glossy walls, and the deposits of red dust gave the reflection a reddish tint, like the light of a fire. But this light provided no warmth. Even through my compression suit and parka, I could feel the temperature drop as I descended.

Some twenty meters down, the sunlight had faded to the barest glow. High above me, through the mouth of the crevasse, I could see the Martian sky, an irregular curve of salmon pink. I could see the silhouette of three heads peering down: three jagged teeth in the pink grin.

"How's it going?" Maria asked.

"Fine," I said.

"I can still see the light of your headlamp. It looks like you're making steady progress."

"Sure. It's a piece of cake."

The rusty stripes of dust captured in the ice walls formed

patterns. The history of Mars was painted on the walls. I climbed down through the ages, past summer and winter and summer and winter and summer again, descending through time.

The light from my headlamp cast shadows on the wall: ghostly repetitions of my own image, created by reflected light. When I moved my head, the shadows shifted, stretching and changing. Other shadows—vague shapes—were keeping pace with me just out of reach of the headlamp's beam. I turned my head to try to catch them, but they were too fast, hurrying away before the light could touch them.

I looked up again, but the crevasse was curving. The smile was thinner now, a line of glowing pink.

"How are you doing?" Nan asked over the suit radio.

"Fine," I said, impatient with the interruption.

"I wanted to make sure you were paying attention."

Climbers had been known to become lulled by the easy rhythm of rappelling and rappel right off the end of the rope.

"I'm about 100 meters down, nowhere near the end of the rope," I said. "And I am paying attention."

"Tell us what it's like." Maria's voice now. "What do you see?"

Light from my headlamp glittered on the walls. "Red streaks on smooth white walls. On the northern face, they run horizontally. On the southern face, they run upward at an angle of maybe ten degrees."

"The face must have shifted as it pulled away from the moberg. What else do you see?"

I knew that Maria was trying to keep me focused on the task at hand, keep me talking. "More of the same. A whole lot of darkness below me. Above me, the crevasse has curved and I can't see the opening anymore."

"I know. We lost sight of your headlamp a while back."

"Maria, there are shadows down here." I hadn't meant to

say it. I had barely admitted my concern about the shadows to myself.

A moment's hesitation. "What do you mean?"

"Shadows. Just beyond where the light reaches. They're moving. I can't get a clear look at them." I stopped, catching myself.

"Sita, are you all right?" The question was asked in a matter-of-fact tone.

"I'm fine. Seeing a few yeti, I guess." I laughed then, trying to turn it into a joke.

"Why are you worried about the shadows?"

I did not want to tell Maria anything more about the shadows. That had been a mistake. "I was joking, Maria."

"Sita—listen to me. Check your air. Are you having a hard time breathing?"

I glanced at the air supply gauge. The tank registered as full. "Everything's as it should be." I was breathing heavily, but I blamed that on the exertion of the climb.

"Tell me about what you see."

"More of the same. White walls. Red streaks. Darkness. Cold. It's very cold and dark."

"Sita, I think you'd better come back." Maria's voice was calm and soothing.

I hesitated for a moment.

"Sita, do you hear me?"

"My receiver must be malfunctioning. I can't make out what you're saying, Maria. You're breaking up."

"Sita," Maria said. "Turn back."

"Maria? Are you there?" I managed to sound concerned. "All I get is dead air."

"Sita. Come in. Can you hear me? Sita!"

"Maria—I can't hear you, but I'm going to assume that you can hear me. I'll keep talking to let you know what's going on. I'm going to continue down—I'm so far down now, that

I might as well keep going."

"God damn you, Sita. Get back up here."

I ignored Maria and continued my descent. And I talked to Maria as I went. "You know, Maria, it's not as cold as it was before. I feel much warmer. The temperature's rising, I think."

The shadows were below me now, leading me down. Sometimes, I thought I could see the glitter of eyes—but that might have been ice crystals, catching the light.

"You know, those shadows are still here," I said. "I bet they are yeti. You know, it makes sense that the yeti would be here. We brought them with us. It would be so empty here without them."

The shadows stayed with me, always beyond reach of the light of my headlamp. Once, I stopped my descent and switched off the light. The darkness was complete: as if I were wrapped in black velvet, as if I had gone blind. I turned off the radio to shut off Maria's attempts to contact me, and I listened. The whisper of my breathing merged with the silence all around me. I waited, not sure what I was waiting for. After a time, I switched the headlamp on again and continued my descent.

When I looked down, I saw a jagged line on the far wall. The ice gave way to the rough stone of the moberg.

"Almost there," I said, forgetting that the radio was no longer on. "I can see the side of the moberg." According to the computer map, the bergschrund continued down for about fifteen meters beyond where it reached the moberg. "I'm continuing down."

I descended a few more meters, then saw a patch of darkness on the wall of stone. On the map, it had been an insignificant shift in shading. A lava tube, a vent formed by gases escaping the moberg during its last eruption, opened into the bergschrund. The shadows were the thickest at the mouth of the lava tube.

The bergschrund narrowed to a little more than a meter across. I reached the bottom where, for the first time in almost an hour, I could release my grip on the rope to relax and stretch. I reached out and ran my gloved hand over the basalt. The rock had been polished smooth by the ice, but a thin crack ran from the bottom of the bergschrund to the lava tube, the entrance to the hidden lands.

By Martian standards, the air was warm. I shrugged out of my parka, glad to be free of it. I removed the ice spikes from my boots and began the climb to the mouth of the lava tube.

The crack provided handholds. I climbed carefully and slowly. It was a short climb but my body was stiff and my right hand was tired from gripping the rope.

The mouth of the lava tube was as wide as I was tall. I could stand upright. The tunnel sloped slightly, a gentle incline. I shone my headlamp down the slope and caught a glimpse of movement where the tunnel turned. A shadow, fleeing the light. I started after it.

I was the first person to ever walk in this place: I knew that. Yet the tunnel was familiar from my dreams of the yeti. The light of my headlamp glistened on the red rock walls. Liquid water dripped down the walls, having percolated through the stone from somewhere overhead. The air in my helmet—oxygen from the tank on my back and air from the tunnel—carried the sulfurous scent of the Martian dirt. The tunnel floor was smooth, polished over the centuries by the trickling water.

I followed the tunnel downward, a straight course into the center of the moberg. I kept to one side of the water, where the rock was rougher and offered better traction. As I walked, I thought about mapping this place. On Mars, where the water was frozen into permafrost or ice caps, surely the trickle at my feet could be called a river. Only here, far below the surface, was the air pressure great enough to allow liquid water.

As I continued down, I talked—not to Maria, but to myself. I liked talking; the words kept me company. "It's a long hike down to the underworld," I said. I almost slipped on a patch of smooth rock, but caught myself and continued. My legs felt odd and rubbery. "I'm not myself. I haven't been myself for some time now. If I'm not myself, I wonder who I am."

I shook my head at that, and concentrated on placing my feet carefully and keeping my balance. If I fell and broke a leg, I would die here. The thought did not disturb me. If I did not turn back, if I kept walking downward into the secret lands, I would run out of oxygen and die. That thought came as no surprise. I kept walking.

The tunnel opened outward into a cavern. I looked up. The beam from my headlamp shattered against the crystalline ceiling to make patterns of broken rainbows. Elaborate ice formations hung above me: lunatic tangles of icicles; delicate networks as intricate as lace; flowing curtains of water, frozen in place; glistening ribbed structures that seemed organic, like the internal organs of some frozen giant. The floor of the cavern was a wide pool—an underground lake. I could not see the far side: the water extended away into the darkness. I stood on the edge of the secret lake, alone at the heart of the world.

I sat on the shore of the lake, watched the dark surface of the water, and waited for the yeti to come. Surely they would know where to find me. This is the place I was meant to be.

The light from my headlamp played on the water of the pool. The smooth surface was marked by ripples, spreading, I thought, from waterdrops falling into the pool from overhead.

While I was watching the ripples, the yeti came to me. A broad face filled my field of vision. A dream ape, with the enormous eyes of a cave dweller. I reached out to the beast, but it stood just out of reach. My fingers moved through empty air. I pushed myself up onto my knees, still reaching for the yeti, but it wasn't there anymore. I was alone.

My headlamp reflected from the dark water of the lake. Ripples laced the water's surface. Dark water and ripples—nothing more. But perhaps there were more ripples than there should have been from the drops of falling water. I peered into the pool.

A ribbon of translucent jelly snaked through the water. For a moment, I thought that this thing—whatever it was—was carried by a current in the pool. But then it changed direction abruptly, heading away from me. The headlamp's beam revealed a pattern of scarlet stripes and dark shapes that might be internal organs.

A jellyfish-like creature with a body the size of my thumb and tentacles the length of my little finger pulsed across the headlamp's beam. The edges of its translucent mantle fluttered, changing color with each movement, shading through pale blue, green, indigo, violet, dark blue, and back to pale blue again. As I watched the jellyfish pass, a school of pale red guppies—they swam like fish, anyway—swarmed into the light, feeding on something too small for me to see. I reached out, and they darted away, shimmering in the headlamp's beam.

Mars had never been balmy by human standards, but hundreds of millions of years ago, the planet had been warmer. The atmosphere had been denser then, and it helped hold the sun's heat in, warming the surface. Liquid water had flowed on the surface then. The plains still bore the traces of those ancient rivers.

These creatures had lived in those rivers. Perhaps there had been rocks slippery with primitive algae, soft-bodied animals grazing on the new growth, jellyfish and jellysnakes swimming against the current.

Then the air had grown thin and the world had grown cold. Ultraviolet radiation, once blocked by the atmosphere, made the surface dangerous. The water that once filled the rivers became a part of the permafrost. The creatures died—except here, where the ice protected them from ultraviolet and heat from the planet itself warmed them. I wondered what they fed on. Perhaps there were chemosynthetic organisms, like the ones found in the deep ocean trenches on Earth.

I sat by the pool and watched the creatures swim in and out of the beam of my headlamp. The yeti was gone. But I was not alone. The life of ancient Mars swam in the water at my feet.

I thought that I should tell Maria and Yukiko and Nan about the jellyfish. It seemed like a tremendous effort, but I switched on my radio. "Hello, Maria?" No answer. My signal was blocked by 300 meters of rock. "Maria?"

My thoughts seemed exceptionally sluggish. Maria would want to know about this. Life on Mars. A tremendous discovery. I should go back. With an effort, I got to my feet. Reluctantly, I started up the lava tube. My feet slipped on the smooth rock, and once I fell, but I caught myself on my hands and did not hurt myself. "Maria," I said on the radio. "You know what? There are these jellyfish, and fish, and sort of snakes. You've got to come and see them." I was babbling, but I could not seem to stop. "We're not alone after all, Maria."

"Sita!" Nan's voice in her helmet. "Where are you?"

Ahead, I could see a glimmer of yellow light at the mouth of the lava tube. I stumbled forward, drawn to the light.

Nan found me at the mouth of the lava tube, where I had collapsed. She replaced my regulator and gave me a fresh tank of oxygen. My regulator had malfunctioned and the resulting oxygen deprivation accounted for my rubbery legs, lack of judgement, and talk of yeti. But the jellyfish, the jellysnake, the little red guppies—those were real, as Nan discovered when she explored the lava tube at my insistence. Those were real.

Snapshot: a portrait of me. I regard the camera with a steady gaze, not smiling. My hair is gray and unfashionably short. Nowadays, women grow their hair to shoulder length, but I still favor a crewcut that would be easy to slip into a pressure suit helmet.

This is the picture that appears in the history books with the caption: "The woman who discovered life on Mars." I look at this woman who discovered life beneath the polar cap. Her face is a map of all the places I have been. The haze of lines beside her eyes (like the chaotic terrain of the Martian canyonlands); the set of her mouth (something stubborn about that mouth); the darkness of her eyes, shadowy in their sockets. It is the face of someone who hides secrets, hides them well.

When interviewers asked me about my first expedition into the lava tube (the first was followed by many more; by a full-blown biological research expedition), I told them about oxygen deprivation and how it affected my judgment. But I didn't mention yeti. If you asked me, I'd would say that I don't believe in the yeti, no sensible person does. I'm a cartographer, and I draw the world in black and white, changing ambiguities into certainties.

But at night, in the darkness of my dreams, I believe in the yeti, the messenger from the secret lands who led me to the underworld, the dark-eyed dream beast that haunts the crevasses and moves as softly as the blowing snow. I believe in the yetiá—as I believe in myself.

The map is not the territory; the world is not all that it seems on the surface. We have not answered all the questions. Dragons still lurk in the corners of our maps. I am my grandfather's child, and I know how to follow the holes in the snow that are not quite footprints.